Astra

Astra

CEDAR BOWERS

McCLELLAND & STEWART

Copyright © 2021 by Cedar Bowers

Trade paperback original edition published 2021

McClelland & Stewart and colophon are registered trademarks
of Penguin Random House Canada Limited.

Library and Archives Canada Cataloguing in Publication
data is available upon request.

ISBN: 978-0-7710-1289-1
ebook ISBN: 978-0-7710-1290-7

Lyrics from "Bloody Mother Fucking Asshole," written by
Martha Wainwright, are reprinted with permission,
courtesy of Martha Wainwright.

BOOK DESIGN BY LISA JAGER

COVER IMAGE: IGOR USTYNSKYY / GETTY IMAGES

TYPESET IN ARNO PRO AND BUTLER BY M&S, TORONTO

PRINTED IN CANADA

McClelland & Stewart,
a division of Penguin Random House Canada Limited,
a Penguin Random House Company
www.penguinrandomhouse.ca

1 2 3 4 5   25 24 23 22 21

Penguin
Random House
McCLELLAND & STEWART

For Mike

I will not pretend
I will not put on a smile
I will not say I'm all right for you
For you, whoever you are
For you, whoever you are
For you, whoever you are

—MARTHA WAINWRIGHT,
"Bloody Mother Fucking Asshole"

CONTENTS

RAYMOND

RAYMOND BRINE DOESN'T want to think about the coming baby. He doesn't want to think about it, or about Gloria, or his role in it all. He doesn't want to think about a creature so mewling and helpless. Not about its cord, its first cry, or its delicate newborn skin. He doesn't want to think about shared blood, or familial lines, or humanity's relentless compulsion to overpopulate this weary planet either. What he wants to do is work. To toil away on Celestial Farm's lands with his comrades under this vast expanse of sky. To focus on soil, irrigation, crop yields, and building more housing for the commune—but this baby is coming as fast as a hurtling comet and already it's made a mess of everything.

Gloria arrived with the influx of spring workers in March, and after a long winter alone in the one-room fir cabin that he'd built his first winter at the Farm, Raymond found himself drawn to her quick laugh and broad shoulders, so he let her spend a few nights in his bed. When it soon became clear she was interested in more, he requested she move into the yurt with the others, carefully explaining that he didn't believe in monogamous relationships, that he treasured his independence, that he never planned on being tied down. Gloria cited this as the reason she kept the pregnancy from him until June, and why she announced the news publicly during the morning breakfast meeting rather than talking to him one-on-one.

After the women finished their congratulations, running their fingers over her small, taut belly and kissing her full cheeks, Raymond pulled her aside to explain yet again that he wasn't *that* kind of man. Not the kind who got married or provided or believed that A and B led to C. He wasn't going to move to the city, cut his hair, get a job in a bank, or some other bullshit like that. He wasn't going to buy a house or a stroller, because on and on it would go. He'd been called to Celestial for a reason, and nothing was going to distract him or slow him down. If Gloria was hoping he'd build a family with her, or that she'd get a declaration of love, she'd set her sights on the wrong man.

Despite Raymond's unwavering stance, Gloria stuck around Celestial all summer long. Sometimes she searched him out by the river or in the gardens; or she bravely knocked on his cabin door to show him a sweater she'd crocheted for the baby, or to update him on the kicks she felt at night. When he encountered her like this, both vulnerable and stubborn, Raymond looked anywhere but into her wide, hazel eyes and pointed out that it would be better if she left and got her mother's help. He had no business getting involved with her child.

"Our child," Gloria reminded him firmly.

"If you say so," he said, closing the door.

Summer turned to fall, yet even after most of the seasonal workers had returned to the city to luxuriate in the convenience of electric heat, Gloria showed no sign of going anywhere. So in October, long after her belly began protruding through her embroidered dresses, the hems riding up her thighs as the baby swelled, Raymond took further pains to avoid her. First, he removed his few belongings from his cabin and set up camp by the river. Then he stopped leading the morning meetings and hiking up the hill for the communal meals. Instead he foraged kale, carrots, fennel, and zucchini from the gardens, and he grew even skinnier.

In November, Doris, his childhood friend and the co-founder of Celestial, informed him that she and Gloria's friend, Clodagh, had moved Gloria into his cabin where it was warmer, and that even though everyone else had gone for the winter, they were going to stay on until the baby arrived— they didn't want the poor woman to be all alone. Though this bothered him, he was still confident that with time, Gloria would realize what a mistake she was making, and so he soldiered on. He spent his nights on the slate-rock riverbank, head resting on his rolled-up jacket, gazing up at the flickering light of the stars scattered across the sky. And when the weather grew too cold for that, he began sleeping in the small hayloft in the animal shed with the nanny goats, holding out for the morning he'd wake to discover that the woman and her pregnant belly had finally gone. Or, even better, he'd wake up to discover the whole fiasco had been a terrible dream.

Now it's mid-December, and Raymond is at the top of a tall wooden ladder while the new kid, Wesley, clings firmly to the lower rails, steadying the contraption over the rocky soil. They are framing a twenty-foot-high, geodesic greenhouse that only needs five more windows before it's completely winterized, and in the distance the sparrows and thrushes are singing, and the river's winter-swollen waters are gurgling under the thin ice. Nature's cacophony is normally the only soundtrack at the Farm, but today something else has been drifting down from the Encampment since dawn: the women are singing. With determination. Raymond can make out their wavering harmonies in the breeze.

Hooking his hammer in his back pocket, he begins his descent, when from below Wesley lets out a holler and the ladder careens to the left. Raymond's tread-bare gumboots lose their footing, and the rails start sliding through his gloved hands. Thankfully, after falling only a few feet, he manages to grab ahold of the ladder again and maneuver his way to the ground in one piece.

Shaken, he rubs his jaw through his long, tangled beard as the boy watches him closely.

"I'm real sorry about that, it's just those women up there are driving me crazy," Wesley stammers, his face red and worried-looking, like he expects a beating.

"No problem. No one died."

Wesley points to the hill. "Can't you hear them? What do you think that's all about? They're going on and on, singing the same song."

Raymond shrugs. "I couldn't tell you," he says, though he's pretty sure he knows the reason behind it.

Leaving the boy to put away the ladder, Raymond zips his jacket up against the cold and wanders towards the paddock, still a little shaky from the fall. As he goes, he surveys his surroundings: the ten acres of vegetable gardens, waiting for spring planting; the fledgling apple orchard; the almost-done geodesic dome; and all that land on the other side of the deer fence, patiently waiting for Celestial to retain enough people to tend it. Physically, the Farm hasn't changed with the coming baby. But it *feels* different. In jeopardy. Raymond pulls a toothpick from his pocket, and tucks it in his cheek.

Inside the paddock, Brave, their best milk-goat, clops across the packed earth towards him. Raymond squats and allows her to root in his pockets for corn. He strains his ears, and is relieved to find he can't hear the women singing anymore. Besides the goat's eager grunts, Celestial is eerily quiet now. It's possible there's a high wind blowing the women's voices down the other side of the hill, away from the valley. Or maybe Gloria has been lying all along. Maybe under that dress she's only been hiding a large balloon. The knot: her belly button.

Raymond closes his eyes. Prays to the emptiness. Then to the stars, to the cosmos, to all of Mother Nature that surrounds him, because what else can he do?

Hearing the sound of distant feet crunching through the frost, he lifts his head and is surprised to see Doris heading his way. She's been pissed off at him since the summer because of this business with Gloria, and then when Wesley showed up a few weeks ago—skinny, pale, and obviously weaning himself off some concoction of hard drugs—she only grew angrier. Doris insisted that they turn him away. She didn't want Raymond distracted by some messed-up kid when clearly there was other shit he needed to deal with. But by that point there were only women left at Celestial, and, truthfully, Raymond wanted someone sympathetic to his side of things, so he went behind Doris's back and told the boy he was welcome to stay. This, of course, proved to be a mistake, and for the first time since they were kids he and Doris found themselves at odds—they've gone almost two weeks without speaking. Never before in the Farm's history has such a clear line been drawn in the sand: women on one side; men on the other.

Reaching the paddock, she climbs over the top rail of the fence in her stained overalls and steel-toed boots. She is breathing heavily and her face is pinched. "You know why I'm here, right?" she says, stopping before him.

"Possibly," Raymond answers, talking at the ground.

She flicks her thick braids behind her shoulders and grimaces. "Well then, is there any chance you could stop being a selfish prick for just a few hours? Just for today? I'm not up for more arguing, and I need you to pull yourself together."

Raymond picks up a pinch of dirt, grinds it between his fingers. "I'm only trying to stay true to my path," he says. "You understand that."

"It's your path now to be an asshole?" she asks.

This hurts quite a bit, and he has to bite his lip to keep from saying so. "What exactly do you want me to do?" He keeps his voice near a whisper. "I honestly have no idea. I'm breaking apart here."

Clearly this was the right thing to say, and Doris sighs, softening a bit. "What *I* want is for you to wake up. *I* want you to be a decent person again. You think this is hard for you? Imagine how Gloria feels."

Wesley emerges from the goat shed and rests his forearms on the top fence rail. He spits on the ground. "What's going on?" he asks.

"We're having a private conversation," Doris answers, coolly.

Raymond dusts his hands off on his pants and stands. "Actually, Wes and I are taking off. We have some work to take care of," he says, careful to avoid Doris's glare.

The boy pushes his greasy hair from his forehead. "Oh yeah? What are we up to?"

"We're going to get the last windows for the greenhouse."

"Oh my God," Doris barks. "You *can't* be serious, Raymond. That will take you hours. Leave it for another day."

"Why? I'm not a midwife. What good will I be if I stay here?"

Doris squeezes her eyes shut in frustration, then opens them again. "You can't leave me to deal with your mess all on my own. I didn't sign up for this. This was *not* the deal."

"Clodagh's around, isn't she?" he asks. Gloria's friend has a two-year-old son, a bug-bitten, serious kid who spent the summer eating off everyone's plates and running around without pants—apparently a method of potty-training. "She'll help you. Didn't she stay for this very reason?" he says.

"So this is her responsibility? Because she's a woman? Because she's a mother?" Doris has her fists clenched at her sides now; she's visibly seething.

Raymond can only bring himself to shrug.

"I don't get it. What's the big deal here?" Wesley asks.

"Gloria is in labour," Doris explains.

The boy scowls, then he turns his wind-chapped face to Raymond. "And what's that got to do with you?"

Raymond tosses his head. "Go get in the truck, I'll be right there," he orders.

Watching Wesley skulk away, Doris lowers her voice and continues her rant: "I can't believe you let him stay. There's something off about him. I don't like how he talks to me. With that smug look on his face? He doesn't respect me at all."

"He respects you fine. And anyways, I asked Gloria to leave and you never had my back about that," Raymond mumbles, perfectly aware that these two situations are not comparable in the slightest.

"So some random junkie *kid* is welcome here, but the woman up there having your baby isn't?"

"I don't know—maybe? Possibly?" Raymond says, and then, sensing that things are about to get uglier, he starts towards the gate. When he opens the latch, he glances back at his friend once more. "I told her to go to Vancouver to have it. It isn't my fault she stuck around. I'm not capable of being anyone's father, Doris. I'm not built for it. I'm doing her a favour by being honest right from the get-go. Can't you see that?"

"No, you're being like every other deadbeat who doesn't take care of his kids!" Doris is nearly shouting now and she's shaking her fist in the air. "You're not some guru, free to do whatever you want. This is *your* fucking problem, Raymond!"

As he reaches the truck, he can hear Gloria and Clodagh singing again. Setting his jaw, he climbs into the driver's seat and slams the door shut.

Wesley is slumped against the passenger seat window, a straw hat placed over his face. "I guess that's what's been eating you, eh?"

"What do you mean?" Raymond turns the key and then switches the radio on.

Wesley lifts the hat from his face. "I didn't know Gloria was having *your* kid."

Raymond shrugs.

"She's a bit young for you, isn't she? Can't be much older than I am."

Raymond's face reddens, and through clenched teeth he says, "She's older than you."

"Sure. Just not by much."

Already drowning in conflict, Raymond decides to let this go as he drives slowly across the rough, rutted fields towards the main road. Wesley lowers the hat over his face again, and a woman on the radio starts singing a folk song Raymond hasn't heard before. Again, his thoughts return to Gloria. How last month, when she'd found him down by the river fixing the irrigation system, she told him that, in some cultures, women sing all through labour; that voices can guide a child into the world peacefully.

"I want that when our baby is born," she said, with her hands clutched over her straining stomach, her face flushed and lovely.

Although he's relieved to get away, Raymond finds that with every additional mile he drives, the more concerned he becomes. Because it's not like he wants to hurt Gloria and her baby. He doesn't want to harm them in the least. He simply doesn't want to get involved.

The old quarry is seventy klicks out, and Wesley manages to sleep the whole ride. After the radio dissolves into static, Raymond switches it off and turns his attention to the repetitive rhythm of the tires bouncing over the rutted road.

When they arrive, he finds another truck parked at the rusty yellow gate. He pokes the boy in the ribs to wake him.

"We're here. Unfortunately, there's company," he says, looking back over his shoulder and reversing down the road until they're out of sight. "We'll have to wait them out."

"We're not allowed in there?" Wesley asks, as they pull under a canopy of balsam.

Raymond cuts the engine. "Nope. This is a secret mission."

Wesley rearranges his limbs and stamps his feet to warm them, while Raymond fishes a metal, ten-sided dice from his pocket. He shakes it, then tosses it across the bench seat, where it rolls over and over before coming to rest on the burnt orange upholstery. He picks it up, runs his thumb over the number 7, and throws it again.

Wesley frowns. "What are you doing that for?"

"Killing time. Meditating."

The boy holds out his hand. "I've never seen anyone meditate that way. Can I try it?"

"I'm only trying to figure out what's next. If I should even bother sticking around," Raymond says, returning the dice to his pocket, away from the boy's possibly thieving fingers.

Wesley lets his hand fall to his lap. "So you're going to leave? Just because of some girl?"

"Might do. Seems she thinks Celestial is where she belongs, and I don't have the authority to say otherwise," Raymond says, although it isn't so much Gloria but the baby that's making him feel like the real world is nipping at his heels. Like he's being dragged under. How will he accomplish his goals with it around? He'll surely end up compromising his beliefs, every single vision; he witnessed his father do the same.

"I didn't think you'd let a woman scare you off so easy. I thought you'd live here forever. Turn into some old stinky guy who never changes his overalls."

Raymond finally allows himself to laugh. Occasionally the boy can be funny. "That's the dream, isn't it? But that's not up to me. Legally speaking, it's Doris's name on the title. She paid for the place," he says, though this is just a small part of the story.

The idea for the Farm came to Doris and Raymond when they were only sixteen. They wanted to get away from the city, to do some good on this planet, to create an oasis for anyone who wanted to join them. At Celestial you could love who you wanted, and dress how you wished. There would be no boss, no "man," and no government dictating your every move. They imagined the Farm growing and growing, until one day it became a town of its own, completely self-sufficient and democratic, with a bakery, a dairy, a children's nursery, and a communal hall where famous musicians and writers would come to visit and perform. Making all this happen had already proved harder than they'd expected, but they'd always understood that such an enormous project would take dedication and time.

Doris was the one who fell in love with this region, surprising Raymond after her father passed away with the purchase of the two low plateaus of rock divided by the hundred acres of fertile valley. Together they directed the excavator as it scraped out the driveway that wound up the hill. Then they cleared the building site that eventually became the Encampment, towed in the old school bus, raised the yurt, and plowed the fields for the gardens. For a whole summer, they picked rocks and ripped out the roots of blackberry and Scotch broom, their muscles burning as though with fever. Then, at dusk, they lit the towering slash heaps and watched the sparks file up into the night sky.

Doris owned the land, but Celestial Farms was a place they were building as a team.

"I don't know if Doris thinks much of me," Wesley says. "That woman never smiles."

"She'll come around if you put in the hours and earn it. She's loyal through and through."

The boy stops biting his thumbnail. "Honestly, I'd rather take off with you if you go."

Raymond looks across the cab, at the purple hollows under Wesley's eyes. If he chooses to take off, the whole point would be to rid himself of responsibility, not pick up more along the way.

When the other truck finally leaves, they drive up to the gate only to find it secured with a thick new chain and a large padlock. "It's fine," Raymond says. "We've got legs. Let's use them."

As they stroll up the dirt road, Raymond explains that the owner of the General Store in Lunn had told him about this abandoned mine. He lists for Wesley all the treasures he's scavenged so far: a toilet seat and screen door for the Celestial outhouse, lumber for the greenhouse, a few folding chairs, a woodstove, and the chains to hang the loft in his cabin.

"If Doris is so rich, can't she pay for all the crap you need?" Wesley asks.

Raymond smiles through his beard. "Whatever *we* need. And sure, she could. But that's just it: you can *buy* anything under the sun, but when you scavenge and recover an item of value, or when you work really hard and build something that's tangible, that's lasting, there's nothing more satisfying. Anyways, that's what we're trying to do at the Farm. Sure, we have a long way to go, but one day people are going to write books about the place, I swear it."

Their conversation dies off when they round the last bend and the jumble of empty outbuildings comes into view. The site is abandoned as usual, but there are new, bright yellow NO TRESPASSING signs stapled to the siding of the double-wide trailers.

Raymond takes off his rucksack and hands Wesley a crowbar. "Let's get to it," he says.

It takes two hours to remove all the windows. And afterwards, labouring in silence, they carry the panes down the road through the falling light, before wrapping them in wool blankets, and tucking them carefully into the bed of the truck.

"I'm going to head back up to make sure there's nothing left we could use," Raymond announces, once they're done. "By the looks of it, this might be the last time I get in."

"I'm really hungry. And I'm cold," Wesley whines, clapping his hands together.

"Oh, come on, you'll survive. I won't be long," Raymond says, slamming the tailgate shut and walking away before the boy can think to follow.

At the quarry again, he takes out his flashlight and slowly wanders through the buildings, kicking at rubble and garbage, opening closets and desk drawers. He finds a Phillips head screwdriver under some old newsprint, a receipt book only half filled out, and a metal bucket with a solid bottom. Back outside, he sits on the splintered steps and lays his finds at his feet. There's no going back to the truck until he's come to some decision about what he's going to do.

When they first spoke about the pregnancy in the summer, Gloria asked if he'd consider moving to Vancouver with her to give their family a go—an idea he flat out refused. Just the thought of being pushed back into civilian life scares him.

The Farm is his sanctuary, his purpose. But the truth is, he doesn't want to cohabit with her at Celestial either. Imagine the three of them, squeezed into that cabin all winter long, pretending to be something they're not? This is what his parents did—compromised, settled—and it left them depressed and broken-hearted. No. That isn't the life he wants.

His other option is to take off. Cut loose before the baby fills its lungs for the first time. Never lay eyes on it. Never hold it. Never learn its name. Simply dematerialize. He could drop Wesley off at the Farm and keep driving towards the highway, alone. He could find some other raggle-taggle crew, in another sad town, and start up something like Celestial Farm from scratch.

The problem is, no matter which way his mind turns, Raymond keeps coming up with the same result. Whether he shirks his responsibilities or commits to them, there will still be a baby, one he'll never escape knowing about. And before too long, this baby will become a real, thinking, spiritual being exactly like he is, and it will resent him. It will tally his absence or his presence, his love or his lack of it, and it will wonder what it did to deserve him as a father. And this is what terrifies Raymond most: that this child is going to end up in some amount of pain because of him. One day it will hate him, or worry about him, or feel the need to forgive him. Time does not bend. Clocks cannot be reversed. Their family story has already begun.

He finds himself humming a version of the song he'd heard earlier on the radio. The woman's low voice had reminded him of the singing at Celestial that morning—strong, imperfect, yet persistent—but it had brought to mind his mother's voice too.

His memories of her are hazy: the itchiness of her woollen sweater pressed against his cheek, the raised veins on the backs of her brown hands, the smell of her hair as she galloped around the lawn imitating a horse while he rode on her back, clinging to her braid. She owned a guitar, when none of his friends' mothers had the imagination or the audacity to be so artistic. And she played for him. Her music is still there, inside him—warm and alive—it trembles in his bones.

Before he was born, Raymond's parents had been vicious critics of bourgeois culture and capitalism, but with a new baby on their hands his father argued that they needed a proper home. Charles Brine moved his family across town from their one-room apartment in East Vancouver into a carriage house tucked beside an ostentatious stone mansion where he'd obtained employment as the groundskeeper. This is where Raymond met Doris (it was her father who owned the place), and even though they attended different schools—Doris's being private and waterfront, and Raymond's public and rough—they spent every spare moment together, roaming the grounds, building forts, and playing cards at his kitchen table.

While Charles enjoyed his job and their newly acquired stability, the estate made Raymond's mother restless. She believed her husband was squandering himself on what she called "frivolities," by tending flowers no one bothered to smell or appreciate, and mowing the golf course–worthy lawns no one ever walked on. She joined the Socialist Party of British Columbia, and spent most evenings out, protesting and pamphleteering. Eventually, she grew prone to throwing dishes and bottles at her husband on the nights she stayed home, and once Raymond cut his heel on a shard of crockery that she'd failed to sweep up from the floor after one of their rows. Raymond's clearest memory of her is when she pulled out the shard with her teeth as he sat on the counter—how she didn't mind the taste of his blood.

He shivers and clears his throat. He rarely allows himself to think back on his early childhood. Because, when he turned six, his mother kissed his forehead one morning, packed her bags, and left.

Over the years, Raymond has tried his best to forgive her for this. To believe that, in leaving, she had done what she needed to do to survive. To save her spirit. To fight for what she felt was right in the world. She'd been a woman before her time, and he—her son—was what she'd had to sacrifice. He needed to believe that she was brave for leaving, not a coward for doing so. But the truth is, he can never know what she felt the day she left, or the day after that. Maybe she had regrets. Maybe things didn't get any better for her. Maybe if she'd stayed she would have had it all: love, work, purpose, and her son.

Goddamn it. Maybe he shouldn't make the same mistake.

Hearing a noise down the dirt road, Raymond wipes his eyes and itches his beard, sure that Wesley has come searching for him. Instead he spots a large, eight-point buck. Its neck thick and muscled, coat puffed up against the cold. Either it doesn't register Raymond or it doesn't fear him—it strides nearer, its head low under the weight of its rack.

At first Raymond is only impressed with the animal's enormous size but as it draws closer he notices that it has a wound on its hindquarter. A long line of torn flesh, almost an inch wide, swollen painfully and bubbling with pus; possibly from where a bullet grazed its flank. The deer is dragging its rear foot and heaving deeply through its nostrils. But the wound doesn't seem to be its only trouble; there is a deep sadness about the animal as well, and Raymond can't help but take its presence as a warning of some kind.

"Get," he shouts, scrambling to his feet and hitting the bucket and screwdriver together with a clang. "Get the fuck out of here."

The deer regards him once more before it turns and lurches off into the thick brush. Only once it's gone does Raymond accept that it's time to gather his things and return to the truck.

After they pass through the gates at the Farm, Raymond veers towards the steep driveway that leads to the Encampment rather than back across the fields towards the goat shed.

"I thought you didn't want to get involved with all that?" Wesley says, still a little grumpy about being left out in the cold at the quarry for so long.

"I figure I should at least check in on everyone," Raymond explains.

"Well, I don't need more of Doris today. I'd rather hang out with the goats."

"Suit yourself," Raymond says, stopping the truck and letting the boy out.

At the top of the hill, he takes a moment to stare out through the windshield at the dark Encampment: the rocky clearing with the birches lining the edge; the school bus, trailer, and yurt; and the outdoor dining hall with the wind-tattered tarp roof. It isn't much to look at yet, but it's theirs.

He and Doris chose to start building in this particular spot because when they first sat on the westerly cliff edge and gazed out over the valley, they could picture the Farm laid out at their feet. They promised to end their days there, growing old together, in friendship and peace. Raymond might not want to conform, and he might not want to have a baby, but he can't bring himself to abandon Doris or this dream either.

The sky has clouded over completely now, a few flakes have started to fall, yet Raymond knows that Venus is above all that darkness, with Orion's Belt neatly arranged nearby. That morning, when he woke to the sound of the women singing, he searched for his astrology book in his bag, to discover that tonight the Geminids will be arriving too, and for the next week meteors will rain overhead. Can a newborn see that far? Can it see the sky? He's surprised to find that, now that he's made his decision, this thinking about the child isn't as difficult as it was before.

He wonders if Gloria has decided on a name for it already. Her friend Clodagh calls her son Freedom, but Raymond dislikes the label. It's too much pressure for a kid. Freedom is something you have to seize or earn. It can't be handed to you. Besides, one shouldn't impose their beliefs on their offspring in such a way. Nor should a person change themselves just because they become a parent—he sure won't. He's decided he'll orbit around the baby and its mother like one of Jupiter's distant moons. If they choose to stay on here, he'll give them the cabin permanently and he'll build another near the river for himself. Maybe the child will visit him some afternoons, and he can teach it how to swing an axe and hoe corn. Gloria is fully capable of managing the rest.

Raymond removes his dice from his pocket, runs his fingers over the numbers, and considers the weight of it in his hand. Though not normally sentimental about material belongings, this is the one thing he always carries with him. He'd found it in his mother's bedside drawer the evening of the day she moved out, and it's the only memento of hers he has left. He brings it to his lips, kisses it, then returns it to his pocket.

Candlelight casts across the Encampment, as the cabin door swings open with a bang. Then Doris is outside, rushing over to the truck.

"I wasn't sure I'd see you again," she is saying, as Raymond cranks down his window.

"I wasn't either. Is everything going okay in there?" he manages to ask, though his throat is very tight.

"Going okay? No, actually, I don't think it is. I swear, Gloria's been waiting for you to get back to have this baby. It's like she's clenching it in. I kept telling her you'd come, though I'd no idea if that was true or not. It's the only thing that brings her any comfort. Though I can't imagine why."

"Shit," he says slowly through his teeth. "Well, what do you need me to do?"

"I need you to get into that cabin, tell Gloria you love her, and that you want the child, and that your family is going to be fine until the end of time."

Though none of this is a joke, Raymond nearly laughs. "I can't do that, Doris. Come on."

"I know you can't, but you have to."

Taking the steering wheel in his hands, he becomes aware of the keys dangling above his knee and briefly considers his escape again. Then he forces his attention back on his friend. "Look, I'll stick around. I'll stay. But I'm not going to pretend to be somebody I'm not. I can't lie like you want me to."

"Yes, you can. And being out here, with no hospital for miles, we need to do everything we can," she says. "Please, do this part my way, then do the rest however you want. Nobody's telling you how to raise your child. I don't care the slightest bit. But tonight, I need you to lie. Start telling the truth when the sun comes up tomorrow."

Raymond stands just inside the door of the cabin that he built log by log, plank by plank, window by window, with his own two hands. In the centre of the room, on the piping hot woodstove, the kettle is rattling madly at full boil, and the sudden warmth makes his skin tingle all over. The air is thick, humid, and it doesn't smell as it did before. Now it's all sweat and metal, sedimentary rock, and freshly broken ground.

He tries his best not to draw any attention to himself; he simply watches the three women from the entrance. Their brows beaded with sweat, their sleeves rolled up to their elbows, their faces fierce with concentration. They aren't singing any longer, and he supposes the time for that has passed. Or it hadn't helped the way Gloria had hoped. Or it's too late now—who knows.

"You came back," Gloria says, looking up. Her eyes are large, intense, and full of what must be fear. Raymond meets them straight on and nods.

"And you're going to stay here with me?"

This, at least, is something he can promise. "Yes, I'll be staying," he tells her.

And with these words, her hands grip the blankets, her eyes droop, and slowly she begins to groan. And it's as if the room expands along with the intensity of her process. The rafters rise, the floor planks lengthen, and the log walls stretch. The cabin he built to live in alone, instead becomes a cathedral—a shrine to what he can't control. And Raymond lets his whole being finally surrender to it. His shoulders fall, his hands drop to his sides. Why fight? He's just a man. Small. Insignificant. As scared as everyone else. The only difference between yesterday and today is that now he can't say he's the only one in this story.

KIMMY

KIMMY'S MOTHER HAS rules for everything now. For instance: bedtime is always at seven o'clock, hand-washing is required both before and after meals, and Kimmy isn't allowed to pick up, hug, or kiss her baby sister Stacy. Quiet Time is yet another rule, and during those two, achingly long hours each afternoon, Kimmy has to stay in her bedroom while the baby naps. This is a problem because she hates this room. It's white, bare, and smells like new carpet and paint, while her old room, in her old house, had wooden pirate-ship walls, a dark adventurous closet, and a shaggy aquamarine carpet that swallowed marbles, puzzle pieces, and bits of popcorn. That old room was a thousand times superior.

When they moved into this house three weeks ago, Kimmy had all her toys with her of course: her ponies, doctor kit, Barbies, Raggedy Ann collection, and her pink wooden dollhouse. But in her new room they look different—shabby, even. As if, during the long drive in the moving truck, all the sparkle they possessed before had rubbed off. Her mother doesn't understand what the problem is. She believes Kimmy should stop all her whining and be grateful for a house that doesn't have other people's fingerprints smeared all over the walls.

Really what Kimmy wants is to bring her toys into the living room. If she could play under the big window, beside the grandfather clock, with her mother nearby, maybe her dolls would come to life again. Maybe the days wouldn't drone on so long either, each second ticking around the clock at tortoise-speed. But this is a rule too: under no circumstances can Kimmy's toys leave her bedroom.

"What if the baby gets her hands on one of your doll's high-heeled shoes, or on a bead, a button, or a marble? What if she chokes?" her mother always says. As if Kimmy has forgotten her seven siblings that didn't make it out into the world alive. As if she doesn't remember how much her mother's eyes had leaked each time she lost one. Or how she always kept the lights low. How her hands shook. How she sat for hours on the couch even though there were piles of dishes in the sink, and how, damp-eyed, she tried to explain, "I'm just a little sad, that's all," when it was obvious she was much, much worse than that.

It was a whole seven years after Kimmy was born that Baby Stacy finally came out perfect and healthy, but that's when the rules doubled, cinching around Kimmy like a belt done up too tight. And now, even though her mother should be happy, she is terrified of everything. She's scared the baby will break a bone, get a rash, or suffocate in her blankets while she sleeps. And she's always puréeing apricots and peas in the kitchen, or wiping down every surface in the house with bleach, and she never wants to go anywhere in case a germy stranger tries to touch Stacy's cheeks with their icky hands. She seems to think her only job is to keep the baby alive, even if it means forgetting about everyone else. Even if it means forgetting about Kimmy altogether.

Usually, during Quiet Time, Kimmy hides from her dead-eyed toys under her covers. She scoots down to the bottom of her bed, finds the deepest black where the blanket is tucked under the mattress, and sniffs around for any lingering smells of her old room in the seams of her comforter. Down there, time gets strange, her sister gets unborn, the air grows hot, and only when she's dizzy and about to suffocate does she untuck the blanket for a breath of fresh, new-room air. But today, bored of always doing the same thing, Kimmy decides to grab some paper and a pencil, and to tally all the animals she sees through her window instead. Ducks, birds, skunks, deer, whatever there is out there she'll note down. She will do what her mother does when she plays Scrabble: she'll make four marks, and when she gets to the number five, she'll put a slash across the lines so it looks like a picket fence.

She isn't allowed to open the window because they don't know how Baby Stacy's lungs will react to pollen or dust, so she stares out at the beautiful summer's day through the glass. Unfortunately, her window is only three feet above the ground, and so the view isn't great. Their gravel driveway passes below, beyond that is a skinny strip of brown lawn, and a few feet further on is a split-rail fence that divides their property from their neighbour's fields of tall, shimmering hay. In the distance, she can just make out the top of two squat mountains studded in scraggly trees.

After twenty minutes, Kimmy has only six lines on her paper—all birds. She is about to give up and climb under her comforter when she notices movement behind the fence. It's an animal. Large and brown. *Deer can be brown,* she thinks, *but so can bears.* She marks it down on her paper, readjusts her headband, and then focuses on the gaps in the fence. There's no mistaking that something is shifting back and forth, half hidden. Then the animal stands up on its hind legs and waves. A girl. In a funny-looking corduroy dress. And beside her is a black and white dog with a bubblegum pink tongue swaying from its mouth.

Kimmy peers both left and right. *Where are her parents?* she wonders. Kimmy isn't allowed outside alone, not even on the deck to water the pansies. Before she can think to wave back or even smile, the girl shrugs, says something to her dog, parts the hay, and disappears into the field.

The next morning, Kimmy wakes up hoping the girl will come back. She goes to the window and stares out—all she sees is a mouse scampering across the gravel. She gets dressed and checks again: the sun is a little higher, but no girl. It takes forever for the morning to go by, and when lunch finally arrives, Kimmy fidgets, picking apart her sandwich, nibbling her carrots, and twisting strands of her hair.

"Stop swinging your legs and sit still," her mother says.

"Sorry." Kimmy jams her toes firmly on the linoleum. Baby Stacy bangs her tray with her rubber-coated spoon and gurgles. "Can I try feeding her?" Kimmy asks, although she knows what the answer will be.

"You're not old enough, sweetie."

"It's like you think I'm still a baby too," Kimmy mutters under her breath.

"What was that, missy?"

"Nothing."

Baby Stacy is watching them. She starts to laugh, then her laughs turn to piercing, joyful squawks, and she throws her spoon on the floor. Their mother clucks, scolding her, and then starts clearing the table.

When Kimmy rushes into her room for Quiet Time, she grabs the string on the window blind and pulls it all the way up. There! Just as she hoped, the girl is squatting behind the fence. When she sees Kimmy, she stands, and this time she doesn't wave but beckons with both hands for her to come outside.

Could I? Kimmy loses her grip on the string and the blind drops to the sill with a crash. As she flops herself onto her back on the floor to think, her mother flings the bedroom door open.

"Shhhhhh," she says, clutching the baby over her shoulder. "What are you thudding around in here for? Can't you be quiet while I put Stacy down? Is that too much to ask?"

"Sorry, Mommy."

The door clicks shut again and her mother starts singing in the next room, the floor creaking beneath her feet as she rocks the baby to sleep. Kimmy can remember when she was held the same way, when the lullabies were sung for her. Once upon a time, she made her mother so happy that she tried over and over for another baby, for a bigger family. "You were so easy and good. You were my inspiration," her mother told her. But Kimmy doesn't like the word *were*. It only confirms what she already knows: these days, she's pretty much as good as forgotten.

During each of her mother's pregnancies, Kimmy lovingly pressed her ear to the bulge of her mother's smooth belly and listened to the creature roll and slosh inside while planning what she would teach it: somersaults, dancing, and how to braid hair. But even though this baby came out fine, Kimmy still hasn't been allowed to show her anything. So when her parents told her they were moving up to northern B.C., where her father, an RCMP officer, would patrol the 200 kilometres of highway that winds between Barkerville, Lunn, and Hixon, Kimmy had cried for days. She worried about leaving her friends behind and she was sure she'd hate the country, but her mother told her not to be silly. "You have your sister," she added. "You'll always have someone to play with." Yet the truth is, Kimmy is even lonelier than before.

But maybe this girl outside could fix everything? Once, Kimmy saw children on TV make a telephone out of tin cans and string. They strung the cans between two neighbouring houses and leaned out their windows to chat. Maybe Kimmy could try that? The girl could stay hidden behind the fence while Kimmy sat at her window, and their words could tight-rope across the driveway on cotton twine.

Kimmy gets onto her knees and flips one of the blind's bottom slats up, only to find the girl right there: forehead pressed against the window. It's as if Kimmy is peering into her mother's zoom-in makeup mirror, but these eyes are not hers, and this face is different. There's a twist to the girl's features, almost as if she'd been pieced together like a patch-work quilt. Kimmy understands that these are scars she's looking at. Bright red ridges that run from her nose and over her lips, before cutting across her jaw, all beautiful and scary at once. For a moment, she lets herself imagine this *is* in fact a mirror—that she's staring at her own reflection, that she's the one outside, that she isn't scared of anything, that she isn't like her mother at all. The feeling is so intense that when the girl furrows her thick eyebrows and pulls her face away, Kimmy jumps to her feet and slides the pane all the way open before the girl has a chance to take off again.

"Hi," Kimmy whispers, breathless. "You can come in, but you've got to be very, very quiet."

The girl grins, shimmies over the windowsill, and then drops silently to the carpet. She's wearing the same brown corduroy dress she had on yesterday. And Kimmy notices that her legs are covered in bruises and bug bites, and her ragged hair looks as if it has been sheared with a bread knife. When she tucks a chunk of this near-black bob behind her ear, Kimmy really notices her scars: the tissue tight and shimmery. She's like a character from a book. Like Gretel or Tinker Bell or Little Red Riding Hood. Brave. Courageous. This girl wouldn't blink if she ran into a wild animal, or a witch, or worse. She isn't scared of strangers. And Kimmy can't help it: she already loves everything about her.

The girl walks around Kimmy's room, inspecting her toys and tracing her fingers along her shelves, her filthy bare feet leaving prints of silver and gold on the carpet like fairy dust. Remembering her mother in the next room, Kimmy quickly pushes her desk chair against her bedroom door, and then whispers, "I'm Kimmy. What's your name?"

The girl cocks her head and squints quizzically, but remains silent.

"What's your name?" Kimmy asks again, taking a step closer.

The girl plucks a Raggedy Ann doll off the shelf and sniffs its hair before she finally answers. "Astra," she says, as her mouth splits into a grin that exposes two missing front teeth.

"Oh, that's a nice name," Kimmy says shyly, remembering to give a compliment just as her mother has taught her to do whenever she is introduced to someone new. "But you *have* to be quiet if you want to stay. I didn't tell my mom about you, and she never lets me play with anyone before meeting their parents."

"Raymond."

"Who's Raymond?"

"He's just Raymond." Astra takes a seat on the edge of the bed and bounces a little on her bum. Kimmy wonders if Raymond is a fairy tale character too. "You know, I really like your house," Astra says. "It's kind of weird and super white."

Kimmy smiles and, hoping to impress her some more, takes down her backpack from the top shelf in her closet and dumps the contents out onto the bed.

Astra fans through one of the notebooks. "What's all this stuff for?"

"School, silly."

"Oh, I don't go to school. Raymond doesn't believe in it. He thinks kids should learn real skills. He says school only teaches you to be a sheep." Astra's expression is very serious, and Kimmy wonders why anyone would think that's what children learn at school. But before she can ask, Astra continues: "And I want to be friends with you, I really do, but I have to tell you something important first. I have to unburden my conscience."

"Okay," Kimmy says hesitantly, adjusting her headband.

"When they were building this house, I cursed it with a raven's skeleton." She clasps her hands on her lap, lowers her eyes to the floor, and goes on to explain how, right where Kimmy's room is now, there'd been the tallest hemlock with long, battleship green branches that drooped nearly to the ground. "I watched them cut it down and rip up its roots. And the murderers didn't even plant a single tree after. They did nothing to replenish the Earth! So I used a stick to push the bones into the wet cement after the construction guys went home. I swear, I wouldn't have done it if I'd known *you* were going to live here."

Kimmy's mouth is hanging open in the exact way her mother hates, but she doesn't care. This here is proof that Astra *is* magic. And the raven explains why the house doesn't feel like her old house in Vancouver did, why her toys aren't as good as they used to be, and why her mother hasn't gotten any better since they moved in.

"How long will it last?" Kimmy asks, curious. Because although living in a cursed house is a little disconcerting, it's kind of exciting too. Like an adventure.

"I couldn't tell you. My guess is it will wear off eventually. So can you forgive me?"

"Oh yes, I forgive you completely," Kimmy says.

Astra gets up from the bed, goes to the closet, and begins sliding hangers across the bar. "This house has a great clothing collection," she says, taking Kimmy's new white sweatshirt off the hanger, the one she's been saving for her first day at school. On the front, there's a picture of a grey kitten with a glittery bow between its pointy ears. Astra pulls the sweatshirt over her head. "I'll take this one for now."

"Like for forever?" Kimmy asks.

"Is it your favourite too? We can take turns with it then. That's fine."

Kimmy doesn't know what to say to this. What if her mother discovers it missing from her closet?

Settling herself on the floor, Astra drags the dollhouse over and suggests they turn it into a stable. Without asking first, she trims orange yarn from the Raggedy Ann doll's hair with craft scissors and pretends it's hay, feeding it to the horses, chattering quietly the whole time. Eventually, Kimmy finds a box of animals in the closet, and she adds the pigs and goats and wooden snakes to Astra's game. She sits back and watches her new friend organize everything on the carpet, happy to see that, in Astra's hands, her toys have come back to life.

As they play, Astra asks about Kimmy's "flushing toilet," her "hot water shower," and her baby sister's room. She asks about Kimmy's mom and dad, and what it's like to sit and eat in an "inside" dining room. When Kimmy tells Astra that she isn't allowed outside by herself, Astra declares it "oppressive." And although Kimmy has no idea what the word means, she loves the way it sounds, and how much Astra talks, and all her strange words, and so she agrees, "Yes. It's very oppressive."

"Well, what would happen if I was caught in here?" Astra asks. "Would you get in trouble?"

"Oh, I'd be grounded for sure."

"What's that?"

"It's when you're not allowed to leave your house or visit your friends." Kimmy pauses. "But wait. Maybe I'm already grounded?"

Astra collapses on the carpet, laughing, and through gasps she says, "I sure wouldn't want to be you! Your life sounds horrible." When she sees that Kimmy is hurt by this, she goes on: "Come on. Do you even want to be you? Always stuck inside? I can't imagine it."

Kimmy thinks for a moment. "Maybe not."

When they hear the baby wake, Astra jumps to her feet and goes to the window. "Should I come by around the same time tomorrow?"

"Yes, please. And then it will be my turn with the sweatshirt, right?" Kimmy asks, because now she's decided she's okay with sharing it if it'll guarantee Astra will come back.

"Sure, that's fine," Astra says, jumping from the window and landing in the gravel driveway with a crunch. She scrambles over the fence and pets her dog, who is waiting patiently for her, before she turns to wave goodbye.

Kimmy laughs, her heart racing, because although her mother would be extremely angry to know she'd snuck in a stranger through her bedroom window, it doesn't matter. She'll break this rule over and over and over again if it means she and Astra can stay friends. Because, for the first time since moving in, Kimmy is finally happy.

The next day, before Quiet Time starts, Kimmy stands at her window, with the blind all the way open, waiting for Astra to come back. No matter how hard she stares, she can't see the cabin, the greenhouse, the bus, or any other part of the place that Astra calls "Celestial," so Kimmy figures it must be a long way off. She gets dizzy imagining what it would be like to walk out into that field alone, and her tummy goes funny thinking about being so far from her mother. What would she do if she got stung, or sprained her ankle, or saw a snake? She wonders how Astra ever became so brave.

Kimmy has almost convinced herself that she'd only imagined her new friend, when she notices a stirring in the field. Astra pops out from the tall grass, and even though it's midday and the sun is scorching, she's wearing Kimmy's kitten sweatshirt over that same dress. The sparkly bow catches the sun.

"How long does it take you to get here?" Kimmy whispers, when Astra flops onto the carpet.

"Maybe twenty minutes? Celestial is up the river a bit."

"There's a river over there?"

"Of course, silly. How else would we get water?"

Kimmy has never thought about this before. She has no idea how they get water, or electricity, or heat their house. It just happens.

Today Kimmy asks Astra to play doctor, because with all her heart, that's what she wants to be when she grows up. After her mother lost the babies from her stomach, a doctor had invited her to live at the hospital for two months before Stacy was born. Ever since, her mother has called him a "miracle worker," and so that's what Kimmy wants to be too.

While Kimmy opens her medical kit and puts on her stethoscope, Astra says, "I love hospitals too, you know. I've been in a real one before. All the nurses were squishy and they smelled like medicine and they were always hugging me. They gave me ice cream too—did you know they have that there?"

"Oh, I don't want to be a patient. I want to fix people who are sick and dying and stuff," Kimmy explains.

"We all get sick, Kimmy. And we all eventually die. It will happen to you too. You can't avoid the inevitable."

Kimmy grows quiet for a minute, and fiddles with the stethoscope in her ears. The "inevitable"? What does that even mean? "If you want ice cream, why don't you buy some and eat it at home?" she asks.

"Oh, Raymond says sugar is poison. I've only eaten ice cream the one time. And anyways, we don't have a freezer."

"What about the one in your fridge?"

Astra looks at Kimmy as if this is the dumbest thing she's ever heard, before rolling onto her back. "Can you just sew up my face now? Make sure you pretend I'm still bleeding. Dab the blood away with the cotton."

Not knowing how Astra got her scars is almost better than knowing, because it means they could be from anything: a pirate's sword, a bear's claws, or they could be wounds from fighting crime. So instead of asking her friend what happened, Kimmy copies the doctors she's seen on TV, and begins numbing the area with the syringe from her kit, plunging the needle into Astra's cheeks and jaw again and again. After Astra's face is completely frozen, Kimmy sews up the very real, wine-coloured ridges. In and out. In and out. She works gently around the scars, stitching across Astra's lips and down her chin. She finishes the job by tying a knot under her earlobe.

"How many stitches did you give me?" Astra makes her words round and clumsy from all the freezing.

"Eighteen."

"That's not enough. Do more. I got forty-six," she says, this time forgetting to mumble.

A little later, when they hear Stacy start to cry in the next room, Kimmy finally finds the courage to ask if she can have her sweatshirt back.

Astra bites her lip, thinking. "No. There are lots of nice clothes in that closet. I'm going to keep it a bit longer."

Kimmy doesn't like this change of plan. The cuffs and collar are already getting dirty, and there's a purple stain over

the kitten's ear. "But it's still mine, right?" she asks carefully.
"You *will* give it back?"

"What do you mean, 'yours'? Don't you share it with
everyone who lives here?"

Kimmy hesitates. "No . . . it wouldn't fit anyone else."

"Oh," Astra says, her face falling.

Then, when she starts pulling at the sleeve to take it off,
Kimmy stops her. "Never mind. I don't care. Just bring it
tomorrow."

For the rest of the week, when Astra arrives at Quiet Time,
she's wearing the kitten sweatshirt over that grubby dress,
but Kimmy doesn't ask her for it back anymore. All that's
important is that Astra pulls herself up through the window, and they can pick up exactly where they left off the
day before.

Astra uses lots of complicated words, like *consumerism,
democracy, protest, organic, composting, oppressive,* and *vibe,*
and because Kimmy doesn't want Astra to think she's stupid,
she never asks her to explain what any of them mean. Astra is
different from Kimmy's old friends in Vancouver. She's always
gnawing on the skin around her thumbs, and she keeps
strange food in the pockets of her dress—overripe berries or
hunks of stale bread. Once she even offered Kimmy a piece of
cured elk meat.

Astra plays differently from regular girls too. She makes
the Barbies walk around naked, she's been trimming their
hair shorter and shorter each visit, and she likes to draw tattoos on the ponies' soft, plastic skin. What's even stranger
is, whenever Kimmy adds a mother into one of their games,

Astra immediately invents elaborate ways for her to die—falling off a cliff, or drowning in a lake, or simply by having a "massive heart attack"—and then she proceeds to "bury" her, by shoving her under the dresser. But this, Kimmy thinks, only proves how imaginative her new friend is. And because of Astra's visits, Quiet Time always flies by.

Even though they've only ever played in Kimmy's bedroom, the way Astra describes her farm, and the people who live there, and the work she does, is so vivid that Kimmy can't help but feel transported. Now whenever she opens her bedroom door and goes out into the rest of the house, it's like stepping into a strange world. Everything is too clean. The plastic-covered couch is too crinkly. The air is spiced with cleaning products and hairspray. And the kitchen cupboards are overflowing with items Astra's never heard of: Cheerios, Pop-Tarts, Hershey's Chocolate Syrup, Old Dutch chips, and Famous Amos cookies, all of which Kimmy sneaks into her room for Astra to try.

Kimmy has also begun to notice that her mother never sits still for longer than a minute; she's always busy, always rushing around nervously. And if she really thinks about it, she realizes her mother has always been this way. Yesterday, when Kimmy begged for a cuddle on the couch, she looked nearly cornered—like she was terrified of getting that close. And today, when Kimmy kissed her on the cheek after lunch, she pulled back and wiped at the spot where Kimmy's lips had touched her skin.

One of the rules in the house is that everyone must get dressed before eating breakfast, yet lately her mother only manages to get changed right before her father pulls up in the driveway at 6 p.m. Kimmy understands that this is proof of something between them. Maybe it means her mother doesn't want him to know how she spends her days, or to know that she's still just as sad as before. Or maybe it means it's more important to act like you're doing okay than to actually *be* okay.

And so Kimmy has started thinking differently about the rules too. How yes, the one about the toys in the living room might be for Stacy's safety, but the rule about Quiet Time isn't for the baby at all. It's because her mother doesn't want her around. Her mother invented Quiet Time so she could be alone.

When Astra next climbs through the window, she isn't wearing Kimmy's sweatshirt, her brown dress is soaking, and she has grass seeds stuck to her damp legs.

"Why are you wet?" Kimmy asks.

"I was doing laundry in the river. I left our sweatshirt drying on the rocks."

Kimmy crinkles her nose and stares at her feet, her belly suddenly stinging like she's just drunk a glass of malt vinegar. She's not going to see her sweatshirt again, she realizes.

Still, because she wants Quiet Time to go well, she pretends to be perfectly fine, and asks, "Why do you do your own laundry?"

"I do laundry, and I cook, and I work in the gardens. I'm not like you, I'm not shut up in a tiny room like a factory chicken," Astra snaps.

This is almost too much, and Kimmy has to force back her tears. "I'm not a chicken."

"I'm not saying it's *your* fault you are. You were just born into the wrong situation is all." Astra raises her thick eyebrows, her eyes gleaming. "I brought something to show you though. It helps me when I'm in trouble, so I thought it might help you with your family." She slips her hand into her dress pocket, pulls out a little silver object, and passes it to Kimmy. It's cold, heavy, and oddly shaped, similar to a board game dice only with more sides.

"What is it?" Kimmy asks.

"It's called a decahedron. It's my magic talisman. Raymond gave it to me, but it belonged to Gloria first."

"Who's Gloria?"

"My birth mother."

"So Raymond *is* your father?"

"Of course. Who did you think he was?"

Kimmy shrugs. She wants to ask where Astra's mother is now, because even though her own mother is strict and pays too much attention to Baby Stacy, she can't imagine not seeing her every day.

"Anyways," Astra goes on, "I always keep the decahedron with me, because Raymond told me it knows all the answers in the universe. All you've got to do is ask it a question. Come on, try it."

Kimmy glances at the dice. It seems too small a thing to be so powerful. "I don't really want to," she says.

"I'll do it then," Astra snaps. She snatches it back and closes her eyes. "If I roll a two, Kimmy's parents love her with all their hearts. But if I roll any other number, they don't care about her at all, and that's why they never let her play outside or be free."

Horrified to hear her complaints about her family come out of her friend's mouth, Kimmy shouts, "Don't!" and tries to grab the dice from Astra's hands. But she's too late. It flies from her fingers and falls to a stop on the carpet: 10. Kimmy bursts into tears.

"It's okay." Astra puts her arm around her waist. "You don't even need them now that you have me."

"How do you know it's telling the truth?"

"It always does," Astra says.

Kimmy rests her cheek on Astra's bare shoulder, and her nose fills with the smell of river-damp hair. Astra smells nothing like Kimmy's mother. Not a bit like strawberry shampoo. If anything, she smells slightly of rot.

Eventually, Astra pulls *The Tale of Peter Rabbit* from the shelf and shimmies under the comforter. Kimmy curls up beside her and watches the large pages turn. Astra can't read yet, but she makes up the story as she goes along by looking at the pictures. The bunnies are invited into the garden to help the farmer glean his onion crops. They befriend a cat, play hide-and-seek, and then the bunnies are freed from the restriction of their clothes. They say goodbye to the gardener, and then sleep in their little bunny hole as wild rabbits should.

When Astra closes the book, Kimmy is surprised to see her eyes brimming. "What is it?" she asks.

"It's just your bed is so comfortable, and I don't think I've ever been so happy."

Kimmy wants Astra to stop crying, so she says, "I'm happy too."

"I'm glad we're best friends." Astra sighs. Then her tone becomes almost scolding: "But I want you to love *me* as much as you love your sister. That's what I really want."

"I do," Kimmy says slowly, though this isn't exactly true— they are friends, yes, but not sisters.

Astra rubs her cheeks dry with the back of her hand. "You're sure? Because now that I have you, I don't ever want to *not* have you."

"I'm sure," Kimmy answers, although in truth she's starting to wish Astra would leave early today. She'd rather spend the rest of Quiet Time by herself than be with Astra when she's acting so strange.

"You know, I've been thinking, and I've figured out a way to save you," Astra says, getting up from the bed.

"Oh, I don't need saving."

Astra rolls her eyes. "Yes, you do. And we need to be together more. Not just during your weird Quiet Time."

Kimmy swallows. "You could start school in September? My mom thinks you can only learn stuff like math and science from a teacher."

"Well, she's wrong." Astra groans, as if disappointed Kimmy would say something so stupid. "I need you to get a diaper and some of Stacy's clothes for tomorrow. We're going to practise with them. And I'm going to take this book with me."

"You already have my sweatshirt," Kimmy reminds her.

"I know. But you should learn not to hog your belongings. Where I live, we share everything. It's better that way."

Kimmy opens the front cover of her book. Under the title, her mother's handwriting. *Happy Birthday, Sweet Kimmy*. She doesn't want to, but after Astra drops out the window, Kimmy passes it into her waiting hands.

The next day, Kimmy gives Astra the small pile of clothes and the two diapers she took from Baby Stacy's drawer. As Astra tries to fit a diaper between a Raggedy Ann doll's legs,

Kimmy reminds herself that she too has a plan. If she keeps Astra happy, keeps reassuring her they are best friends, and doesn't let her use the decahedron again, their friendship will go back to how it was at the beginning.

"Is this how big your sister is?" Astra asks.

"No. She's kind of bigger."

Astra stomps her foot and throws the diaper on the floor. "Shit. Let me think."

Kimmy takes a step back. It's against all her mother's rules to swear. "Do you want to play hospital again?"

"No," Astra says. "You don't get it. This is important. I'm going to rescue you from this house. You and your sister are going to be my sisters too."

"We can't be your sisters for real. We can only pretend."

"No, we *can* be sisters. I asked the decahedron and it said this was the perfect solution. I have plenty of room for you at Celestial." Astra goes on to describe her cabin in detail, the bed above the woodstove where they'll all sleep, and the quilts they'll use to keep warm. She lists recipes and her favourite soups and the clothes they will share. She reminds Kimmy how easy it will be to move in, since her kitten sweatshirt and rabbit book are already in the cabin waiting for her.

"Have you talked to your dad about this?" Kimmy asks, trying to change the subject, trying to be reasonable, trying to think about anything but her sweater tucked in an old, rotten-smelling drawer, in a cabin she's never seen.

"Anyone's allowed to join us. Raymond has an open-door policy. I don't have to ask him," Astra says as she starts pacing the room. Kimmy notices a new tear at the hem of her dress and a scrape down the back of her thigh. The cut isn't bandaged, although the wound is deep and fairly fresh. Astra stops. "What's your problem, anyways? Don't you want to be my sister anymore?"

She is speaking too loudly, and Kimmy puts her finger to her lips. "Shh, you're going to get me in trouble."

"I can find out how you really feel." Astra digs in her pocket and pulls out the dice. Kimmy can't even look at it, her eyes are burning. There's nothing she hates more than the decahedron.

"If you want to be my sister, if you really love me, then I will roll an eight." Astra shakes her cupped hands for what seems like ages. She stops, blows into the crack between her thumbs, and then, finally, she lets the dice roll across the carpet. "Oh!" she cries.

Kimmy eyes the shiny lump on the floor, first with terror, and then tremendous relief: 8.

Instantly forgetting how angry she just was, Astra starts planning again. "I know what we have to do. We'll practise on Stacy. Let's borrow her for a bit."

"We can't do that."

"It'll be fine," Astra says. "You need to trust me."

Sneaking into the nursery is easy, but Kimmy hesitates once she's inside and looking down into the crib. Stacy's small chest rises and falls. *How heavy is she?* Kimmy wonders. Will she be strong enough to lift her over the bed rails?

Suddenly Astra is there at her shoulder and Kimmy follows her gaze: over the alphabet decals, the zoo-animal wallpaper, and then at the slowly turning mobile above Stacy's bed. Astra reaches out and touches a pair of patent-leather baby shoes on the dresser. "Well? Are you going to get her out or not?" she asks.

"I don't think I can," Kimmy whispers, still peering into the crib.

Astra elbows her aside, leans over the rail, and effortlessly lifts Stacy from the mattress.

After sneaking back into her room again, Kimmy pushes her desk chair against the door while Astra sits on the bed with the baby. Used to seeing Stacy on her mother's hip, Kimmy is struck by how much longer and floppier she appears in Astra's slight arms. Kimmy cringes at Astra's dirty, nail-bitten fingers and her filthy dress. She remembers how Astra talked about dying, like it was no big deal, how it would happen to all of them. Not only has Kimmy broken all of her mother's rules, now she's put Stacy's life in Astra's hands. She must get her away from the germs. She must get her back in her crib where she'll be safe again.

Astra smiles as if nothing in the world is wrong. "Want to hold her?" she asks.

Kimmy opens and closes her mouth like a fish. Because even though she should be screaming for her mother, Astra is right. What she really wants is to hold her sister, and she's overcome with jealousy that Astra has had the first chance. "I don't know how. I've never done it," she admits. The springs in her mattress squeak as she positions herself at Astra's side.

"Put your arms out like you're trying to catch a ball," Astra explains.

"How do you know this stuff?"

"I raise goats."

Stacy's eyes flick open once she's settled on Kimmy's lap, and she gazes straight up at her big sister. Kimmy tenses. *Is she going to cry?* No. She only gurgles. Her skin is pale and delicate. Kimmy bends down and kisses her forehead.

For the first time ever. She presses her cheek to Stacy's velvety soft skin and breathes in. Powder, laundry soap, their mother's shampoo. This is real magic. It hits her with such force: Stacy is *her* sister. And she will be for each and every day of her whole life. Kimmy feels crushed with luck. And no, she doesn't want to take Stacy back to the crib just yet. She wants to hold her a little longer, because who knows when she'll be allowed another chance.

Astra gets up from the bed and takes the doctor kit down from the shelf. "We should make sure her body is working properly. We can feed her too." She pulls out a grimy-looking bottle from a canvas bag that she left by the window, and Kimmy understands that this has been Astra's plan all along.

"She's not hungry," she says quickly.

"You're right. Not yet," Astra agrees. "Why don't you bring her here."

She kneels on the carpet, and Kimmy lays Stacy on the ground between them. Astra carefully unsnaps Stacy's purple pajamas, then pulls the diaper from her bum. Her sister is laughing, waving her arms and legs, arching her back. Kimmy grins. If her room was cursed before, it's all better now. It only took having Stacy in here to cure it. To fill it with joy.

The girls take turns looking into the baby's belly button with a magnifying glass. They listen to her heart, hit her dimpled knees gently with the wooden hammer, count the rolls cascading down her thighs. When Kimmy tickles Stacy's hips, her laugh is hard and unstoppable.

"Okay, it's time to feed her," Astra says, taking the bottle from the floor and pushing it against Stacy's mouth. Stacy keeps her lips sealed and turns her head away.

"Where did you get that?" Kimmy asks.

"The barn," Astra answers firmly. "I use it on the animals."

"Is it formula?"

"What's that?"

"It's what you feed babies."

"Well, I was raised on goat's milk. It will be fine for her too," Astra says, trying again to shove the nipple between Stacy's lips.

Kimmy knows she must stop Astra. She knows that what's in the bottle could make her sister sick. And she needs to tell Astra they'll never be sisters, that she'll never move into the cabin on Celestial Farm, and that she thinks her mother should meet Raymond before they play again— but before she gathers up the nerve, a shriek comes from the next room. It sounds inhuman. A pitch of pure terror. Because of course, in the rush, Kimmy had forgotten to close Stacy's bedroom door and now she's been discovered missing. Her mother's worst fears have come true, and it's all her fault. Her mother had been right to protect the baby from Kimmy. To make all these rules, to be strict, because look at what she's done!

Stacy begins to howl along with their mother, and their cries squeeze painfully at Kimmy's temples. Desperate to fix what she's done, she lifts her sister off the floor and holds her securely, away from Astra, who has already jumped to her feet, the dirty bottle clutched in her fist.

Kimmy bends over Stacy's tiny worried face. "Shh, my love," she says, and at the sound of her big sister's voice, Stacy's cries quiet a little. She reaches up and grabs a lock of Kimmy's hair in her clammy fist.

There's a shout and Kimmy's bedroom door flies open and the desk chair hits the wall—it doesn't slow their mother in the least. Of course it doesn't, nothing could. Their mother might be sad, but she's fierce too.

As she dashes across the room towards them, Kimmy finds herself clinging to her sister even tighter. She bends down and kisses Stacy's forehead protectively.

Seeing this, their mother stops short. "What are you doing?" she cries, staring down at Kimmy in bafflement. "Why is the baby out of her crib? I don't understand what's happening," she adds, dropping to her knees.

The open window lets in the soft summer breeze, which is full of the aroma of dust and hay. And off in the distance, already far, far away, Astra is sprinting across the fields. And Kimmy is so glad she's gone. Because Astra doesn't know anything at all. She thinks kids can survive on their own just because that's what she has to do. She thinks rules are "oppressive," whatever that means. And that some hunk of metal can know anything about love. Kimmy is loved; it might not always feel good, but she has proof of it every day.

"I'm just holding her, that's all," she says, as tears start to run down her cheeks. "I need her to love me as much as she loves you. And I think she does, Mommy. I really think she does. You just haven't given us a chance."

CLODAGH

CLODAGH DRIVES FAST along the August-hot gravel road, hurricanes of dust swirling into the ditch behind her van. The passenger seat is piled to the ceiling with bags, and the floor is cluttered with puzzles, records, cast-iron pans, and a basket of mismatched kitchenware, the cutlery clattering on and on over the rough road like cymbals on a never-ending track of music.

Though she's moved countless times, she is still anxious. Being a mother is hard when you're dragging your kids to another new place. When you're terrified and broke and your safety depends on who you meet when you get there. And this van is running on borrowed time too, weary under the weight of their belongings. Any minute it could simply die on the side of the road, subjecting them to the mercy of the first man she manages to flag down for help.

Since leaving her last foster home at sixteen, Clodagh has always had a van like this one: used Chevrolets big enough to sleep in or to haul off everything they own at a moment's notice. She's had them in rust-pocked white, wine, navy, steel grey, and army green with wood panelling. She likes to name them: Bob, Charlie, Winona, and Grandpa—after her own, who raised her until she was twelve. But this van, Janice, is one stall away from the scrapyard, and every hour Clodagh has to pop the hood, hang her face over the oven-hot engine, and pour water into the steaming radiator. Now on the back roads, the temperature gauge is reading red again and the water jug is empty. She pats the dusty dash. "Come on, Janice," she says. "Don't you dare give up on us."

She looks over her shoulder into the back, which is brimming with boxes, framed paintings, and garbage bags of clothes. Her eight-year-old daughter, Sativa, has slipped from her seat and is asleep on the floor with the cat, her sweaty orange hair plastered across her face like tea-stained lace. Next, Clodagh checks the side-view mirror and spots Freedom's car following closely behind. She loosens her grip on the steering wheel. *It's okay. As long as I've got my kids with me,* she thinks, *I have everything I need.*

For the past three years, Clodagh and her two children have lived in Nelson, B.C., with a man with long red hair and work-hard hands. Dale made his living growing weed in his barn, and he kept a shotgun slung over his shoulder at all times, claiming it was for the thieves who were always trying to steal his shit, though Clodagh never saw anyone suspicious nosing around. If she's honest, she never really liked Dale, but she ignored his rages and his conspiracy theories because Freedom was enrolled in the local high school, and Sativa loved Caterpillar—Dale's auburn tabby—and the house reminded Clodagh of her grandfather's, with its front porch and sturdy plaster walls. She stayed because she'd already moved twenty times since having Freedom, and she was exhausted. They'd lived in attics, in communes, in damp teepees, in one-room cabins on the Gulf Islands, on creaking sailboats, in women's shelters, and even once in a converted train car that a professor of neuroscience installed in his backyard in Vancouver. But none of those places ever truly fit or felt safe, so she'd decided to stay in Nelson with a man she didn't love, because what was the difference, really? She was too tired to care about romance or love or finding the right guy anymore. And Dale wasn't terrible. He was only nasty to her when he was in one of his "moods." Besides, she'd long ago convinced herself that her kids wouldn't be affected. That they couldn't see it. That they'd never know.

But then last night, when the mewing of Caterpillar's new kittens kept Dale from falling asleep, he got out of bed, woke Sativa, and made her watch as he plucked their impossibly soft bodies from the cardboard box, tossing them in a pillowcase and tying it shut with a knot. Clodagh said nothing as Dale dragged her daughter outside, kicking and screaming down the rotten front steps, across the mossy yard, and knee-deep into the glistening duckweed-covered pond, where he submerged the pillowcase until the kittens stilled. That's when—fists clenched, fingernails cutting into her palms—Clodagh finally woke from her despondency. *You stupid woman*, she thought. *You weak woman. You're going to fuck them right up if you don't put your head on straight.*

She looked back at the house, dark, curtains drawn, and then again at her daughter weeping and shivering in the water. She had to get them out. Now. Yet with no money, no job, and barely anything to offer anyone, there was only one place she could think of to go.

So here she is, on the road again, plumes of smoke leaking from the hood and funnelling over the windshield, as the van struggles over the last hill and breaks into the valley. The countryside is mostly as she remembers: the low, rugged mountains to the west; the smell of pine; glimpses of the Willow River, jet black. She stops before the wooden slat gate, the Farm's name faded but still hanging on the arch overhead.

When Freedom pulls up beside her, Clodagh climbs out and walks barefoot to his open window. "Well? Do you remember it now?" she asks, poking her head inside. The back of his car is full too, although he's far more organized than she is. Books in careful piles on the floor. Two laundry baskets of folded clothes and stacks of shoeboxes arranged on the seats.

"I was five when we were last here. Stop trying to get me to remember this place," he says.

"All right, fine. I only thought the view might trigger something, and then you'd feel better about being here."

He eyes her suspiciously. "I feel fine, Clo. I didn't just leave my boyfriend. How do you feel?"

"Great, it was overdue," she chirps, though she's not being entirely honest. Is she scared? Absolutely. Excited? Possibly. But did she act too hastily? Dale had supported them, that much was true. And isn't she too old for all this hunting and searching and longing for a home? She's in her mid-thirties now, for fuck's sakes, and her most valuable possession is a worthless van.

Clodagh raises her hands to the sky and stretches, releasing the tension in her back, her bracelets tinkling on her wrists, while Freedom presses play on the stereo and then picks nervously at the steering wheel. His ash-blond hair, which Clodagh kept long and braided down his back when he was little, is now short and hidden under his hat. She should probably stop comparing him to his younger self; he's basically a man already. But sometimes, when he looks at her, he is six all over again: chubby, devilish, and dependent. It's only when he notices her watching that he stiffens, becomes unreachable, turns into a stranger, and she has to stand up tall and breathe deep to keep from crying. Freedom might be the only person left in this world who can hurt her.

She dares another brief glance at him, and then returns her gaze to the fields on the other side of the gate, where the hay is overgrown, scattered with bramble and thistle. "It's possible you'd love it here if you give it a chance, Free," she says.

"What did you say?" he calls over his speakers, which are now thudding with bass.

Clodagh leans in the window again. "You should give this place a chance, is all I'm saying."

"Why? I'll be gone in less than a week."

"Or you could stay?"

"Come on, Clo. Stop it."

"What do they call it? A gap year?"

"When people do that they usually go to Thailand or Goa, not some shitty hippy farm in the middle of nowhere with their mother." Freedom licks a finger and rubs off a smear of dirt from the car door.

"You're right. What do I know."

"I promised to help you and Sativa get settled. You promised you wouldn't keep pushing for more."

"I'm not pushing," Clodagh says, though of course she is, and she'll keep doing so until she runs out of time. Because she needs him. Because it's been the two of them since she was a child herself. Because she's worried that once he's gone he won't ever come back.

At the Encampment, Clodagh pulls into a patch of sun-dappled shade under a silver birch, smoke wafting from the engine. She turns the van off and loosens her grip on the steering wheel, as doubt wraps around her throat.

Years back, there'd been much talk at Celestial of constructing a big, fantastical house for the commune workers. They'd start by building a river-stone oven in the heart, one that they could use in the winter for central heat and all year round for bread baking. Then they'd build out in a circular pattern, room upon room, towers, nooks, dorms, bunks, all the woodwork original and intricate. In the evenings, when the workers gathered around the fire, Raymond sketched construction plans in the dirt with his boot heel while they sat, rapt. Watching, listening, believing. Their irises tracking his every move.

"Here's where the front door will stand. And there," he said, gesturing enthusiastically, "that's where the pantry will be, and the music room, and the dining hall. I envision the kitchen, here, looking off the cliff. You'll all be warm and sheltered. And you won't have to worry about rent cheques or any of that bullshit. Your kids won't be raised by the system, this land will do that for you!"

"Hear, hear," the workers cried in unison.

So she'd hoped to find Celestial still thriving. Instead, the Encampment hasn't changed and appears nearly abandoned. There's no fireplace, no house, no community of like-minded people waiting to welcome them. Boxes of beer bottles and whiskey jugs are stacked by the dining table, and worn tires and garbage bags are heaped everywhere. Beside the flat-black school bus, Raymond's little cabin stands in the shade, bursting with painful memories. And at the edge of the forest sits the yurt that Clodagh and Freedom called home for two summers, although now the canvas is shredded and stained with continents of mould.

"Fuck," she says under her breath, as Freedom pulls up beside the van again. "Fuck. Fuck. Fuck."

"Is this it, Mama? Is this our new home?" Sativa asks, waking to her mother's swearing.

"I don't know," she manages to say, trying her best to sound unfazed. "Let's get out and see."

They shut Caterpillar inside the van, and Clodagh tells Sativa to stick close by. She doesn't want Raymond to catch them nosing around or doing anything that might get their reacquaintance started on the wrong foot, because she'll need a few days to rest and to take Janice to the mechanic before they can go. They won't stay any longer than that. She'd been wrong to come.

Ten minutes pass before she hears someone coming up the path. Then there's the sound of Raymond whistling, crisp and clear, the same tune as always. *Tra-la-la-traaa.*

"Well, shit," he says, voice booming, once he breaks into the clearing, a young woman half hiding behind him. Raymond is still bearded and very skinny, loose linen pants tied around his hips, plaid shirt left unbuttoned, his torso bare. He pulls the girl into view, and puts his hands on her shoulders. "Do you see what I see?" he asks, giving her a slight shake. "Is there a woman standing there, or is that my imagination?"

"No, she's real," says the girl, who appears to be around fifteen. Her hair is waist-long, nearly black, and parted clean down the middle as if she'd copied the style from the back of a folk record. She's wearing a paisley skirt that Clodagh recognizes as one she herself used to choose from the communal closet.

"You're just what I needed today. Just exactly what I needed!" Raymond's eyes are twinkling, as intense as ever. He weaves his way through the refuse, his arms open wide. "I asked for this, Clodagh. I swear, I woke up this morning and said, 'Something's got to change. Something's got to give.' Didn't I say that, Astra?" he calls back over his shoulder.

"Yeah, you said that," the girl agrees, trailing after him.

Clodagh's muscles tense. His daughter, of course. Dark, tall, and thin, exactly like him; no trace of her round, hazel-eyed mother in her at all. It's not that Clodagh had forgotten Astra—how could she? But for some reason she'd blocked her out, assumed there was no way she'd be living here still. That at some point, some kind soul would have swooped in and taken her off Raymond's hands. Clodagh is unsure if she's pleased or horrified to see her again: all knees and bones and baggage.

Once in reach, Raymond pulls Clodagh into an embrace. His stench is multilayered and thick: wood, loam, sweat-salt, and goat milk. The hairs on his chest prickle her cheek, and— never a fan of men hugging her too long—she gently eases him off and takes a step back.

"You should check out the gardens, Clodagh. It's a disaster down there. We're at least a month behind with the weeding. Our runner beans and lettuces are choked in morning glory. The carrots have rust fly again. And I'm getting old. Tell me, how do I look?"

"You look good. Exactly the same," she says, smiling at him in the way he expects. Clodagh knows this man well.

"Well, I'm glad I look 'good,' because I sure can't work like I used to. And the guys we've got up here now, they're shit. No, shit's better. Shit makes things grow. These guys are a waste of food. They should be back by tomorrow, then you'll see for yourself." Raymond shakes his head and a spray of sweat flies from his brow. "What do you think, Astra? Maybe Wesley is all right? Does he pull his weight at least?"

Already, Clodagh can tell that this is their act: Raymond boisterous, the one with things to say; Astra his echo, his shadow. This time his daughter only shrugs in response, twisting a flip-flopped foot in the dirt.

"But Clodagh, people don't just show up here anymore. This is a new era. There aren't many folks like us left kicking around. So give it to me straight." He rubs his callused hands together, the sound like pumice stone over rock. "You help me, I'll help you. What's going on?"

"Okay," she says, scanning the Encampment once more. "Let me try to explain."

Clodagh sleeps fitfully, waking often to the steady whine of mosquitos outside the screen windows. None of her relaxation techniques are working—not counting, or slow breathing, or holding Sativa's limp hand and feeling her pulse. It seems Freedom isn't faring any better at the front of the school bus either, tossing away under the afghan she'd crocheted for him as a baby, on a loveseat much too short for his long legs.

That afternoon, when Raymond said they could make the bus their own, Clodagh didn't have the heart to tell him that now that she'd laid eyes on Celestial again, she didn't plan on staying. Instead, she accepted a beer and watched Freedom and Astra drag out the rotting mattresses and trunks of moth-eaten clothing from the bus and dump them by the rest of the trash in the bush. Afterwards, they scrubbed the grime from the walls and floor, and polished the windows with vinegar. Now Janice is unpacked and they're set up in the bus for absolutely no reason at all.

I'll give us two days, she thinks. *That's enough time to figure out where we'll go next.*

As she tries to empty her mind by focusing on the gentle breeze in the trees, she becomes aware of a new sound: a vehicle. Soon, tires are kicking up rocks on the driveway and then an engine cuts outside. Doors slam. Someone whoops. "Let's get a fire going," a familiar voice shouts.

She listens to the men carrying what must be boxes of food to the kitchen trailer, dropping things, flashlight beams crisscrossing the dark Encampment. Freedom turns over on the loveseat again and Clodagh pulls Sativa close, shushing in her ear to cover the noise.

Someone ignites the firepit with gas, and right away the light flickers across Clodagh's futon. Beers are opened and clinked together, and then the men start to tease one another, talking about some "silly skirt" they met at a bar. It's Wesley's voice that she recognizes. She disliked him even back in the day. All the women did. Now he's the one swearing the most, and his fingers are screeching up the steel strings of a guitar. Always that guitar. Even after all these years, he's still no good at playing it.

"Mama," Sativa whispers beside her. "What's happening?"

"Shh, baby. It's just Raymond's friends. They're harmless," she says, kissing her daughter's fine hair.

Despite the noise, Sativa manages to fall asleep again, but the bus glows bright orange and Clodagh is more awake than ever. Outside the men are growing rowdier, and one of them starts splitting logs with an axe as sparks fly past the bus windows. She can't stop thinking about the dry crunch of the forest and the drought-weary branches hanging over the Encampment, begging to catch. Earlier, as dusk fell, Raymond explained that he still slept down by the river during the summer months, so now Clodagh worries about Astra, all alone in that cabin. Had they woken her too?

Unable to leave it be, Clodagh untangles her body from Sativa, pulls on her dress, and pads past Freedom. As she steps outside, one of the men hollers, "Jesus! Are you a fucking ghost?"

"Not a ghost yet," she replies, keeping her voice level. "I'm worried about this fire, though. I have kids sleeping in there."

"I fight forest fires," says another. This man is sitting on a stump, legs spread wide, a beer hanging between his knees. She notes that his hands are as large as shovels and that he's missing a forefinger.

"You *used* to fight fires," interrupts the first man. "Then you got fired for being a drunk," he adds with a sharp laugh.

These guys are all dressed the same: gumboots, soiled jeans, work shirts torn through at the elbows. Clodagh wants to be calm, to show that she's chill, but their roughness reminds her of Dale, and it's too soon to deal with more men like him.

"I worked in the bush most my life. This one here is fine," the firefighter says, getting up from his stump and throwing on two more logs to prove his point. Sparks funnel up into the night sky and Clodagh's skin prickles.

"Hello, Wesley," she says coolly, turning her attention to the man with the guitar nestled in his lap. "Do you remember me?"

"Nope," he answers, scratching at his sparse beard and looking sidelong at his friends.

"Clodagh," she reminds him.

"Right, maybe," he mutters.

"I don't want to be a nag, but can you ask your friends to put this out and keep it down? Do me this favour, for old times' sake?"

Wesley says nothing as the firefighter gets to his feet again, swaying. "You know, you remind me of my ex-wife. She was a bossy, bossy bitch."

"Well, *I* don't think it's too much to ask that the forest doesn't burn down around us," Clodagh adds. She hears the bus door open and then her son is at her side.

"Can you just put it out, guys? It's really dry out, and that's a pretty big fire," Freedom says.

"Jesus," the firefighter finally says, falling back onto the stump and taking another swig of his beer. "You're all a bunch of killjoys, aren't you? If it's such a big deal, you do it. I ain't dousing my masterpiece for no reason."

Freedom squeezes her hand. "I'll take care of it, Clo, go back to bed."

"Thank you," she says.

Freedom crosses the Encampment to fetch water, and Clodagh turns back towards the bus right as Wesley lets out a long, slow whistle of appreciation. Following his gaze, she finds Astra spying on them from the shadows.

"Well, hello darling," Wesley says, and then all three men burst into laughter.

"We sure missed you, little lady," the firefighter calls out. "There isn't a girl in the big city as good-looking as you!"

Clodagh marches over to Astra and drags her behind the bus and out of sight. This is as close as they've been since she returned to Celestial, and she's sorry to see that, yes, even in the firelight, the scars on Astra's face are clear as day.

"I'm so sorry, sweetheart," she says.

"Why? What's the problem?" Astra asks, blinking lazily and fiddling with a leather pouch that's hanging by a string from her neck.

"Those men shouldn't think they can talk to you like that." Then, unable to help herself, she tucks a piece of Astra's hair behind her ear. "You can tell me. Do they make you uncomfortable? When they pulled up, right away I was worried about you over there in that cabin all alone."

Astra makes a face and recoils from Clodagh's touch. "Why would they make me uncomfortable? They're my friends."

Some friends, Clodagh thinks. "Well, I don't think you should be in there by yourself. Not at all. You're more than welcome to stay with us on the bus."

"There's no room for me in there," the girl says, scoffing. "But Freedom and Sativa can sleep in the cabin if they want. We used to call it the 'Kids' House.' No adults allowed. We just haven't had anyone up here in a long time."

With this, Clodagh starts to recognize the little girl she once knew so well. Her curious near-black eyes. Her yellow-olive skin. Her serious expression. Always such a fierce creature. "That's right," Clodagh says, remembering.

"Unfortunately, Sativa's too young for that. She's still pretty attached to her mama."

Astra drops her gaze to her feet. "What about Freedom?"

Clodagh glances over at her son, now lugging buckets of water from the kitchen to the firepit, leaving a trail of water in the dirt.

"Actually, it's okay. I'll go ask him myself," Astra says, spinning on her heel and heading his way.

Back in bed, Clodagh cuddles up to Sativa and listens to her son put out the fire. The men are still talking, but quieter now. The water hits the flames with a hiss, and the bus fills with the stink of char and steam.

After, Freedom comes into the bus to grab his pillow and blanket. "Clo," he whispers. "Astra says there's space for me to crash in the cabin. This couch is too short, I can't sleep."

Although she wants her son as close as possible during the few days they have left together, Clodagh has no energy to fight this. "All right," she says, resting her head back on the pillow. "Night, night, baby."

"Night, Clo."

The following morning, Clodagh decides to clean up before anyone else is awake. She can't help but imagine what Gloria would think to find her daughter being raised in such a dump, and so she plans to honour her memory by giving Celestial a little tender love and care while she's here. She lights the crusty propane stove to heat water, and Sativa helps her wash the pots and pans, scrape the counters, and sweep mouse turds out of the aluminum door. Next, they begin clearing up the outdoor dining room, loading the empties into a dented wheelbarrow and bringing them to the van, filling it up with foul bottles full of cigarette butts that she will return in town when she goes to find a mechanic. When Clodagh hauls the broken tools and bags of trash away, Sativa tugs on her sleeve and starts to complain, so they string their old woven hammock between two sturdy trees, and the girl settles in with a book.

Eventually, Astra emerges alone from the cabin and Clodagh follows her into the kitchen. "Did you guys sleep okay after all that racket?" she asks.

Astra shoots her a guarded look. "Yeah, but Freedom snores super loud."

"That's true, he does," Clodagh says, while wondering just how long it's been since Astra's spent any time with a woman. She's clearly uncomfortable, clearly a girl raised by men.

Astra pulls a box of potatoes from a cupboard and takes up a knife. "I suppose I should be making you guys breakfast too?" she asks.

"That'd be great, thank you," Clodagh says. Then, remembering how the girl had done all the work the evening before and wanting to establish a bond, she adds, "Do you always do the cooking for the Farm?"

"Yeah. It's sort of my job."

Clodagh leans against the counter. "Doris used to make sure the cooking and cleaning was split between everyone, men and woman equally. It looks like Raymond didn't keep up with that."

"I don't mind. He says cooking is a political act. I only use whatever we can't sell. We're really anti-waste here. In the city, people won't buy a vegetable if it has the tiniest scab or imperfection. It's so ridiculous."

"I'm sure he appreciates you trying so hard."

"Doubt he really notices. He'd forget about eating altogether if I didn't put something down in front of him. I have
to sort of keep track of him."

This makes Clodagh cringe. Raymond might consider
himself progressive, but here is his daughter, doing all the
"women's work," serving both him and his friends. She can
picture him shovelling up Astra's feasts while she watches,
wondering what he thinks, taking note, planning the meals for
the next day. He's never seen much past his own two hands.

Clodagh looks out at Sativa swinging in the hammock.
"How is it growing up here anyways? Do you like it?"

"Of course. Why wouldn't I?" Astra says. The potatoes are
browning in the pan now, and she is breaking up a block of
tofu in a bowl. She stirs in sea salt and red pepper flakes.

"Do you have friends nearby, or maybe in Lunn?"

"I did before. The neighbours had a girl my age, but she
moved years ago. I had a dog too, but then it died."

"Oh, God. I'm sorry. How did it die?"

"Raymond had to shoot it. It caught rabies from a coyote
or a bat or something."

"You couldn't take it to the vet?"

Astra ignores the question and pours the tofu scramble
into a pot. But Clodagh is determined to get to know this girl,
even if she intends on making it difficult. Gloria would want
Clodagh to try. "Did your dad tell you that I was really close
with your mother before she had you? That I was right there
in the cabin when you were born?"

The girl shrugs. "And then you left. Just like the rest of
them. None of you old-school workers were ever tough
enough for Celestial."

"Some of us were pretty tough. Your mom was, that's for sure."

Astra snorts. "Do you know how cold it gets here in the winter? No one can take it."

"I *do* know, actually. I was here until February that year," Clodagh says. "And Winter is one of your names, isn't it? Astra Winter Sorrow Brine? Am I remembering that right?"

"I hate my names. They're embarrassing."

"It was your mom who wanted to call you Winter. She wanted that to be your first name. Doris made sure Raymond put it in somewhere."

Astra glares at her again. "You can stop bringing her up. We're not going to be close just because you *knew* her," she says, dropping the spoon on the counter. "And I don't have to like my name, just because she picked it. Raymond is the one raising me."

"I guess that's true," Clodagh says, though really she's thinking: *Oh, Raymond. What have you done? Why did you have to erase her?*

Because this is what bothers Clodagh most: in all the houses, in all the communes, in every goddamn place she's lived, she's met girls exactly like Astra, and women just like herself. Invisible, doing all the hard labour: the cooking and cleaning and the raising of children, often without a cent to their name or a home to call their own. Meanwhile, the men sit around discussing liberation and free love and what a glorious new world they are creating, because now everyone can truly be "free" if they have the balls for it. And it's such bullshit. Clodagh has met hundreds of free men over the years, but she can't say she's ever met a free woman.

She places a hand under Astra's jaw, runs her thumb over the scars. They are rubbery, vicious, so red they still look sore. Clodagh isn't cold at all, and yet she shivers.

"What are you doing," Astra snaps, jerking her head away. "Why do you keep touching me?"

"I'm sorry. I'll try to stop," Clodagh says. "But you know, you should tell Raymond when those guys talk to you like they did last night. This is your home. It's important you feel safe. You're a child."

The girl turns her black eyes on Clodagh. "I told you it was *fine*. What you should do is stop talking about stuff you don't know anything about. You don't even belong here."

"And why is that, Astra?"

"Because I said you don't."

It happened the summer Freedom turned five, when Doris and her girlfriend—desperate to recruit more women—had convinced Clodagh to come back and give the Farm one more try. Astra was only two then. It was late August, early evening, the air humming with dragonflies, and all the workers were either swimming in the river or lazing nude on the bank. Clodagh was letting the current rush over her flesh and sweep the day's sweat from her hair, while the children entertained themselves by ducking in and out of the twilit grasses. No one spoke, and the silence felt powerful, spiritual even, like an accomplishment of some kind, as the sun slowly fell behind the mountains. That's when, through the water, Clodagh heard Freedom screaming.

She remembers the dry hay slicing her bare legs as they ran to find the children, and thorns lodging in the soles of her pounding feet. The kids were so small, not even as tall as the grass, and the field was endless, an impossible thing to make sense of. But then their luck changed, and at the sight of Raymond—growling, yelling, and running right at it—the cougar loosened its jaws, dropping Astra before it fled towards the sage and shale that staggered up the ridge. And there she was at their feet: silent, bleeding, limp as a doll.

While the workers surrounded Astra, Freedom stood with them, large sobs racking his ribs, but there were no tears on his face. Just that horrible noise coming out of him. Clodagh hated that he was crying in such an intense and unnerving way. She hated what it meant, and what it said about her as a mother. She remembers looking at his contorted face and wishing they'd found the children dead instead. Because she was only twenty-two, and life would be so much easier if she didn't have to be responsible for anyone anymore, if she could go back to the river and let it wash her out to sea.

Raymond, needing something to stop Astra's bleeding, noticed Freedom was the only one wearing clothes, and that's when everything got worse. Clodagh was rough as she tried to rip the T-shirt off her son's shaking body. And he fought her: pinning his thin arms to his sides, howling the whole time. So she slapped him. She needed to stop that wretched noise. She needed him to stop being so stupid and defiant and making her life so difficult. But he refused to be untangled from his clothes, and so she hit him again. On his shoulders. On his face. Across the back of his head. She hit him until Doris shoved her away and she fell back in the trampled, bloody grass.

Then as Doris kissed Freedom's forehead, touching his face lightly, Clodagh saw this gentleness change him. He put his hands up and allowed Doris to carefully tug the shirt over his head. And that's when it struck her. These children would pay the price for this life at Celestial. They would pay for their parents' experiments and mistakes, for all their stupid dreams. Because Raymond was wrong. This land wasn't all good and peaceful, it couldn't save them or erase the past, and it definitely couldn't protect their children. And that's the day the vision for Celestial first began to tatter and fray. There in that field, with Raymond binding up his daughter's face under that sky.

Soon after that the workers started to leave, one by one. Some moved back to the city. Some moved home. Some who promised to return to the Farm the following summer made new plans. And Clodagh did the same. She left, vowing to become a better mother, to be gentler to her son, to always put him first. She left, vowing to never set foot on this godforsaken land again. And what happened to that moment of clarity and strength? Because look, she'd come back, hadn't she? She was still stupid enough to think it might work out.

On their fourth morning at the Farm, while Astra and Freedom tend the hothouse plants in the geodesic greenhouse, Clodagh works alongside Raymond on the western slope, covering the carrot beds with black plastic in an attempt to kill the rust fly. Though she knows she can't stay at the Farm, she can't help but love the smell of it here. The gardens, the bracken, the goat manure, the rich soil, and dust. Every so often she pauses, just to appreciate the beating of her heart or to adore the wisps of cloud overhead. After all those wasted years with Dale, she is thankful for this respite, for this chance to wake up again.

At noon, the kids fill a basket with beans, zucchini, and chard, selecting the ingredients from the garden's bounty, and Astra prepares their lunch with a pocket knife under the willow. Afterwards, Wesley and his friends head to town in the truck, and Sativa lies down on a wool blanket under the swaying branches.

Leaning her work-weary back against the tree, Clodagh watches the teenagers, pressed shoulder to shoulder as they squat on the riverbank, scrubbing the bowls clean. Astra smacks Freedom's hand, splashes him, flips her hair—but she isn't the only one flirting. When she rips off Freedom's hat and pulls it low over her brow, he grabs for her waist and then runs after her up the path, yelling her name the whole way.

"Astra tells me Free has big plans," Raymond says, as he takes a seat beside Clodagh and hands her a mug of water.

"Yes, he does." She takes a long sip and then adds, "I'm kind of in shock, though. In a few days my kid is starting university! He's studying finance, if you can believe it."

"Well, they're bound to move along at some point."

"Yeah, but for more school? I think his teachers really pressured him. They were always going on about his potential and claiming he was a genius or something."

"No such thing as a genius."

"Exactly," Clodagh says, fiddling with one of her bracelets. "Did you know that Freedom was his school valedictorian? When he gave his speech, it was like listening to a stranger. All he talked about was achievement and success. And come on, is that how a seventeen-year-old kid should think? But the whole auditorium got to their feet when he finished." Clodagh pulls her hair back behind her shoulders, watches a breeze rustle the branches overhead. "He keeps saying most parents would be proud. And he's right. But I'm not a normal parent. And I *hate* how materialistic he is. Sure, his childhood was a little all over the place and kind of messy, and I get that he doesn't want to be poor like me. Fine. But why can't he see that money and a fancy job won't fix anything or make him happy? Yet that's what he says he wants. A 'conventional' life he calls it."

"His childhood was an adventure," Raymond cuts in. "One day he'll recognize that. Don't be so hard on yourself."

She smiles briefly. "I'm not so sure he will. And if I'm honest, I wish he'd change his mind and stay with me a little longer. I'm not ready to lose him."

Raymond pulls a toothpick from his pocket and grips it in his teeth. "So," he says, "does that mean you've come to a decision? Are you going to stick around and be my right-hand woman this time?"

"Oh, I don't know. What ever happened to Doris? Wasn't that her job?"

"She comes around here and there, but I'm in the market for someone new. Someone willing to work their ass off." He chuckles softly.

Clodagh looks at the river—sun-splashed, silver, and swift—and then down at Sativa, asleep, arms hugging her bony legs to her chest. "It's hard to make such big decisions for your kids. I want her happy, that's all."

"Don't worry about her," he says. "Kids can survive anything. They're tough as nails. Whenever Astra's all worked up, I tell her, 'You're the star of the cosmos, ruler of the skies!' You should see her face when I say that. I swear she lights right up. Astra is the most capable person I know."

Oh, I wish I'd been born a man, Clodagh thinks. *To have that sort of confidence.* "You really think that's all it takes?"

Raymond grins. "Yup. I sure don't see any evidence otherwise."

Clodagh is busy weeding when Sativa runs up, a handprint of raspberry juice smeared across her cheek.

"Free and Astra are kissing," her daughter says.

Clodagh stands and rubs her lower back. The windows of the greenhouse glint in the sun. It's hot, but there are ominous clouds building above the hills, and an electric tightness hangs in the air. "Were you spying on them?" she asks.

"No." Sativa's smile is coy. "Or maybe I was, a bit."

"Well, I suppose they're old enough to decide that sort of thing on their own," Clodagh says.

"Am I old enough to kiss someone?"

"Absolutely not. You have years to go, baby," she says quickly, because just the thought turns her stomach to knots.

Later, even though the sun is choked behind cloud, she takes Sativa down to the river and teaches her to hang in the centre of an old inner tube. They push off the bank and kick out into the lazy current. Under the water, their treading limbs look like ribbons: graceful, silky, and smooth.

Eventually the older kids wander over, hand in hand. Today Astra's hair is brushed into a high ponytail, she's in very short cut-offs, and she has one of Freedom's white shirts knotted at her belly button. No longer wearing cast-off hippy garb, she looks like one of the girls from Freedom's school; a bit grungier maybe, with no makeup, legs unshaven, but similar enough.

"It's nice in here, Freedom. Why don't you come swim with us?" Clodagh says, eager to spend some time with her son. "You should hang out with your sister a bit too."

"Maybe later. We're going into town now," he says.

"Really? What's in town?" Clodagh asks.

"Astra wants some nail polish and we're going to vacuum the car. I want it to look good if I go," Freedom answers.

If, Clodagh notes, not *when*.

As the teenagers disappear up the trail, a roll of thunder cracks above. The clouds split and rain sweeps over the parched fields with a religious hush. The downpour crosses the river, and drops the size of nickels bounce off the surface, littering it with bubbles and froth.

Clodagh pulls Sativa to the shore and they run naked up the steaming path to the bus, clothes clutched to their chests. Inside, with the rain pelting heavy on the metal roof, they flop onto the futon to catch their breath.

"I love it here, Mama," Sativa says. "This bus is way better than our old house. It's cozy. And I love the sound of the rain too. Don't you think it sounds like people clapping?"

Clodagh remembers the standing ovation and cheers in the theatre when Freedom gave his speech. She hadn't been completely honest with Raymond—or with her son for that matter. That day, sitting on one of those hard metal chairs, watching him talk onstage, she *had* been proud of him. More proud than she ever thought possible.

"You're right. It does sound like applause," she says softly, her voice nearly drowned out by the noise.

Sativa sits up as Caterpillar jumps onto the bed and starts licking her muddy legs. "Mama," she says, "you aren't listening. I'm saying I want to stay here! I like Celestial."

It takes effort for Clodagh to hold back her tears. "I *am* listening. I just haven't figured out what's best for us. I need more time."

"Well, I want to stay, and we each get a vote," Sativa says, falling back on the pillows again.

Clodagh sighs. "I know, baby. You're right. You get a vote too."

When Clodagh wakes, it's to the bus roof banging as it expands in the heat. She pulls on her sandals and heads for the outhouse. On her way back, she spies Wesley through a thicket of alder near the yurt. Over the past few days, he and his friends haven't warmed to her at all. They ignore her when she talks, and every night they light a fire, stoking it higher and higher, as if agitating her is a game. Now, as she draws closer, she tries to come up with something civil to say, something to get this day started with a little less animosity between them.

She's about to call out and say hello, when she realizes Wesley is not alone. Astra is with him. He has her pinned up against the exterior wall of the yurt. One strong forearm across her chest. His other hand somewhere else, somewhere Clodagh can't see.

She watches as he pushes his face right up close to the girl's, and then he starts whispering madly. And even though Clodagh can't make out what he's saying, she has no problem hearing the hiss in his words and the spit in his mouth. Astra's face is flushed, and her eyes are pinched shut.

"Hey," Clodagh finally yells. "What the hell are you doing?"

"Not you again," Wesley says, letting the girl go and holding his palms up as if to prove his innocence.

Astra adjusts her clothes as she starts to run, her black hair hanging in her face, her shoulders crumpled forward. She doesn't even look up as she pushes past Clodagh on the path.

By the time Clodagh reaches Wesley, her whole body is vibrating. It's possible all the anger she's been bottling up for years is about to erupt. She wishes she could hit this man who is laughing nervously now as his eyes dart around. She wishes she could beat on him until she feels calm. Until she's sure everyone she loves is safe.

"What the fuck were you doing?" she shouts.

"Oh Jesus. Stay out of my business, will you," he says, wiping the back of his hand across his pathetic beard. "You act like you own this place."

"Wesley. You've known Astra since she was a baby."

"I know how long I've known her," he grumbles. "And I know her better than you do. She's not some little girl. She's not all that innocent."

Back in the Encampment, Clodagh finds Freedom and Raymond sitting at the dining table, and Astra standing beside her father, asking, "Should we get to work? I'm ready."

"Soon enough." Raymond picks up his coffee and takes a long sip.

"I kind of want to start now," Astra says. "I need to do something, I have all this energy."

Raymond doesn't seem to notice the rasp in her voice or the frantic look in her eyes. "Go ahead then," he says. "Remember who you are, Astra. Child of the cosmos, ruler of the skies. You're in charge of you. I don't get a say."

As Clodagh watches them, she's reminded of what happened in the hospital after the cougar attack, when Doris pulled him aside and offered to take Astra back to Vancouver.

"Why don't I raise her in the city?" she said. "Bring her up to Celestial to visit in the summer? I feel like you're not dealing with this all that well."

Raymond had this dice that jangled around in his pockets with his toothpicks. He used to roll it in the dirt when assigning the workers their daily tasks at the morning meeting, or deciding who would stay in the bus or the yurt, or who got to go into town for supplies. He claimed the randomness of the roll was fate, and all he had to do was throw the dice to reveal it, but Clodagh knew it was just a way for him to avoid making any decisions himself. To her horror, Raymond pulled it out that day and tossed it across the foot of Astra's hospital bed. When it landed, he turned to Doris and said, "Looks like she's supposed to stay with me."

Astra rounds the table and then tugs Freedom's sleeve. "Get up. Let's go for a drive then. I want to get out of here."

"Sure," Freedom says with a clueless grin.

After watching them pull away down the driveway, Clodagh takes a seat across from Raymond. "Something weird is going on," she says. "I just saw Wesley with Astra behind the yurt. He was holding her in this way . . . I don't know, it didn't seem right. She was upset." She glances down at her hands; they're still trembling.

"Oh, don't worry about those two."

"What do you mean, 'those two'? What the hell are you talking about? What did you let him do?"

"I didn't *let* him do anything. Who they like is their business. I can't control them. I can't control her," Raymond says, pushing back from the table and getting to his feet.

"Yes, you can!" Clodagh finds herself nearly shouting. "That's all we have, the tiniest bit of control. Why do you keep refusing to keep an eye on her? Why didn't you learn your lesson years ago?"

"Astra is very capable. She can take care of herself."

"She's not capable yet, Raymond. And you shouldn't tell her she belongs to the cosmos. Because she doesn't. She's *your* kid."

He rounds the table, but once he's beside Clodagh, he stops in his tracks, and his chin falls to his chest.

Clodagh continues, softly now that she can see he's listening. "She told me she doesn't like sleeping alone. That it was better when there were other kids up here, staying with her in the cabin. At first I thought it was normal fear-of-the-dark stuff. But now, after seeing Wesley with her like that, I'm not so sure. Why do you sleep so far away from her? She told me you camp down at the river all summer long. Why do you want her to grow up so fast? It's not good. It will make her vulnerable to all kinds of people. Wesley won't be her only problem."

Raymond slowly sinks to his haunches, then he presses his forehead against Clodagh's hip. On closer inspection, she notices his tangled hair is now mostly grey. She pats his back and sighs.

"What exactly are you doing here, Raymond? What has this place become? I don't think you and Doris wanted this, did you?"

"No," he mumbles. "It's supposed to be good here. That was the whole point. But then everyone gave up on it. Everyone gave up on me."

Clodagh turns her gaze to where Freedom's car was only moments before, wishing more than anything that she hadn't let them go. She doesn't want that girl around her son anymore. He's susceptible to Astra's exact kind of damage. He'll think it's his job to take care of her; Clodagh has cursed him with that.

Next, she glances at Sativa, who is swinging in the hammock and hanging on their every word, and then she turns to Raymond again. "All right, if you want my help, if you want me here, I'll stay, but I have one condition."

He sits back and meets her eyes. "Oh yeah? What's that?"

"You have to tell Wesley and his friends to leave. I won't raise Sativa around people like that. We have to run this place the way you and Doris intended at the beginning, before everything got so complicated."

"Wesley has been at Celestial a long, long time."

"I understand that, but it's him or me."

Raymond shakes his head. "I can't turn people away. I don't have the spine for it."

"Well, you're in luck because I do," she says. "I've been turning people away all my life."

When Freedom and Astra return after lunch, the three men are already gone. Astra disappears into her cabin, and Clodagh, taking her son's hand, explains that it's time for him to pack up too.

"I *am* going."

"No, not in a few days. Right now. Today. I was wrong to make you follow me up here in the first place." She hands him a slip of paper. "Do you remember Doris? This is her address in Vancouver. Raymond says she's always home, and that she'll let you crash with her until your dorm is ready. All you have to do is show up."

"After all your fighting it, you're suddenly okay with me going?"

"I shouldn't have dragged you up here, Freedom. You're right to want to start your own life. It's time. I'll be okay."

He laughs. "You sure about that?"

"I'm sure."

Freedom looks towards the cabin and his face falls. "What about Astra? What will I tell her?"

"Nothing. I'll take care of it."

"I can't just leave without talking to her, Clo."

"Of course you can. You're just kids. You don't owe each other anything. Don't make things more complicated than they need to be."

"We're not *just* kids. Astra needs me, and I need her. We *understand* each other. You don't get it. You always act like you're the only one with stuff going on."

Clodagh laughs and touches his cheek. "Oh, baby. I *do* get it. And it makes sense that you like her so much, of course you do. She's a little like me when I was young. She's a bit helpless, and desperate for someone to take care of her. And you're so good at that. You've been taking care of me your whole life. But I don't want that for you anymore."

Freedom shakes his head, his eyes fixed on the dirt. "No. You're wrong. Astra's not like that with me. Not at all."

"Trust me, Free. She is. And I know that new love can feel like everything when you're in it, but you've only been together for what? A week? She won't mean anything in the long run, you'll see."

Clodagh watches as his eyes fill, a child again in this moment. Her poor son. Always her son. No matter how far away he goes. "Okay," he finally whispers. "Fine. I'll just go."

"Good. And I'll tell her you'll stay in touch, but right now, let's take proper care of you."

"Yeah, do that. Tell her I'll write. Tell her I promise, and that I don't break promises."

"I know you don't, Free."

After Freedom loads up his car and Sativa waves him off, Clodagh stands before the door of Astra's cabin. She's avoided going in all week, but now she steps over the threshold for the first time in years. The room is cavelike and musty-smelling: damp ash and incense. The same old black woodstove, the same kettle, and the same table and chairs. The shelf by the door contains a few empty canning jars, a hardcover volume of *Peter Rabbit*, a torn-up edition of the *Joy of Cooking*, and a lone book on astrology. The rest of the room is bare and dark, as if still in mourning.

She climbs up the ladder and is pleased to find the loft is a bit more like a regular bedroom. Astra's bed is messy, the futon piled with quilts and matted stuffed animals, and the walls are covered in tacked-up clippings from magazines: lipstick advertisements and groups of teen girls laughing.

"Go away," Astra says, her voice muffled by the pillows.

Clodagh pulls herself the rest of the way in, and Astra sits up and scowls. She's rolling something between her fingers.

"What is that?" Clodagh asks, making sure to keep her voice very light.

"A dice. It was Gloria's. Raymond gave it to me," Astra says, briefly holding the silver object in her palm before closing her fist around it.

Clodagh exhales. "I see."

When she was last in this cabin, Raymond sat downstairs with the wailing newborn in his arms, trying to get her to latch on to a bottle of goat's milk, while the snow fell heavily outside. It was only after Doris confirmed Gloria was no longer with them that Raymond took out his dice and began rolling it on the rickety table. In just one day his whole world had changed twice over, and the only question left was, what was he going to do? The room was very quiet, except for the clatter of the dice as it landed on the table again and again and again. It wasn't until the sun crawled through the small windows, and the baby finally grabbed the nipple, that he gave it one last roll. Then, looking at Doris, he said, "What do you think of the name Astra?"

The dice was never Gloria's, but, Clodagh decides, this lie is the least of the girl's problems. Maybe this lie is the perfect gift. The only thing Astra will ever know of her mother, even if it's not true.

"You don't have to worry about the fires or Wesley anymore. I've sorted it all out. Those guys are gone. They aren't coming back. Freedom left too."

Astra sits up straighter. "You sent him away?"

Clodagh gives her a weak smile. "I'm sorry, baby. But he's starting school soon and it's just time for him to go."

"I don't care about Freedom. I'm talking about Wes."

Clodagh drops her hands to her lap. *No, she can't be serious.*

"You don't know anything about him," Astra cries. "He's the only person who's ever nice to me here. He gives me stuff. He talks to me. But then you show up for five minutes and chase him away? Why would you do that?"

Clodagh tries to conjure Gloria. How would she want her daughter guided in this moment? Because Astra is obviously hurting. And she'll need help processing this pain or else she'll weaponize it. Clodagh can see the whole topography of Astra's life ahead: the highs and lows, the stretches of lonely desert, and all that deep, deep ocean where, if she's not careful, she will drown.

"Can I give you some advice, baby?" she eventually says, putting a hand on Astra's calf.

"Please don't." The girl's eyes are two steel pins in the dim light.

"Don't look for the kind of attention Wesley was giving you. Because it's not real. It's not the kind you want or the kind that lasts. Wesley isn't your friend. He isn't even a good person."

"You don't know what the hell you're talking about."

"Sure I do, and you deserve more than that from this life, baby."

"Stop calling me *baby*!" Astra shouts. She kicks Clodagh's hand from her leg. "I want you to go. Get out of my room."

"Okay, I'll give you some space. But Astra, Sativa and I have decided to stay on at Celestial. Your father needs help, so we're here for the long haul. You're going to have to get used to me."

Astra falls back on the bed with a groan. "God. I hate you, you know? I barely know you and already I hate you."

"That's okay," Clodagh says. "I've survived my fair share and I expect I'll even survive that too."

BRENDON

THE GIRL PAUSES under the store's blinking neon sign, the white brilliance of the mall's concourse at her back. There she shuffles her feet and keeps checking over her shoulder, as if hoping someone will come along and save her. She retreats a bit, peers into the neighbouring shops—the Reitmans to her right, and the hair salon to her left—but just when Brendon is positive she's about to take off down the corridor, she surprises him by stepping forward through the security gates.

Usually on weekday mornings there's nothing to do in the store. The teenagers are in school and so the mall is empty apart from the security guards, who cruise by checking on Brendon expecting to find trouble, and the seniors who march circuits around the mall in their runners on doctor's orders, trying to get their heart rates up. And so Brendon hopes that this girl will at least stay and entertain him for a little while.

"Can I help you with anything?" he calls out from behind the till.

The girl shakes her head, but she braves another two steps in.

Street Stylz sells only men's clothing, the kind young guys buy hoping to look like the rappers and pop stars they idolize. Adidas. Dickies. Jordans. The stereo is constantly playing hip hop, the walls are painted with graffiti, and all the furniture in the store—the shelves, the displays, even the seats in the change rooms—is constructed out of corrugated metal. The aesthetic is masculine, cool, and it's not uncommon for Brendon to see women customers hesitate at the entrance. While men can appreciate a hard sell or direct comment, an aggressive approach only encourages a woman to scurry off like a field mouse, so he refrains from saying much until they're at the back wall near the change rooms. If he manages this, fifty per cent of the time he lands a sale.

But this girl is a strange specimen: inspecting the shelves and displays the way one would in a museum with strict rules against touching things. She stops and gazes up in awe at the chrome mannequins in their brand-name underwear, hanging from the walls like chiselled gods. She is out of place here, wearing those gumboots and a canvas hiking pack, her purple down jacket stained at the cuffs. It crosses Brendon's mind that she might be homeless and only hanging out in the mall to get warm. Regardless, once she reaches the back corner of the store he pulls out one of his most trusted lines.

"So," he says, "are you shopping for a boyfriend?"

Missing the joke, the girl apologizes and explains that she doesn't have one before disappearing behind a rack of socks. Amused, Brendon busies himself behind the counter with some papers, leaving the girl to circle the store once more. This is another of his sales tactics: acting preoccupied allows female shoppers to relax a little. It's best if they don't feel like they're being observed.

When she passes the counter again, he notices a sheet of paper hanging from her fingers for the first time. *Ah!* he thinks. *Even better.*

"Can I see that?" he asks.

"No. It's okay," she replies, hiding it behind her back.

"Why? Isn't it a resumé? Don't you need to hand them out to get a job?"

"You only sell men's stuff though, and I'm not a man," she says, boldly meeting his eyes. "I'm gonna go next door."

"To Reitmans? No, don't do that. You'll die in there."

"Why would I die?"

"Boredom. And men love buying clothes from a girl. There's a good chance I'll even hire you if I like you," he says. Because it's true: female staff have always helped with the sales numbers, and he could actually use someone else.

Shyly, she passes him the crinkled resumé. Then, once he has it in his possession, he lets it drift to the counter. "On second thought, I don't even need to read it. I already know everything about you."

She frowns. Her face is sharp-featured and her black eyes are wide-spaced, like Bambi's. She's pretty, despite the fact she isn't wearing any makeup, and she has some nasty facial scarring that screws up the left side of her mouth.

"Oh yeah? What do you know about me?" she asks, shrugging off her pack and placing it at her feet. Brendon spots a sleeping bag poking out from under the top flap.

"Well," he says, taking on a fatherly tone, "you don't have a job, a boyfriend, or a home." He still hasn't smiled at her.

Girls will lean in closer if they think you're disapproving; they're always eager to change your mind.

"Are you a psychic or something?" she asks.

He points to her overstuffed pack. "You're an open book, carrying your whole life around with you like that." She squares her shoulders and narrows her eyes at him. "And I bet you're only sixteen," he adds, though he's just guessing. She could be any age between fifteen and thirty. There's a blankness about her, like you could paint whatever you wanted across the canvas of her skin.

"Wrong. I'm almost eighteen."

"Close enough," he says. "And did you grow up on a farm?"

"What? You can't possibly know that."

He snorts. "Only cow-folk wear boots like those."

She lifts a rubber-booted foot and then stomps it back on the floor. "Whatever. What else?"

"Your fingernails. They're disgusting. You have working-man hands." He gazes at her directly now, wonders if he's gone too far. When she meets his eyes again, he releases his first smile. No, today his timing is impeccable, and this girl is perfectly equipped to handle his games. If anything, she wants more. "What's your name?" he asks next.

"Astra Winter."

"Liar. That's not a real name. It's a toothpaste flavour or something."

She laughs finally. "I'm not lying. That's my name!" Then, as if remembering what he said about her hands, she peers under her nails and starts trying to dig the dirt out. "Okay," she says, still focused on her manicure. "I think I *do* want a job here. You're kind of funny."

———

Because Brendon is a softy, he holds a very brief interview—only asking questions that concern Astra's favourite foods—before he hires her on the spot and instructs her to dump her pack in the back room. As he shows her around the store, he tries to piece together her story. She doesn't divulge much, only that, yes, as he'd guessed, she'd been raised on a cattle farm, she has a mother and a father and five younger siblings, she arrived on a Greyhound bus the night before, alone, and she doesn't know a soul in town or have a place to stay. Brendon can't help but think this is sort of worrisome, so as they close up the store at the end of the day, he offers her his couch after telling her she's out of her mind to think it's "totally fine" to sleep in the bus station again.

The entrance to his building smells like piss and cigarettes, but Astra doesn't seem to mind. While he checks his mailbox, she flops into one of the brown armchairs in the lobby and waits.

"If I was your father, I don't know if I'd be okay with you staying with a total stranger," he says as he pockets two take-out menus. "You don't have to worry, though. I'm not a creep."

"I don't get worried. It's a waste of energy," she retorts.

Is she for real? Brendon wonders, not for the first time. "Well, you can call your folks once we're upstairs, if you like. I'm sure you want to tell them you've found a job and a place to crash?"

"Nah. It's fine," she says, picking up her bag and following him to the elevator.

Inside his apartment, Brendon orders pizza, cracks a beer for himself, and pours one for Astra into a large plastic juice glass with a picture of a lemon on the side. After she takes her drink to the window to admire the glittering city, she claims the view is the most beautiful thing she's ever seen, as though he lives in some grand palace, and not a bland, 1950s stucco apartment building.

"I never really thought about city lights at night. It kind of looks like we're standing on stars," she says dreamily.

The total decor in Brendon's living room consists of two racks of CDs, a brown leather couch, a stereo, and a glass coffee table with a chip on the edge—white as a crescent moon—where he once slammed a beer bottle down too hard. He's lived here for twelve years, yet he still hasn't hung any art on the walls. But Astra isn't like other girls; she isn't fancy or picky, and she seems completely pleased by what he's offered her so far. It's been a long time since he's had anyone over. It's been even longer since anyone has wanted to come. So he appreciates the sound of Astra's voice in his apartment; it's like wings dusting each and every surface, brightening up his home.

Brendon takes a seat on his couch with the TV muted on The Sports Network and tries to get his body to relax. "Why did you want to work in the mall?" he asks, eager to keep their conversation going.

She turns away from the window and faces him. "In his last letter, my ex gave me a bunch of tips for when I moved to Calgary. He said the mall would be the easiest place to get a job because you can hand out a ton of applications at one time. It ups your chances."

"Your boyfriend was your pen pal?"

"It's complicated," she says, returning her gaze to the window. "He might come visit me in the spring, though. Which would be cool."

When Astra removed her jacket at the store that morning, Brendon was horrified to find her in wool tights and a men's x-large Led Zeppelin T-shirt that was belted around her middle to make it into a dress. All day long it'd taken considerable effort to usher her behind the counter whenever a customer came into the store—he didn't want anyone to notice her horrendous style. Tomorrow he plans on taking her shopping; he'll even offer to advance her some pay if she hasn't got any money. He can't wait to see her in normal clothes.

"Do you like working at the store?" she asks, talking over her shoulder again.

"I don't know. I've had the job for ten years already."

"You say that like it's a bad thing."

"Maybe it is, maybe it isn't." Brendon clears his throat and digs his fingers into the sides of his beer can with a slight crunch. He's not going to admit that he's been trying to find the nerve to leave and get a job elsewhere, but at some point over the last little while he'd become a chickenshit.

Astra sighs dramatically and her breath fogs across the cool glass. "Do you have lots of friends?" She draws a heart on the window and writes her name inside.

"Of course I have friends."

"I can't wait to meet more people," she says. Then, turning away from the window to look at him, she adds, "What about a girlfriend?"

He can tell she isn't asking because she's interested, and for a moment he finds this annoying. "Not currently. But I've had many. I was married once too," he replies stiffly, though he never has been, not even close. It's just that when he uses this line, it often earns him a little pity.

"Really?" Astra is nearly laughing. "*You* were married?"

Brendon doesn't like her reaction at all. Here he gives this girl a job, and a safe place to crash for the night, and she laughs at him? He grips the beer can in his hand even harder, crumples his fingers into the thin metal again and again, trying to think of something perfectly awful to say in response.

Then she's walking away from the window, settling down on the couch beside him, talking non-stop the whole time. "That's amazing," she says, apparently oblivious to the fact she'd just insulted him. "Like, getting married and stuff. I want to hear all about it. I've never known anyone who's actually done that."

Now Astra is only two feet away from him. He noticed her smell earlier in the day—or lack of smell, he should say. No products. Just soap. Like stepping outside on a crisp fall day. And she is so skinny; her weight barely leaves an impression on the beat-up leather cushion at his side. He feels his anger evaporate as quickly as it came.

"Your parents must be married," he reminds her, leaning back again.

"Oh, right. Sure. I've just never had a *friend* who was married. I'm from a really small town. Like, tiny," she adds, blushing. She takes a sip from her glass and a bit of beer runs from her mouth over her chin. Although she wipes it away with the back of her hand, her damp skin continues to glisten. "I want to do that someday too," she goes on. "All of it. Get married. Have a baby, maybe? It would be amazing, wouldn't it? I mean, I'm sure you were happy for a while."

"It doesn't always work out," he mutters.

"Oh, I don't need it to work out. That's not what life is about," she says, emptying her glass in a final gulp. He can hear the beer in her voice, and he's well aware that he shouldn't give her any more. God, she's so young. "I don't even mind being alone," she continues. "I just want experiences. I want to know what all that feels like. Love. Breaking up. Even hating someone. I don't care."

"You just want experiences," he repeats slowly. He really wants to say the right thing; he doesn't want to blow this. "What about bad ones? You don't want those, do you?"

"You can't control what comes," she says. "And you can't have any good in this life without getting some bad."

"I suppose that's true. You know, you really remind me of this girl I dated once. She worked in the Aldo right below my store," he says, though now he wonders if he could legitimately call three nights with someone "dating."

Jessica had a large, pigeon-like chest, an orange, tanning-salon complexion, and a stud in her tongue. When she spoke, that tiny ball of metal flashed at Brendon and made it so he couldn't take his eyes off her mouth. He told her that once, that the tongue thing made her look slutty, and she stuck it out at him. Back in the day, the mall hadn't been so bad. He'd been popular even. Of course, telling Astra that she and Jessica are alike in any way is a lie; he only wants to see what form her face takes when he says it.

Her expression gives nothing away. She doesn't flinch or smile. All she asks is "What's Aldo?"

"Wow. You don't know anything, do you?"

"I guess not."

"It's just a crappy shoe store."

"Okay. Well, how was she like me?"

All day Astra has been asking questions like this. He isn't sure if it's flirting exactly, but she definitely enjoys it when he talks about her. She likes being teased. "She was about your age," he says carefully. "She had the same large brown eyes, like an old sad cow."

Astra smirks and plays with a hunk of her shabby black hair. "So what happened?"

"Pfft," he says, jerking his thumb back over his shoulder. She is watching him expectantly, and her scars make her smile complicated.

He adjusts his pants and puts his beer down on the coffee table. "Anyways. You don't have to worry about Jessica. I like you better."

All week Astra proves to be completely unlike the girls Brendon has hired in the past. She is keen to clean and organize, and she listens carefully to all his instructions. Brendon shows her how to make the shirts hang properly, tightly buttoned to the collar, spaced an inch apart on the rack; how to compliment the customers when they step out of the change rooms so the men think she's interested and buy twice as much; and how to mop the floor at the end of the day so it shines bright under the lights. Astra asks thousands of questions: about bus tickets and bank accounts, about his high school and the mechanic shop where he used to work with his father before he passed away. And she's always laughing, like she did when he mentioned being married, but now he understands she isn't making fun of him—it's just that she's young and nothing in her life has ever been hard and so laughter still comes easy.

She loves the punch cards from the coffee shop downstairs and wastes her money on mochas with extra whipped cream, as if the purpose of life is to receive a free drink and start over again. She enjoys the weird, damp concrete tunnels that maze under the mall where they take the trash, but she isn't comfortable wandering into the other stores to kill time on her breaks. She says she doesn't like the girls there, she hates how they stare at her and whisper, and Brendon knows exactly how she feels.

Astra transforms quickly. She spends her advance exactly as he instructs: on shiny tank tops, tight jeans with a subtle flare, and high boots with a chunky heel. When she befriends Tabitha—an overly pierced and tattooed hairdresser from the salon next door—the woman irons Astra's long hair flat, and litters it with tiger stripes of blond and orange. She shows Astra how to cover up her scars with makeup and line her eyes periwinkle blue. By her second week at the store, Astra looks like she's been raised in a mall, like all Calgary girls.

At first, Brendon doesn't mind these changes, because of course they are only surface. He's just happy to have finally befriended a female who, for the most part, totally understands him. The only time it gets difficult is in the evenings. When they are alone together in his apartment. When Brendon shuffles through the drawer of takeout menus and Astra sits on his kitchen counter, drumming her bare heels against the cabinet doors. Some nights he pays for dinner, sometimes she insists, always asking him first how much she should tip because she appreciates his direction. And then they eat together: Brendon on the couch, the TV muted, while Astra stands by the window, fork in the box, gazing out at the city lights.

Because they are friends. They are friends, they are friends, they are *best* friends. And this appears to make Astra extremely happy because she is constantly saying so. And it's true that during the day that's exactly what they seem to be. She always manages to position something between them: a rack, a shelf, a person, or just a few feet of air. Even when she buys him coffee and hands it to him, her fingers don't brush his. But back home, every night, right before she goes to sleep she hugs him.

The first time was in the kitchen, while he stood at the sink washing up their few dishes. Another time he was in the bathroom, toothbrush clutched between his teeth. Suddenly she was behind him, her gentle voice whispering, "Thank you so much. Thanks for taking care of me." Her small breasts pressing against his back, her arms reaching around and tightly squeezing his ribs, always trapping him in an embrace when his hands are too busy to return it, when he is helpless. And then before he can respond, she lets go, flees the room, and he's all alone again. This is what's tough for Brendon, the waiting for it, the wanting it, and mostly the not knowing what it means.

Afterwards, in his room, he lies on his back under his navy comforter, and listens to Astra through the thin walls. He hears her feet pad down the hall to the bathroom. Her toothbrush scrubbing her little pearls of teeth. Her spit hitting the basin. The trickle of her pee. Then the hall cupboard opens and there's a nylon swish as she unpacks her sleeping bag from its sack. Listening to her is like being on speed—he can't sleep.

Most nights, once the sounds of her have stopped and it's been quiet for a time, Brendon goes to the living room. The winter winds beat at the windows and it's never that warm in the apartment, so he slowly folds Astra's stray limbs inside the sleeping bag and zips the cocoon up to her neck. Brendon wants her warm. He wants her safe. It takes a lot of effort to limit his wants to those things, but he manages.

On Friday, after running an errand at the bank, Brendon returns to Street Stylz to find a man chatting with Mo and Colin, the two part-timers who spend most of the day discussing how fucked up they're going to get after work. The man is wearing a mall-cop shirt and he has a walkie-talkie clipped to his hip. Brendon changes direction and is about to head back towards the food court, when Mo spots him and waves him into the store.

As the man introduces himself as Chris, the new owner of the security firm that patrols the mall, bile shoots into the back of Brendon's mouth. Every time he thinks he's finally overcome his misunderstanding with these pretend cops, they catch him doing something harmless, like chatting with a new girl selling sunglasses at one of the kiosks by the food court, or they notice him inadvertently sitting near the exit of the women's washroom, and suddenly they amp up their patrols of the store again. Since Astra started working at Street Stylz, they've been extra attentive, and it was only a matter of time before they paid him a visit. At least they waited until after she went home for the day.

"I'm just making my introductions. Getting the rundown on all the staff I should know about," Chris says, giving Brendon a deliberate nod. "And by the way, maybe she mentioned it to you, but I met Astra earlier today. Very nice girl." The radio on his hip crackles and he turns the volume down.

"I'd like to discuss your probation too. Call me next week and we'll arrange a time," he adds, handing Brendon a business card.

"It'd be my pleasure," Brendon says, jaw clenched.

When he returns to his apartment, Brendon finds Astra sitting cross-legged on the living room floor, folding clothes and shoving them in her backpack, the knobs of her spine rippling under her T-shirt like the keys on a piano. At the sight of her packing, he assumes Chris must have said something to her, but when she spins around she's grinning, just as clueless as ever.

"I've got good news," she says, as he removes his gloves and shoves them in his jacket pockets. "You don't have to put up with me on your couch anymore. I'm moving into Tabitha's place tomorrow. Her roommate just left and she's only charging me one fifty a month."

Brendon stares at her blankly, barely able to swallow. So she isn't leaving because she heard some stupid rumour, she's choosing to go all on her own, which is even worse. He tosses his bag into a corner, heads to the kitchen, and starts rooting through the takeout menu drawer.

It takes a minute, but eventually Astra follows him. She doesn't hop up on the counter to chat like she normally does; instead she stands, fidgeting, adrift in the middle of the floor.

"Don't be sad," she finally says, addressing his back. "You'll still see me every day at work."

Brendon sets his shoulders, flexes his arms, and imagines he's a bull as he rummages in the drawer. He still hasn't said a word since coming into the apartment, and he can sense her growing panic and unease. *Good*, he thinks. Because then she does it: her arms are around him, clasped tightly over his stomach, only this time he's ready. Quickly, he turns around within her embrace and pulls her in so tight he can feel the hard swirl of her ear against his collarbone. He notices her smell. Different after all these weeks. Like antiperspirant, cakey makeup, fabric softener, and sweat.

Astra goes limp in his grasp. She lets her hands fall to her sides, waiting for whatever he's going to do next. It makes Brendon recall being seven years old, catching a small bird and holding it in his cupped hands. Fear had stopped it from twitching as well. The only evidence of life: the rapid-fire ammunition of its heartbeat, but then that ceased too. He hadn't meant to crush it, he just didn't know how tight was too tight. Sometimes, at thirty-five, he still doesn't.

Appalled with himself, Brendon pushes Astra away with such force that she nearly topples over backwards. Once she regains her footing, she backs up slowly to the counter, and laughs nervously.

"I'm really grateful for all you've done for me, Brendon. Please understand that," she says, eyes wet. "And even if I don't live here, we can still be friends, can't we? We'll still work together."

What he doesn't like is that she talked to Tabitha behind his back, that she didn't consult him about leaving—that she didn't think she needed to. He liked her better when she didn't wear so much makeup, when her scars and her faults were easier to see. But Brendon refuses to think about pinning her down. He refuses to think about what she should give him after all he's given her. Because he remembers what she said about experiences, and he doesn't want her to end up thinking of him as a "bad" one. He's better than that.

"Brendon. Please," she says.

Turning away from her, he focuses all of his attention on the takeout drawer. "Of course, Astra. There's no problem. We'll always be buddies."

The next morning Brendon makes coffee. And then, even though it hurts him to do so, he offers to help Astra bring her belongings to Tabitha's. He carries a straining garbage bag full of Astra's clothes and shoes, while she staggers under the weight of her hiking pack, holding her sleeping bag to her chest with her mittened hands. They don't say much, and Astra seems cheerful, almost as if nothing had happened the evening before, so he doesn't bring it up either.

They take the train a few stops into an industrial area, then they cross the highway on foot. Astra stops in front of a large parking lot with a plain, two-storey building plopped in the centre of the cracked pavement. There's an auto rim shop on the ground floor, chrome spinners in the windows catching the sun. "This is it," she says, pointing at the apartment above. "Home sweet home."

Tabitha has an extensive cactus collection, three mangy rescue cats, and she's painted the walls a deep burgundy. Under the living room window there is a shelf made from milk crates and splintered boards that's crammed with books and magazines. The apartment faces south and has better light than Brendon's, but the area is probably sketchy at night. Outside, a semi-truck filled with cattle stops at the intersection, rocking under the weight of the animals trapped inside, steam from their body heat billowing out of the vents.

While Tabitha tells Brendon about her salon, he watches Astra drift away from them and enter the bedroom adjoining the living room. Through the open door, he continues to watch her intently as she throws her bags on a yellow-tinged mattress that the old roommate must have left behind. As she sits on the bed. As her face explodes into a childish grin.

"Did you know, I used to have a bit of a crush on you?" Tabitha is saying to him.

He tears his eyes away from Astra. "No, I had no idea."

Tabitha is dressed in all black, her short hair is dyed a vampire red, and she has crinkles starting round her eyes. They are around the same age: growing older, fading. He supposes this is the sort of woman he should be attracted to.

"Don't get too excited," Tabitha continues. "I'm over it. You're not my type."

"Obviously," he says. "You're not mine either. And it's kind of weird that you want Astra living here. Isn't she a little too young to be your friend?"

"You think it was *less* weird when she was staying with you?" she asks, before bending down to pet the cat that's busy winding through her legs.

He looks at Astra again. She is already unpacking, clothes scattered across the mattress, Brendon the furthest thought from her mind.

His apartment feels different with Astra gone. Emptier. Sadder. As if she'd swooped in just long enough to highlight all its shortcomings before leaving. But the way she moved out, not hating him, left him with some hope too. As they said goodbye at Tabitha's door, Astra gave him her new phone number and kissed him on the cheek. Believe it or not, it seems she still considers him a friend. This is because he managed his time with her properly. While she stayed on his couch, he was completely respectful. And when she told him she was leaving, he reined in his disappointment before it was too late. It'd been close, but he hadn't done anything irrevocable.

Brendon sweeps his apartment, wipes down the counters, then takes the elevator to the basement storage and digs out the old paintings he kept from his father's place. Back upstairs, he hangs two in the living room, one in the kitchen, and one in the hall outside the bathroom. Afterwards, he goes through his takeout drawer and throws the majority of the menus in the trash.

The next morning, he pulls on a toque and walks to a new coffee shop near his apartment. It's crowded, and he's happy to note that a few people are sitting at tables alone, so he won't stand out when he does the same. The woman behind the counter is round-cheeked and cute, her nails chewed and sparkly. When she accidentally drops his change on the floor, her shirt pulls up at the back as she bends over, revealing stretch marks on her waist. *She's probably a mother*, he thinks. For a moment he fantasizes that this is his imaginary ex-wife, that her child is their child, that he has a chance to make amends, and even though it's ridiculous, he's struck with such emotion he ends up dumping all his change in the tip jar before taking his latte and muffin to his seat.

After he finishes his coffee, he walks down the crisp street to the twenty-four-hour gym that he's passed a million times on his way to and from the train. Inside, he signs all the paperwork for a monthly membership. Then, on an exercise bike facing the street, he watches cars pass while thinking about the woman from the coffee shop. How she was polite but not needy. How her stretch marks made her seem strong, and he's surprised that this is something he genuinely finds attractive all of a sudden. He'd noticed her name tag, *Marigold*, which he decides is the most beautiful name he's ever heard.

That evening, Brendon scans newspaper headlines while eating at a small diner around the corner. When he gets to the jobs section and the personals, he reads the ads closely. He decides he will have a meeting with Chris. He will be honest and remorseful. If that doesn't get security off his back, he'll quit and finally get a job elsewhere, maybe at a mechanic shop again. Then, if Marigold doesn't say yes when he asks her out, he'll take out his own personal ad. Why not?

After dinner, he falls asleep quickly and dreams of nothing at all.

On Monday morning, he gets off the train and looks at the rising sun, a piercing orange, behind the mall. He is excited to tell Astra about the rest of his weekend. To tell her about the gym and how he has a new crush. He wants to thank her for staying with him for a while, and then for leaving the way she did.

When he gets to the mall's revolving doors, he spots Astra climbing out of the passenger side of a Toyota truck. She leans back inside, talks briefly to the driver, and then slams the door closed.

"Morning," she says when she reaches Brendon, tossing her hair over her shoulder and stomping her feet against the cold. It's only been two days since he last saw her, but already she seems different, older. She's wearing a scarf he's never seen before and her nails are painted purple.

"Was that Tabitha?" he asks, trying his best to sound casual.

Astra doesn't meet his eyes. "No. It was Chris. He's just parking."

Brendon swallows. "Security Chris?"

"Yup," she says, pushing past him to get inside.

All morning Astra is quiet while she focuses on her tasks, unpacking new orders and ticking off the items from the invoices. She tears the soft plastic covering off each shirt with a static crackle, and folds or hangs the clothing accordingly. When Brendon asks her about Tabitha's apartment, she answers curtly and in as few words as possible. When he asks her about her commute, she only shrugs and says it's fine. So he doesn't tell Astra about his weekend. He doesn't tell her about the gym or about Marigold. For hours they barely speak to each other at all.

After the store closes, Astra starts cleaning the glass cabinets by the till as Brendon is cashing out. "You know, if you're ever in trouble, or if you need somewhere to go, you're always welcome back at my place," he says, not looking at her. He's completely aware that she doesn't need a place to stay. He wants only to remind her of all the favours he did for her. How he gave her a job, let her sleep on his couch, and never asked for anything. How he never—except the once—touched her.

Astra doesn't respond.

"So, I guess you're seeing Chris now?" he goes on, unable to help himself. "I don't like that guy at all. He's a loser."

"I'm not dating him," she answers, coolly.

"Then why did he drive you to work?"

"We're friends. He's watching out for me, that's all."

Brendon laughs. "That's one of your talents, isn't it? Finding guys to take care of you without actually dating them?"

Astra puts down the rag and the bottle of Windex. She is close to him now, but the tension between them is different than it's been in the past. Her expression is cold, brittle. "Brendon, I only came to work today to tell you that I'm not coming back," she says.

"Oh yeah? Why's that?"

"Chris is getting me another job."

"Where?" Brendon asks, though he's perfectly aware she's not going to tell him.

Later, when he thinks back on this conversation, on his whole relationship with Astra, he'll tell himself that he wasn't the only one in the wrong. That first day, after Astra told him about sleeping at the bus station, she knew he would offer her his couch. She wanted him to. And it was wrong of her to have manipulated him, when all he wanted—all he needed—was a little affection.

Astra steps closer, almost spitting as she speaks. "Did you know they have your picture up in the security office? It's up there beside the photos of shoplifters and the other criminals."

Brendon has seen it. His face, printed in colour, a few notes dashed underneath. Where he's allowed to go. What stores he's been banned from. The conditions to his being allowed in the mall at all.

He puts the daily deposit in the little zippered bag with the bank slip, the same task he's been doing for ten years. He wonders if he should even come back tomorrow. After locking up, he could slip his keys under the gate and never set foot in this place again. This could be the moment he's been waiting for: the push.

The girl from Aldo with the stud in her tongue—she had been the first to file a formal complaint at the mall. He dated Sammy from the Le Château next. Took her out to dinner twice, then they had a misunderstanding when he tried to persuade her to come into his apartment. He visited her at work the following day, called her frigid, maybe used a few other poorly chosen words, and the manager had to ask him to leave over and over again before finally she called security. And there were others. Girls who said nothing. Girls before Jessica and Sammy. Girls after. Of course, he'd hoped Astra would never find this out.

"Chris thinks the old security company was unprofessional, handling the complaints the way they did. If he'd been in charge, he would have called the cops," Astra says.

"And what? Send me to jail for having a few girlfriends?" he scoffs.

"That wasn't the issue, and you know it." She pauses for a second and then smiles. "You used to watch me sleep," she goes on. "I could feel you there."

Brendon's face falls. "You were in *my* apartment. I'm allowed to look anywhere I want in my own fucking place, aren't I?"

"Did you take photos of me too?" As she speaks, her lips pull back over her teeth, and Brendon sees that she can be very nasty.

"No. No, I didn't . . ." He hates that he's mumbling when here he is finally telling the truth.

"Is it true that you like to follow girls around? That you go in the women's washrooms with a disposable camera and take photos of them peeing." It's almost as if she's taking pleasure in this now. In watching him crumble. "So, tell me the truth. I really want to know. Do you have pictures of me too?"

He is trying to breathe. He is trying to move slowly and think before he acts, but then her ponytail is in his fist and he is yanking her head back. Hard. The rope of her hair inside his hand is so satisfying. Thick. And her shiny, overly made-up face is under the hot pendant lights, upturned, an inch away from his. And he holds her there. Neck kinked. So close. Strawberry lip balm. Vanilla shampoo. Ugly. Pretty. Stupid. Brilliant. Girl.

But Astra is quicker and stronger than she appears. She slams her shoulder into his chest, and she twists from his grasp just before he can press his mouth over hers.

"Don't you fucking touch me," she says.

Her eyes are flat and cold as she takes a step back. She holds her hand out in front of her, stopping him in his tracks. He's surprised that she knows how to do this—as if she's been in this position a million times before. It's disturbing. *Who is this girl, really? How did she get this way?* And there he is, both amazed and worried about her all over again.

SATIVA

SATIVA AWAKES TO the sound of knocking and a muffled, distant voice. She blinks a few times; then, after adjusting to her surroundings and remembering where she is, she kicks the covers away and sits up in her outrageously comfortable and still off-gassing bed. Back at Celestial, the nights are so pitch-black, you can barely see your own hand. But here in Calgary, they keep the world illuminated. The streetlights blaze outside, and the neighbourhood's curling avenues lie bright as day between the boulevards of plowed snow. Even now, a couple of minutes past midnight, she can see her reflection clearly in the large, round mirror on the other side of the room.

The knocking is not on her door; it's coming from the far end of the long hall. And although she finds it very strange, she isn't surprised. Chris works late, and when he gets home, he always goes to the door of the master bedroom where Astra sleeps, and asks to be let in. Or, at least, that's what

Sativa assumes he wants, since she can't actually hear what he says. But the larger question is, why doesn't he just walk right in? Or, just as pressing, why do they sleep in separate rooms in the first place? Chris and Astra may inhabit the same house, but as far as Sativa can tell, they pretty much live separate lives.

Fully awake now, Sativa opens her bedside drawer to get the small leather pouch she found in Astra's cabin years ago. At the time, she'd convinced herself it wasn't stealing to take it—Astra had left it behind when she moved away from Celestial, and she'd given no indication she was ever coming back. But it *feels* wrong to have it here, in Astra's new house, right under her nose, so Sativa only takes it out when she's alone in her room. She opens the pouch—the necklace string broke off ages ago—and removes the tiny silver dice. She doesn't play with it or ask it questions the way Astra used to; she's simply comforted by having it in her possession. With her attention fixed on the drama unfolding down the hall, she turns the precious object methodically between her fingers.

Now, there's only a murmuring, Chris's voice coming in fits and starts, so she presumes they're holding a conversation through the door. Then, after another ten minutes, this ceases too, and Sativa hears him pad back downstairs. But where does he go? This house is room upon room, most of which Sativa hasn't been in yet, and she hasn't figured out where exactly he sleeps. Once the house falls quiet again, she tucks the dice back in the drawer. And though her mind is alive with questions, she pulls a pillow over her head to shut out the streetlights and tries her best to sleep.

———

Her mother claimed the reason she was sending Sativa to stay with Astra and her boyfriend for the winter was so she could help with their five-month-old baby and try living independently now that she was eighteen. "*I'd* been on my own for years at your age," Clodagh told her. But Sativa knows the real reason her mother wanted her to go to Calgary, and not to Toronto to stay with her brother, or to Vancouver to stay with Doris, was because Clodagh is still obsessed with Astra and she's been sent to spy.

"Well? How does she seem?" her mom asked, when Sativa called home her first evening here, without even bothering to inquire about her flight, or to ask if she was okay or feeling homesick for the Farm—but this was normal. Sativa is always relegated to second place whenever Astra is being discussed. Yet that night on the phone, she refused to let this upset her as much as it had in the past. Because Sativa wasn't *only* in Calgary as a pawn in her mother's agenda; she'd embarked on an adventure of her own. She was in a new city, Celestial was far behind her, and nothing could dampen her excitement.

"I don't know, Mom. She seems great. Though she looks really different," Sativa said.

"Having a child will do that. My body completely changed when I had Freedom, and then even more when I had you. My face became the shape and colour of an apple."

"No, not that way. I mean, she's glamorous now. She's like a whole new person."

"Glamorous? What do you mean, 'glamorous'?"

"They're really fancy. They even have a swimming pool," Sativa said. Then she went on to describe the house where she'd be staying until June. The three-car garage. The five bedrooms, each with its own cushy king-sized mattress and dedicated bathroom. As Sativa carefully luxuriated in the details, her mother just groaned with disapproval or said, "Jesus Christ." She knew her mother hated extravagance, but she found herself loving every inch of this house, with its vaulted ceilings, the tracks of carpeted halls, the granite kitchen with the floor-to-ceiling windows that had a view over the frozen lake. It was hard to believe that this was going to be her home for the next little while.

"It's a fake lake. They stock it with walleye," Sativa added, knowing the absurdity of this would only annoy her mother further.

"How is it 'fake'?"

"That's what Chris said. There aren't any real lakes around here. They dug it out when they put the subdivision in. He called it a 'large water feature.' There's even a fountain in the middle."

"Well, I don't care about that. Tell me about him. What's *he* like?"

Clodagh, always vigilant around unfamiliar men, had been suspicious of this "new guy" from the day Astra called Celestial out of the blue and announced that she'd had a baby, but Sativa was trying her best not to jump to conclusions. "He's a business guy, I guess. Apparently he owns a security firm and he invests in a couple restaurants. He's nice enough though," she said, remembering how, when he picked her up at the airport, he held the passenger door of his truck open as she climbed in, then let her stare out at the passing city and the grey, dystopian towers of downtown without pressing her for a word of small talk.

This didn't reassure her mother. "He doesn't sound right for Astra at all! Do you think she's okay? We all know what a terrible judge of character she can be. I find this all very worrying."

Sativa bit her lip. "She's fine, Mom. I already told you. She's better than fine."

Sativa was just eight when her mother brought them to live at Celestial, and almost immediately she took on the role of Astra's shadow, captivated by how she spat and talked back to Clodagh and the men, and how she galloped around the Farm as if she owned the place, her tattered dark hair flapping behind her like the flag of a rogue nation. The only time she grew annoyed with Astra was when Clodagh took her aside for "private conversations" that Sativa wasn't allowed to join. They would curl up on the sagging loveseat in the bus and chat for hours, leaving a pouting Sativa to draw or knit under the dining room tarp alone. When she complained to Clodagh about feeling left out, her mother fiddled with her many clinking bangles and, using her "serious" voice, reminded Sativa that they were all Astra had. "*You're* fine, sweetheart," she added. "*You* have stability. I'm basically a rock now, something you take for granted. Astra doesn't have that. She has abandonment issues. So try to be generous with your time with me."

"She wasn't abandoned by anyone. Her mother died. Plus, she *has* a parent already. She has Raymond," Sativa argued.

"That's different," Clodagh said. "You know how he is. He doesn't really count."

During Astra's last few years at Celestial, she began to act up more and more. And although it was fascinating to witness, Sativa understood that this reckless behaviour was calculated. Astra liked—possibly *needed*—to have people worry about her, and since Raymond was too spaced out and preoccupied to bother, she threw this labour into Clodagh's wide and welcoming lap. Astra was always finding trouble: cutting herself in the kitchen, getting gashes on her hands and legs from climbing the barbed wire fences, scratching mosquito and spider bites until they were nearly septic; sometimes she claimed to have headaches that lasted for days—which, from where Sativa stood, appeared completely fictitious. But Astra was a marvellous actress, gifted at embellishing her panic or pain to garner sympathy, or to get Clodagh to open her sewing basket of home remedies that they'd root through for the perfect "cure" for whatever ailed her. Yet Clodagh, blinded by her newfound maternal nature, was oblivious to the fact she was being manipulated by a child who wasn't even hers.

And then it got worse. Astra started ditching her chores and hitchhiking away from the Farm without telling anyone where she was going. One evening, when she hadn't returned by dusk, Clodagh told Sativa to get in the van and they drove an hour into Lunn. Of course, they found her right away. She was on the main drag, perched on the railing in front of the lone bar, laughing flirtatiously with a drunk man in a cowboy hat. He was teaching her how to smoke "properly," by showing her how to pinch a cigarette between her two fingers and tilt her head back when she exhaled. Sativa remembers the snap of Astra's jaw as she endeavoured to form smoke rings— that, and her bare arms rashed with goosebumps.

Once Astra was slumped in the backseat beside Sativa, the first thing she asked was if Raymond had sent them.

"Of course," Clodagh answered over her shoulder. "But you *must* stop thumbing for rides, baby. It's dangerous."

"I'll be fine," Astra said. Then, stinking of cigarettes, she leaned into Sativa's ear and lowered her voice to a scratchy whisper. "Is that true? Did Raymond ask you to come get me?"

"No," Sativa answered, turning away from Astra's dark, probing eyes. "You just made her worried. Like you always do."

"Liar," Astra hissed. "I bet he asked and *you* didn't hear him. You don't know anything at all. You're just a kid."

Astra may have been untameable back then, but when Sativa arrived in Calgary she found that girl from Celestial flushed from Astra's system. These days, her hair was swept back in a smooth, inky ponytail, her clothing was posh and immaculate, and her nails were painted a glossy ivory. The scars on her face, which had always added to her intrigue, were now as fine as a pencil line, expertly concealed under layers of makeup. While they hugged, Sativa's nose filled with the aroma of roses and flour and babies; Astra smelled nothing like home at all. Of course, Sativa was immediately drawn to this reinvented version of her childhood idol. So taciturn, and poised in her demeanour. The complete opposite of the eccentric women who had dominated their childhoods at the Farm. The exact kind of woman Clodagh would dismiss as "plastic," if she were here to make such a judgement.

Yet after that first day, Sativa found herself fighting disappointment. Astra was always busy with the baby: rocking, changing, nursing, bathing, wiping his face or fat little fingers. Often, she simply disappeared into the master bedroom with her son, where they'd hide for hours behind the closed door. Clodagh had implored Sativa to be useful: "When you were a baby, all I wanted was for someone to take you away every once in a while." But each time Sativa offered to help, Astra refused, brushing her off by saying Hugo was ready for a nap, or hungry, or that he was inconsolable because he was getting his first tooth.

Then, when they *did* talk, it was only ever briefly, over coffee and toast at breakfast, or when they took Hugo around the block on the icy sidewalks in his stroller. Unfortunately, during these rare moments, Sativa quickly discovered she shouldn't ask Astra anything personal. Not about Celestial, or Raymond, or Chris, or Astra's friends in the city—if she had any at all—because such subjects made her rise from the table or say that it was time to turn the stroller around and head back home. The only thing Astra enjoyed talking about at any length was the Italian restaurant where she had worked before she had Hugo. It was one of Chris's restaurants, and he had managed to find a few shifts for Sativa there as well; she'd be starting as a hostess on Friday.

Astra gossiped about the waitresses there: some weren't trustworthy, some were "awful," and some consistently tipped out too little. She filled Sativa in on who had dated who, told her about the hilarious line cook who liked to snap the girls' behinds with a dishtowel, and went on and on about one handsy bartender Sativa *must* stay away from. Yesterday, she went so far as to draw out the seating plan on a sheet of paper so Sativa could memorize the table numbers, even though she hadn't set foot in the restaurant yet or met the manager. Now, this topic didn't even begin to scratch the surface of Sativa's curiosity about Astra or her strange life here in Calgary, but she was so desperate for attention by this point, that she would listen to Astra talk about anything—frivolous or not.

Because, most of the time, Sativa was left to rattle around the enormous house by herself. Sometimes she flipped through the channels on the TV, past daytime talk shows and soaps. But mostly she snooped, ambling across the plush carpets from room to room. She opened drawers, cupboards, closets, and medicine cabinets, most of which were empty— this house was half full and barely lived in. She opened the

French doors that overlooked the lake, and stood barefoot on the snow-covered deck until her feet couldn't take the torture. There, she inhaled the icy, prairie air that didn't have a trace of forest or rot or Celestial in it at all. Inside again, she ran her hands along the walls, flopped herself onto one of the large leather sofas, and stared up at the slowly spinning fans on the ceiling, all the while longing for something more. For Astra to become more like she used to be. And for her own life here to hurry up and begin.

The next day, after that interrupted night of sleep, Sativa takes the stairs to the basement in search of the washer while Astra is napping with the baby. She hasn't been down here before, and so with the laundry basket propped on her hip, she saunters along the tile floor, pausing to open doors one by one. Behind the first she finds a home gym, complete with a treadmill and weights. Behind another is a storage room filled with snowboards and bikes and tools. When she opens the second-to-last door, she discovers a gigantic rec room with an L-shaped couch where Chris is sitting and playing video games.

"Oh, shit. Sorry!" Sativa says, making to close the door again.

"Wait. It's okay," he calls out. "Come in and say hello."

Sativa sets the load of dirty clothes down. "I thought you were at work," she explains awkwardly. She can't help but be a little embarrassed for him about the night before.

"I usually do my rounds in the afternoons and evenings. During the day I'm down here," he says, nodding towards some filing cabinets, a computer desk, and a blinking phone. "I'm taking a short break from the paperwork," he adds with a wink.

Sativa tries to visualize how many of Clodagh's buses would fit inside this space—at least four, she decides. Behind the couch, a door opens on to a room where the curtains are drawn and there is an unmade bed. Another door leads into a bathroom, where a fan is running. And in the far corner there's a bar, complete with stools, a dartboard, and a fridge. Well, at least she's finally discovered where he sleeps.

"Sorry about the mess," Chris says. "It's normally neater than this down here, I promise."

"I don't care," Sativa replies, turning now to the large TV where staticky cartoon men are running around after a ball. *Hah!* is the sound they make when they slam into one another. "What game are you playing?"

"NFL. Football," he says, completely focused on what he's doing.

"I've heard about video games, but I've never seen one before."

"Right," he says. "I keep forgetting that you're exactly like Astra that way."

"What way?"

He shrugs. "Just sort of . . . you know."

"Sheltered?" Sativa asks, growing more curious by the second.

"That's one way to put it." He chuckles and points at the TV. "I can teach you how to play if you want?"

"Sure," she says, perching timidly on the end of the couch.

Chris pauses the game, passes her a controller, and then, pointing at each button, he shows her the combinations, the most important being those that made you catch and run and jump.

They play in near silence for some time, Chris only occasionally pausing the game to issue another lesson, although
Sativa can't possibly retain all his instructions. Really, she's
perfectly happy to jam the controller with her thumbs at
random, grateful to finally be doing something other than
wander through the house by herself.

Right as she begins to worry that she's overstaying her
welcome, Chris puts his controller down. "How are you
doing anyways? Are you settling in okay?"

"Oh, yeah. I'm great. It's nice here. Thank you for having
me."

"Has Astra shown you around at all? Have you guys gone
out?"

"Not really. Just to the grocery store, and sometimes we
take Hugo out in his stroller."

Chris adjusts his baseball cap and returns his gaze to the
frozen football game. "I'm sorry about that. Astra is going
through a bit of a rough patch. My buddy who has kids tells
me it's probably hormones. Still, I worry about her a little."

"Everyone always worries about Astra. She has that effect,"
Sativa mutters, forgetting to hide her irritation.

"Yeah, I've seen her like this before," Chris continues,
unperturbed by Sativa's tone. "She'll snap out of it eventually."

"What happened before?"

"She can just insist on being really independent, like she's
always got to prove that she's fine on her own. She's like that
with the baby too. She doesn't even let me help, though I'm
perfectly happy to. At this point, I've basically given up trying. And she doesn't want to talk or hang out anymore. I
understand that Hugo has all these developmental stages, so
things are going to change. But when she first moved in, we

pretty much did everything together. Maybe she's more worn out now? I don't know."

"I've offered to help her with Hugo too. I want to. He's really adorable," Sativa says, jumping in.

"Well, I think it's good for her that you're here, even if she hasn't said so. And Astra certainly has the space up there. But don't give up on her. Sometimes she needs help, even if she can't recognize it for herself. She's pretty good at finding trouble. Trust me, I've seen her do it time and time again. She needs friends, especially when she thinks she doesn't."

The following morning over coffee, while Hugo gums mashed banana in his high chair, Astra asks Sativa if she wants to try on some of her clothes. "You probably need a few outfits for work, right? There's no reason for you to go out and buy anything. I have plenty that will fit you."

"Oh, wow. That'd be awesome," Sativa says, unable to conceal her excitement. This is what she's been waiting for. Back at Celestial, Astra let her hang out in her cabin all the time, so she'd been confused by being kept at such a distance.

A few minutes later, they are in the master bedroom and Astra is rummaging through her underwear drawer, while Hugo is on his belly by her feet, streams of drool running into the carpet. Once Astra finds a bra she believes will work, she wraps the band snug around Sativa's chest. "Don't worry about the restaurant too much," she says flatly. "I remember being really nervous when I started. My first few months here, I was convinced everyone could *see* Celestial all over me. But we'll make it easier for you."

Sativa stares at her reflection. Her skin is as colourless as a bar of Clodagh's homemade soap—not bronzed and freckled like Astra's—her knees and elbows are bony, and her ribs wrap prominently beneath her breasts like the warp of a basket. She feels childish, ridiculous in this fancy lace bra. And what should she say? How should she act? She crosses her arms over her chest and shivers.

When Hugo whimpers, Astra heaves him onto her hip, and they disappear into the closet where she starts sorting through her dresses. Finally alone, Sativa inspects her surroundings and notes that, like all the other rooms in the house, this one is vast, white, and nearly empty except for a bed with a gold crib squatting at its side. She quietly opens each dresser drawer: no men's shirts or boxers, no evidence of Chris anywhere. Yesterday, she'd been tempted to ask him more questions. To ask how long he and Astra had been together. If they were going to have more kids. Why he was camped out in the basement. But she couldn't bring herself to do it. And now she's confirmed what she already suspected: this is not, nor has it ever been, Chris's room.

After choosing a few outfits, Astra ushers her along into the bathroom, where she suggests giving Sativa a makeover. The vanity is cluttered with serums, foundations, pencils, brushes, palettes of eyeshadow, and tubes of lipstick scaling from ebony to carnation pink. Sativa waits patiently as Astra agonizes over the makeup, holding one compact and then another up to Sativa's cheek, as if the decision is of the utmost importance. When Astra tells her to close her eyes and she begins prodding, poking, and buffing away, Sativa surrenders to the sensation: the downy brushes and her gentle touch.

While Astra works her magic, Sativa thinks about her phone calls home each evening. How she's never admitted to her mother that, over this first week, she's felt more alone than she ever did at Celestial. She doesn't describe how shut down Astra is either, or that she's never once seen Chris hold his baby, or how strange it is that he knocks on Astra's door every night. When Clodagh prods, asking over and over if Astra seems "happy," Sativa always answers, "Yes," "Of course," "Absolutely," when really she has no idea. Even here, in her room, Astra is as unknowable as a still, black lake: there's just no way to tell what's underneath or how deep down she goes.

"There. I'll help you again on Friday before your shift," Astra says, snapping the compact shut. She picks up a lip gloss, runs it expertly around her own mouth, then bends down and lifts Hugo up off the floor.

Facing the mirror, Sativa finds her reflection altogether different than the one she analyzed earlier. Her lashes are laden with coats of mascara, her flaws and pimples have been powdered away, and her lips stand out as prominently as two wedges of plum on a white plate. Besides her orange hair, she looks a little like Astra; her younger self would be ecstatic at such a transformation.

Sensing that she'll soon be asked to leave, Sativa finds a sliver of courage. She reaches out, tickles Hugo's toes, and says, "I've been meaning to ask you, how did you and Chris meet? You've never told me."

"We met when I was at work," Astra says.

"At the restaurant?"

"No. At this clothing store. It was years ago."

Astra's walls are already up, but recalling what Chris said the day before, Sativa presses on. "That's cool. I also wanted to say that I've been hearing noises in the middle of the night, out in the hall. Have you heard them too?"

Astra steps back, bouncing her son. "It's probably this guy. He still wants to nurse all night long and he's really loud when he gets going."

Sativa raises her eyebrows and smiles, trying her best to illustrate that she's capable of discussing things that are real. That she's old enough to handle it. "No, I mean . . . I think it might be Chris. Like, at your door," she says. "Are you guys fighting or something?"

Astra's complexion colours and her expression stiffens into stone, but whatever it is that Sativa has made her feel— embarrassment, shame, anger—she contains it. "Huh. I haven't heard that at all," she says with a quick shrug, before turning to leave Sativa alone in the bathroom.

Sativa sets her gaze on the mirror again and glowers at her new face. Honestly, she's had it. Why is she wasting so much energy trying to figure out what's going on in this house? Sure, it's possible that Astra is miserable with Chris, or even miserable as a mom. But why is that Sativa's problem?

She peers out into the bedroom to make sure Astra is out of sight. "Bitch," she says, very, very quietly. Then she looks down at the messy countertop, picks up a tube of lipstick, and tucks it in the waistband of her pants.

Back in her room, pulse racing, she opens her bedside drawer and lays the lipstick beside the dice. There's no deny-ing it now: *this* is stealing. Or it's payback, she decides, for all the attention Astra has robbed from her over the years. She's not going to feel sorry for her anymore. Astra has more than she needs. She has a fancy house. A healthy baby. A rich and handsome boyfriend. But nothing is ever enough for her, is it?

And now Sativa needs something in return; she needs something for herself, so she'll take it if she has to. She touches the dice and then the lipstick one more time before she closes the drawer.

Over the next two days, Sativa returns to Astra's room to take more items: some cover-up, a compact, mascara, and an eyeshadow that she discovers in a makeup bag. Then, because she has nothing better to do, she spends hours in her room copying looks from magazine advertisements, drawing dark lines around her eyes, and pencilling her lips espresso brown.

When she talks to her mom at night, she arranges herself in front of her bedroom mirror, the phone pinned to her shoulder with her ear. She pulls at the cord, sticks her tongue out at her reflection, and rolls her made-up eyes. She's getting used to her face like this now. It's starting to look almost normal.

When her mother asks how she and Astra are getting along, Sativa answers that they are fantastic. When her mother asks about Chris, Sativa tells her he's amazing. When her mother asks if Astra is an attentive and affectionate parent, Sativa barely bothers to register the question. She answers her mother with single words. She says that everything here is "perfect." She lies, and lies, and lies. Because Astra is just one person, no more fascinating than anyone else, and Sativa is sick to death of everyone acting like she's so important.

The restaurant is located in an unimpressive strip mall, sandwiched between a beer store and a service station, the name *Italiana* scrolled across the windows in black calligraphy. But inside, Sativa finds the dining room upscale. Mirrors line the west wall, the tables are draped in linen, laid with precision, and hanging from the ceiling is an extravagant chandelier containing hundreds of miniature twinkling bulbs. The colour palette is gold and cream, better than a sunset in late August, and immediately Sativa loves this place too.

For two days now, she's practised clomping around the dining room like an elephant in her new high heels, yet she's still a little shaky on her feet as she's introduced to everyone. But Sativa delights in this fresh vantage point over her environment, and she doesn't care that she's hobbled and couldn't run if she desperately needed to. *If only my mom could see me now*, she thinks with a shiver of pleasure, because of course Clodagh despises high-heeled shoes. She believes men invented them with the intention of making women much easier to bring down.

With Astra's warnings about the waitresses who work here fresh in her mind, Sativa is briefly nervous when she meets the one who is going to train her that evening, although, thankfully, that feeling quickly subsides. Rebecca is adorned in a short and strappy black dress, nearly identical to the one Astra gave Sativa, and her ironed-straight, blond hair is styled exactly as Sativa had been instructed to wear hers. It turns out that Astra was right: based on appearances at least, Sativa fits in perfectly. Rebecca starts making jokes right away, and when she giggles she covers her crooked teeth with her fingertips. She tells Sativa that the job is simple. She only has to stand at the imposing mahogany desk by the door, cross out names from the leather reservation book, and lead the customers through the pleasant din of clinking cutlery to their tables. It's much easier than any chore Sativa had at the Farm. The most gruelling part is managing to both smile and stay upright at the same time.

Unlike Astra, Rebecca has no trouble talking about herself. During lulls in the evening, she tells Sativa all about her new apartment, and her "sketchy" roommate who labels his milk and only drinks protein shakes. She explains that she was a cheerleader in high school, and that her dream is to one day open her own dance studio, where she'll teach ballet and jazz to children. Ever curious, Sativa peppers her with questions: about the salon where Rebecca gets her nails done, about her neighbourhood, and if she takes a cab home after work. At this, Rebecca tears up, dabbing at her eyes carefully with a napkin so as not to smudge her makeup. Last weekend, she'd gone through a "major" breakup with her boyfriend of six months. He used to pick her up from work, so now she has to find her own way home.

"Oh, that's terrible," Sativa sympathizes, briefly putting an arm around the young woman's shoulders.

Once the dinner rush is over, Rebecca begins asking Sativa questions too. She wants to know about the Farm where Astra and Sativa grew up. About Sativa's mother, and even her brother, who she seems to have heard about—somehow she knows Freedom's name. "And how is it at Chris's house? You're living there, right?"

"It's good, I guess," Sativa says.

Rebecca adjusts the spaghetti straps on her dress while she tells Sativa about the staff party Chris held at his place last winter. He'd hired a caterer and a deejay and everything. That night, Rebecca drank so much at the open bar, she ended up passing out in one of the bathrooms. When she woke up in the morning, she was terrified she'd be fired for getting so messy. Instead, Chris made her toast and an egg and then drove her home. "And Astra? How is she doing these days?"

Rebecca continues, watching Sativa closely. "It's been *ages* since she's been in."

"She's all right, I think."

"You think? Aren't you guys supposed to be friends?"

Sativa, struggling with how to respond, hesitates.

"Wait? You're not friends?"

"No, not really. We just grew up together," Sativa mumbles. "My mom asked her to give me a place to stay for a while."

Rebecca touches Sativa on the arm tenderly. "Phew. That makes me feel *so* much better. You're *so* nice. *So* easy to talk to. All night I've been wondering how you can stand her. Honestly, I hope you don't mind me saying this, but Astra can be a bit of a bitch."

Sativa blushes with the echo of what she herself said only a few days ago.

"She never tried to get to know any of us," Rebecca goes on. "She wouldn't even sit with us at the end of the night for a drink! She can also be pretty mean when she wants to be."

"How is she mean?" Sativa asks carefully. Though she's conflicted, it's satisfying to hear this fresh take on Astra. She's used to people making excuses for her, everyone always reluctant to acknowledge her darker side—a side which seems to have only grown more pronounced here in Calgary.

"One time she told Chris I was stealing," Rebecca says now, arching the sharp, drawn-in lines of her eyebrows into mountain peaks.

"Were you?"

Rebecca laughs, her hand in front of her mouth again. "No, of course not!" she exclaims. "Astra didn't have any evidence. Like I said, *mean*."

For the rest of the evening, Astra remains the main topic of conversation. Rebecca asks what she does all day at home or if she ever has friends over. She asks about her room. She asks about the baby. A couple of times, Sativa considers whether she might be divulging too much, but it's intoxicating to finally speak freely without being policed by her mom. She finds her body tingling with adrenaline, waves of pleasure running up and down her spine, especially when Rebecca urges her to continue, saying, "Sativa! I feel awful talking about her like this, but please go on. This is more fun than I've had at work in ages!" So Sativa does. She tells Rebecca about Celestial, and what Astra was like back home. She mentions that Chris is always knocking on Astra's door at night, how she *hears* him. She even tells Rebecca that he'd said he was worried about her.

At the end of their shift, when the only patrons remaining in the restaurant are larger parties finishing up their bottles of wine, the girls sit in a booth with their complimentary gin and tonics, rolling cutlery in napkins in preparation for the next day. It's then that Rebecca asks if Astra will be coming back to the restaurant after her maternity leave.

"Hard to say," Sativa says, taking a long slurping sip of her drink. "She hasn't said much about it."

"I hope she doesn't. Astra's not like you at all; she only ever talks to the guys in the kitchen or Chris if he's in." Rebecca lines up another knife and fork on a napkin. "I can't imagine having to *live* with her. I feel kind of sorry for you."

"It's a bit lonely," Sativa admits.

Ignoring this, Rebecca slowly shakes her head. "And poor, poor Chris. Imagine how it is for him."

Sativa pictures him playing video games in the basement, sequestered in the rec room even though it's *his* house. "Yeah," she agrees.

"And don't go thinking this is new or anything," Rebecca is whispering conspiratorially. "This has been going on for *years*. Ever since I met them. And why is he still so devoted to her after she had that baby? Why did he let her move into his house? It's almost like he thinks they're together. Aren't they supposed to be 'just' friends? Is he secretly in love with her or something? She's not even *that* good-looking. Her face all fucked up like it is. To be honest, everyone here thinks she's using him. That she's leading him on. Chris is a catch. He's too good for her."

Sativa sits back and frowns. "Wait. They're together though, aren't they? I mean, it's *their* baby."

Rebecca's eyebrows do their dramatic dance again. "Oh, honey," she says. "Did Astra tell you that? Then she's a liar on top of everything else. No, no, no. They've never been together, not for a second. And that's *not* Chris's kid."

Later, in her bathroom at home, Sativa dabs makeup remover across her cheeks, and then rinses her face clean. In the shower she stares at the bridges of her feet, the skin red and puckered from wearing her heels all evening. She wriggles her sore toes and flexes her stiff calves, while going over what she's learned. She thinks first about what Astra had told her about the restaurant—none of which ended up being accurate. When Sativa met the apparently "creepy" bartender, he seemed perfectly harmless; he even called her "gorgeous" as he handed her a second free drink. Then she pictures Rebecca's large and curious stare, and how she squeezed Sativa's hand outside when they were getting in their cabs: "I can't wait for you to meet the rest of the girls. They're going to love your stories." Astra had been wrong about them too. The waitresses weren't cliquey. On the contrary: they wanted Sativa to be their friend.

After towelling off and putting on her old flannel night-gown, Sativa starts down to the kitchen for a snack. She gets a glass of water from the dispenser on the fridge and a bag of chips from the cupboard. In the dining room, she eats slowly, gazing out over the swimming pool and at the frozen lake buried under snow, mulling over the questions that remain difficult to answer or face: Had Astra actually *said* that Chris was Hugo's father? Had she told anyone they were together? Had she lied, like Rebecca said? Or was Clodagh the one who'd made the mistake? Had she just assumed this to be true, just because she liked the drama of the story? Because she thought she knew Astra better than Astra knew herself?

Finishing up, Sativa wanders back into the giant kitchen and puts her chip bag in the trash. Restless and not ready for bed, she tiptoes down to the basement, pokes her head into the rec room, and turns on the light: the papers on his desk are now organized, the controllers are lined up below the TV, and through the open door she can see that his bed is neatly made. The room smells good, like his cologne.

Upstairs, Sativa stands outside Astra's master bedroom, her heart pounding. All she wants is to understand this piece of the puzzle. She needs to hear what Astra says to him.

She raps her knuckles on the door.

Silence.

She knocks harder, this time in the same pattern he uses. *RAP. Rap, rap, rap.* Then she pulls her hand away when she hears Astra say, "Chris, sorry, I didn't hear you. Come in, let's talk."

Sativa swallows. She wants to sprint down the hall to her room, but her sore feet are anchored to the soft carpet. She can hear Astra getting out of bed. Her steps as she approaches. Her hand on the knob.

"Oh, it's you!" Astra says, jerking her head back as the door swings open. Her hair is loose and wild, her face red, swollen, and stripped clean of makeup. This is the Astra Sativa used to know. The Astra from Celestial. The Astra who would run up to Clodagh sobbing and throw her teenaged body into her lap as if she were still a small child. The Astra who wasn't ever put together. The Astra who was never in control. Face to face with her again, Sativa begins to regret everything she told Rebecca.

"Are you okay?" Astra asks, not at all unkindly.

"Yeah. I'm sorry," Sativa stammers. "I don't know why I'm here."

Astra frowns at her. "I thought you were Chris. Sometimes we talk when he gets home from work, but I haven't been up to it lately. Is he home yet?"

"I don't think so," Sativa says.

"Well, come keep me company. This is Hugo's witching hour. He often needs a good play and a nurse around now."

Sativa follows Astra into the dim room, watches her pick up the baby and settle back against the headboard. Usually, she uses feeding Hugo as an excuse to disappear, and so Sativa has never seen them together like this. As she watches them settle snugly in the pillows, for the first time she comprehends the full gravity of Astra being a mother. The momentousness of the task. Of having a *child*. This isn't some joke. Astra isn't

acting out or acting up like she did as a teenager. She isn't trying to be difficult or get attention anymore. And she definitely
isn't an object to speculate about. Yet Sativa has betrayed her.
All evening she told stories. She behaved like her mother,
thinking she had the right to gossip, as if the details of Astra's
life were common property and not her own.

"How was work?" Astra asks, though there's that old,
familiar waver in her voice that betrays her—there are other
things on her mind.

"Okay," Sativa says. "How are you?" Though it's completely
obvious now that Astra is struggling.

"I don't know." Astra sighs heavily. "I guess I'm not great.
And I've been thinking about you too. I've been so distracted.
We haven't really talked, have we? It's just . . . Well, this is just
all so much tougher than I thought it would be. I sleep a bit
during the day, I have these useless short naps that don't make
me feel any better, then Hugo and I are up half the night. I'm
so exhausted in the morning I'm literally feverish. And then
it's the same thing all over again. And that's not even the worst
part. The worst part is not knowing when it's going to end.
Or where we're going to be a month from now, or in a year.
I'm terrified. I'm hoping it's hormonal. Chris keeps telling me
that's all it is."

Sativa tucks her hair behind her ears, and hesitantly she
asks, "Did you know that I thought he was Hugo's father?"

"Yeah, I kind of figured you did," Astra says.

"Clodagh was the one who told me he was."

Now Astra is crying openly, and as tears drip from her
chin they are caught in Hugo's onesie. "God, here I go again.
See! I can't stop. I've been like this all night." She sighs again.
"Please understand, I never *told* your mom that. But I guess

I did sort of let her assume it. I probably shouldn't have. I just didn't want to deal with her fucking questions, or have her compare us again, say we were the same. I didn't want to hear about all the deadbeats she'd dated, or about your dad or Freedom's dad again. I didn't want to hear her say for the hundredth time that there aren't any good men out there. She's told me those stories so often."

"Oh God. Me too."

"I have a son, Sativa. I need to believe there are good men in the world. I can't handle her negativity."

"So you and Chris are just friends?" she asks, needing to hear Astra say it one more time.

"Yeah. But lately things between us have gotten weird and sort of tense. His feelings keep getting hurt when I say I'm too tired to hang out. He tries to tell me it's just because he 'cares' about me, but something feels different. It's almost like he cares *too* much, if you know what I mean. And that sucks. That isn't what I want from him. So I've been trying to put on the brakes and not hang out so much, but that's pretty much impossible unless I stay in this room. I'm living in his house, Sativa. For free. And I *hate* that. I don't like depending on him. I *need* to not depend on him. I figure I probably shouldn't stay here for much longer. And that's been worrying me too. Obviously."

"Can I do something? My mom keeps telling me that I should help you, but I don't know how." Sativa hates that these words expose how young and inexperienced she still is. She thinks back to that night when they picked Astra up in Lunn. She'd been right: *You don't know anything at all,* she'd sneered. And Sativa had deserved it.

"No, no. Don't be silly. What could you do?" Astra pauses, and then she meets Sativa's eyes and laughs sharply. "Unless you can tell me how to be a good parent? I don't have anyone to help me with that. And from this point on, it's all about Hugo. And this might be what freaks me out most. There's *always* going to be Hugo. He's *my* responsibility. That's never going to end. What if I fuck him up?" Astra inhales sharply, then she looks down at her son and her voice softens. "You're lucky you have Clodagh."

Sativa lowers her head. "I don't know. You're right about her questions. I call her every night and all she wants to talk about is you."

Astra wipes what's left of her tears away and laughs again. "Oh, you poor girl. She's too much sometimes, isn't she? She tries her best, but she's *so* intense. When she calls here, I can barely bring myself to answer."

"I used to be really jealous of you guys. I still am, sort of."

"Don't be. She doesn't even like me much. She never has." Astra switches Hugo to her other breast, then she continues: "Do you remember that dice I used to have? The one I used to wear on that necklace?"

With these words, Sativa takes a step back towards the door. Because now everything she's done comes back to her and she's filled with dread. She pictures the drawer in her room. All the makeup. The dice that she stole so many years ago, because she was jealous. Because back then, a little part of her wanted to *be* Astra. "No. I don't remember it," she says softly, hating herself the whole time.

"Freedom was the one who told me to leave it at Celestial. He thought it was 'harming' me. That's how he put it," Astra says, oblivious to how Sativa is falling apart before her. "I wish I had it now. It might sound pathetic, but all I want is something of hers. Something of Gloria—even though I never knew her. So you might hate those phone calls with your mom and listening to her talk about me, but imagine having no one to talk to at all. I think that's worse. I'm sorry."

Sativa is anxious to get back out into the hallway, where she's hoping she'll be able to breathe again. The baby, grunting as he drinks, reaches up and grips his mother's lips tight with his fist. And so Sativa doesn't even bother to excuse herself or say anything. She can't. She backs out of the room, leaving Astra there, her mouth sealed shut in her son's tiny hand.

Sativa stands in front of her bed as cars drive by the house, their headlights sending beams of light across the ceiling. Far in the distance, she can hear the rumble of the highway and maybe an airplane. She thinks momentarily of Clodagh, and then pushes her firmly away. She's determined to be the opposite of her mother now. Tomorrow at work, when the girls ask, she'll talk about Celestial, but she won't only mention the bad things. She won't be so negative. She'll tell Rebecca about how Astra let her sleep in her cabin after Freedom left. How she taught her how to bundle sage and make friendship bracelets. How they walked for hours along the river, chewing on the ends of grass, imagining together what it would be like once they left, once they lived in the city, once they were free from the Farm. She understands that if she wants Astra's friendship again, she'll have to earn it.

Sativa opens her bedside drawer and, slowly, takes out the items one by one, stacking them in a little pile. She removes the pouch last and presses the dice to her lips. Then she gathers everything up in her hands, tiptoes down the hall, and knocks on Astra's door.

DORIS

WHEN DORIS WAS a child, Charles Brine kept the lawn around the estate weed-free and cropped short like a carpet. Her father claimed that Charles was a genius with grass, and that they were lucky to have found such a dedicated man to tend their gardens. But after both men passed and she inherited the house at the age of twenty-four, landscaping was the first extravagance she cut from the payroll. Since then, Doris has mown the lawn herself, though only once or twice a season, primarily as a means to discourage bramble and limit complaints from the neighbours. She adores weeds, anyway: dandelion, daisy, buttercup. The long sticky kind that knots around your ankles and clings to your wool socks. She's always been capable of finding beauty in what ordinary people plow right over.

Usually, Doris pushes the lawnmower in a circular route from the foundation of the house out to where the hedge divides the property from the road. But today, pulling the cord to get the mower started, her arms feel sluggish, the way they do during aquafit class when she makes swirls underwater with her hands. Halfway through the job, it's her bones that require her to stop. Aching as if with flu. Tired in their very marrow. *Well,* she thinks, *looks like Astra and her boy have finally burned up the last of my strength.*

She cuts the engine and removes her ear protection. Down Connaught Drive she can hear the busy street. Car horns. Crows. A dog barking. Glancing at her legs, she notes that her calves are thinner than last year—less muscular, the skin cracked and dry. It's there in her shins that it hurts most these days. She imagines the feeling is similar to the growing pains that cause Hugo to cry before bed. But the pain is all over too. In her elbows and fingers. In the bones beneath her eyes. In the deep roots of her teeth.

Of course, she could have accepted Astra's offer to help with the grass, but Doris didn't want to be owing any favours—especially not today. She's already made up her mind: at some point this afternoon she will tell Astra it's time to move out. That she should fend for herself and grow up a little. Doris knows that this won't be easy. The girl has trouble processing criticism without feeling unreasonably rejected and hurt.

Since coming to stay with her nearly four years ago, Astra has taken Hugo to look at ugly basement suites throughout Vancouver every six months or so, only to return to Doris's complaining about the cost or the light. Once, she turned a place down because at the last minute she realized she didn't want to live alone after all. "You have Hugo. You aren't alone," Doris pointed out, annoyed, and yet she kept allowing Astra to stay. But why? These people aren't her family. She doesn't owe them anything at all.

Doris sits at a picnic table and looks back at the house. Some of the main-floor suites have their windows open and she hopes her tenants appreciate the smell of cut grass—one of the greatest scents—because she's not going to bother mowing again this year. Let the grass turn to hay. Let the neighbours complain. She doesn't have the energy to care about this anymore.

After she tucks the mower away behind her motor-bikes in the back corner of the garage, she passes the small groundskeeper's cottage where Raymond grew up. The woman who rents it now has three small dogs, and they are all yapping furiously inside. Back at the main house, she starts up the front steps, which are well trodden, the planks rising and falling in rough waves. Though Doris isn't a people person, something about the dips in the wood, proof of all those feet—including hers, and her father's, and Raymond's when he was a child—gives her satisfaction every time she climbs up them. She doesn't know why. Maybe she loves the silence people leave behind once they're gone, or maybe she feels akin to the steps themselves, walked all over and worn down, but either way, despite the blatant sentimentality, it's love she feels for this entrance.

As a young woman, she'd been so ashamed of her newly acquired wealth that her first inclination had been to get rid of it. First, she let go of her father's staff, donating the majority of the furniture and shutting up most of the rooms on the estate; and then she spent the remainder of her energy—and a considerable fortune—establishing the Farm with Raymond. It was years later, once she'd tired of dealing with the dynamics of the commune and she'd fallen in love with a woman who preferred city life, that she returned to Vancouver full-time.

There, living in her childhood home again, she found herself reluctant to sell the house. The best solution, she decided, was to become a "good and fair" landlord instead. And so with Jane's help, they converted the estate into apartments—something her father would have been horrified to see. They put two small suites and a laundry in the basement, five one-bedrooms on the main floor, and two larger apartments upstairs, one of which they kept for themselves.

When the renovation was complete, Doris rented the suites out at well below the going rate, housing single mothers, university students, and roommates who published political zines in the basement. The house was crowded: tenants stomped around, fought in the halls, and held potlucks on the lawn that dragged on past midnight. Then, once the late seventies turned into the eighties, long after Jane left, Doris began renting to a different, quieter sort. To older women who grew tulips in their window boxes, or to bachelor men with cats—people who had the brains to appreciate a little bit of peace and quiet, people like her. Her current tenants never bother her, and she pays them the same favour in return. She wouldn't even know their names if it weren't for the cheques they slip into her mailbox at the end of each month.

In Doris's apartment there's a decent view of False Creek and the Cambie Bridge from the kitchen window. In the evenings, she does the dishes there, looking out at the city, before taking a Pilsner to her La-Z-Boy. Or at least that was her routine, before Astra and Hugo arrived. Before her spare room was taken over by the woman and her baby, before toddler toys were strewn all over the floor, before the tantrums of a four-year-old preceded bedtime every night. Doris has let Astra invade her space for far too long, she realizes, climbing the last steps to her apartment, and boy, is she ever ready for them to go.

In her kitchen, Doris finds Astra's newest friend running shears through Astra's hair, and Hugo sitting cross-legged on the table as his mother transforms before him. Only that morning, her hair was down to her mid-back; now she is basically bald, and the floor is a messy pile of her long, damp black tangles which resemble a bed of kelp at low tide.

"Get off the table, Hugo. You know better," Doris says, while digesting the scene front of her.

"Sorry. He never listens to me," Astra says, as Hugo slips into one of the pleather chairs. Then, face expectant, she adds, "Well, what do you think? Jesse won't give me a mirror, so I can't see how I look."

Jesse has her head shaved too, but truthfully this style is dreadful on Astra. Without her hair, she appears a good ten years older than she should, and her scars are suddenly more apparent, puckered and red like the mountain ranges on a globe, and yet Doris is much too tired to reassure her. She dips her head into the fridge to retrieve the milk jug. "It's just hair, Astra. What do I care."

Doris takes her drink to the window, keeping her back to everyone. When she finishes, she turns to find Hugo's face as she expected: contorted in horror over his mother's altered appearance. Sensing the meltdown that's about to erupt, she places her glass in the sink. "Well, enjoy this. I'm off to have a soak."

In the tub, the grass cuttings from the earlier mowing loosen from her legs and float to the surface. On the other side of the window, the branches on the maple tree are sway-ing. She wants to feel that breeze, but she's too tired to heave herself up and pad wet across the floor. When she closes her eyes, she can still see Astra's pleading, worried face. *Poor thing*, she thinks for maybe the thousandth time over the last twenty-nine years.

After Gloria died, whenever Doris drove up to Celestial for a visit, she was troubled by the signs of neglect. The baby's clothing was either too big or too small, her face and fists grimy, her hair a rat's nest. On one visit, Doris had to slam on her brakes as she pulled into the Encampment, because there she was: barely a year and a half old, sitting alone in the middle of the driveway, half-hidden behind the Pontiac's hood. And with all the animals around? It had been terrifying. Then, the following winter, she and Jane arrived to find Astra alone again, running around almost naked. Spotting Doris's car, the girl ran towards them, right through the edge of a dying firepit, and they watched, helpless, as Astra sank ankle-deep in white ash, the hidden red-hot coals blistering her toes and the soles of her feet. That night, Doris wrapped herself in blankets and sat with Astra on the riverbank, as she dipped her ravaged feet into the frigid water whenever the pain grew too intense. That's what it was like at Celestial back then: everyone was responsible for everyone else, while nobody knew how to be responsible at all.

Jane saw what a toll the Farm took on Doris, but it wasn't until the cougar attack that she herself realized just how much of an emotional burden Celestial had become. Unable to stay silent any longer, Doris told Raymond she couldn't be a part of the Farm anymore if these sorts of incidents kept happening, and then she offered to take Astra home with her from the hospital. Raymond said nothing. He just pulled that silly dice out of his pocket, rolled it right in front of her, and turned her down. From that point on, she limited her visits to no more than once a year, and whenever possible she kept those trips brief.

And yet, even though Astra was growing up and becoming more and more capable of watching out for herself, Doris woke up each morning thinking about her. Sometimes she wrote to Raymond hoping for news, but his replies never contained anything specific about his daughter, rambling on instead about his frustrations with the workers he had up there, or with the old, failing machinery, or with another early frost. When Clodagh moved back to Celestial and had the phone put in, Doris started getting calls every once in a while. Occasionally, she'd catch Raymond on the line, and after letting him go on for some time, she always concluded the conversation by reminding him that Astra was welcome to come down to Vancouver to live with her, to get some real schooling, to gather some life experience, or just to give him a break. Of course, Raymond always brushed her offers off, which was fine. It wasn't like Doris *wanted* Astra living in her house either, but this habit of inviting her alleviated some of the guilt she continued to have about the child. It let her feel like she was doing *something*, even if in truth she was doing nothing at all.

Many years later, when Clodagh mentioned that Astra was still living in Calgary and that she'd recently had a baby with a questionable man she hadn't known long, Doris wasn't all that surprised. And after she hung up, she found herself angry—with Raymond, with herself, even with Gloria, because it was obvious they'd all failed her. Here was Astra, twenty-five years old and still no better off than her mother would have been had she lived. Wholly unprepared to parent a child well. Cut off from her family and without any real support. And if that was true, what had been the point? Of Celestial? Of feminism? It was almost the end of the century and women were still struggling and at the mercy of men.

Doris put off calling Astra for a few months, but when her worry failed to subside, she picked up the phone and dialled the number Clodagh had given her. It only took a couple of minutes before Astra was blubbering away on the other end, saying she didn't know what to do, or where to go, or how to make money and support her child. And as was her old habit, Doris instinctively offered Astra her spare bedroom.

"You wouldn't mind?" Astra asked, jumping on the opportunity before Doris realized her mistake. "Maybe you're right. I should just start over somewhere new."

"I didn't say that," Doris added quickly. "Besides, there's always Celestial. You could have a good life there."

"No, no," Astra said. "I'm never going back there. This is a *much* better idea. I'll come as soon as I can."

And that was that. Not three weeks later, Astra and the baby were on her doorstep.

Maybe if the girl had moved in at two, like Doris originally suggested, or even at five or fifteen, she would have had some influence. But it's too late now. Astra has zero interest in processing her issues or getting a handle on her past. Most of their conversations are prickly and loaded, and if Doris ever attempts to set a boundary, it gets blown out of proportion or totally ignored. The few times she's dared to give the girl some advice, she's regretted it right away. Astra can be wickedly defensive. Honestly, there's no other way to put it; she is downright exhausting to be around.

Doris opens and closes her hands under the water to ease their aching. Then she tries to rein in her thoughts to the present: the water, the bathroom, the tree through the window. As her mind settles, she becomes aware of a light knocking on the door.

"Yes?" she says, pulling her head out from the water.

Jesse pokes her head into the bathroom, and through the open door Doris can hear Hugo yelling in the kitchen. Something hits the floor with a crash and then Astra starts talking rapidly: "It's okay, it's okay. You're right. I'm sorry. I'll make it up to you. Please calm down, Hugo."

Jesse grimaces. "I'm going out to pick up tacos. I think that boy needs some food. Can I get some for you too?"

"No, thank you." All she's had today is that glass of milk, but it seems her appetite is gone. Then, as Jesse begins to close the door again, Doris says, "Wait. Could you open the window for me before you go?"

"Sure, not a problem."

Jesse has tattoos across her back, down her arms, and crawling up her neck. On her left forearm she wears the name Sarah; on one shoulder there's a half-naked woman, and on the other she has an American flag. *Why an American flag?* Doris has always wondered if the tattoos are ironic.

Jesse met Astra at the health food store where Astra works as a cashier, and although Doris likes her perfectly fine, she knows that the relationship won't last. She's often tempted to take Jesse aside and tell her to run for the hills, because, any day now, someone is going to get hurt.

Over the past few years, Doris has watched Astra go through people as casually as if she was trying on pants in a change room—discarding them once she realized they didn't quite fit. Every few weeks she has a new best friend, or lover, or "soulmate" who she claims is going to solve all her problems.

Some of these people give her too much room and freedom, which makes her feel unloved and ignored, and she grows so insecure and desperate they end up leaving her. Others barely give her the space to breathe, fussing over her, trying to shape her into who they want her to be, which she suffers willingly until she's nearly out of air. And Doris can never figure out just what "kind" of person it is that Astra likes. She comes home with men, women, conservatives, anarchists, bodybuilders, and bookish punks. Doris asked her about this once, how she decided who to date, only to be horrified by her reply.

"I don't really put much thought into it," Astra said.

Doris laughed uncomfortably. "Well, you should! And you should think about who you're bringing into Hugo's life."

Of course, commenting on Astra's romantic life proved to be a mistake, further fuelling the tension in the house. Astra didn't speak to Doris for days. That's when she finally understood how truly vast and deep the hole in the girl really was. Astra was going to fill it with anything or anyone, regardless of the fact that no human on this planet would ever do the trick. But that was something she'd have to figure out for herself.

All this worrying about her is wearing me out, Doris thinks. *This is why it's time to stop. This is why it's time for her to go.*

When Jesse opens the window, the smell of fresh-cut grass drifts in. "Thank you. You're a good one," Doris says, and then she slips back under the water again.

Dressed in a clean undershirt and shorts, Doris finds Astra consoling Hugo on the couch. This is a common sight. Since Hugo was a baby, he's cried a lot, and Astra is always fussing over him, convinced she's to blame for any discomfort he feels. Yet as far as Doris is concerned, the boy is perfectly fine. Sure, he cries, but let him cry! Isn't that what kids are supposed to do?

What Astra doesn't understand is that this anxiety she has around her son gives him power, and already he knows how to use it. When she talks on the phone, Hugo pulls at the cord and shouts until she gives in and hangs up. He will only drink out of the red cup, and if she gives him another, he swats it to the floor. If she tries to have a conversation with someone else, he puts his hand over her mouth so she can't speak, yet Astra doesn't push him away or scold him for being a little tyrant. She's perfectly content to have him boss her around. It makes her feel important, Doris supposes, and necessary. *We all need a bit of that.*

When Astra glances up, she smiles meekly, and Doris realizes that this new haircut is identical to the one she was given after the cougar incident. Rough and ugly. There's a photo of her from that time somewhere, all bandaged up and bruised.

"He hates how I look," Astra says. "I keep telling him I can grow it back, but he doesn't believe me."

Doris notices now that Hugo has his eyes squeezed shut. She smiles tightly, then takes a seat on her La-Z-Boy across the room. Even after that long soak her body is still sore. "Why did you let Jesse do that to you?"

"She said cutting your hair is a good way to get rid of baggage and stuff. I thought that was a cool idea."

"It's different, that's for sure." Doris turns to the boy. "I find it strange too, Hugo. Your mother had perfectly reasonable hair. She should learn that she doesn't have to change herself every time she makes a new friend." He quickly opens one eye, peers at Doris, and squeezes it shut again. "And Astra, we actually have to have a conversation. I'm sorry if this doesn't feel like the right moment, but it can't wait any longer. For once, I want you to try to hear what I'm *actually* saying before getting the wrong idea. You can be frustratingly sensitive sometimes."

"I'm not sensitive," Astra says. She starts combing through Hugo's hair with her long fingers.

Doris clears her throat. "Well then, you won't mind me saying that it's time you find your own place."

Astra's face falls.

"There are aspects to your staying here that I've enjoyed," Doris presses on, "but I'm getting old, and I'm tired, and I need my space back. I need my *life* back. I had one of those once, you know."

The girl purses her lips.

"I'm not going to throw you out or anything like that," Doris continues. "So don't overreact. I can even cover your first and last month's rent. I'm not being cruel. Now, say something."

"I don't want to say anything." Astra's dark eyes land on Doris's and stay there.

Doris exhales heavily. "Fine. If this is how you want to do this, so be it. I'm giving you two months. Stay until the end of September. Hugo will be in kindergarten then and it's a great time for you to make some changes. This will be good for you once you're used to it. You'll see. You've had a while with me to get back on your feet. For Hugo to get older and easier."

"He's not any easier."

"Well, that's not my problem, is it? It's time for you to figure your life out. And you should work a bit more. You should experience what it's like to be on your own. Because I can't support you forever. You're wearing me out." Doris stops. She's gone on too long, her tone is too stiff, and what she's saying isn't coming out quite right. *Damn it! I'm sick and tired of always weighing my words. Why should I damp down what I have to say? Astra should learn how to deal with honesty.*

They all sit quietly for a full minute, and only when she realizes that Astra has no intention of adding anything further to the conversation does Doris get to her feet. "As far as I'm concerned, you don't get to be mad at me about this. I've given you more than enough. You are a fully capable human being. This is one of those things. Please tell me that you understand. Tell me that you hear me, at least."

"I hear you," Astra says slowly. "I just think you're making a mistake. You're acting like I've never tried to find my own place. But whenever I found one, *you* always came up with a reason for us to turn it down. *You* never thought it was good enough for Hugo. Now you're saying I forced myself on you? It's insulting."

Doris rolls her eyes. "That's an incredibly creative way to rewrite the past four years, Astra. You never put any real effort into finding anything suitable."

"Yes, I did!" Astra snaps. "God, I'm so mad at you right now. And I'm sad too. You don't have to push us away like this. You don't have to blow up our relationship just to get a little space."

At this, what's left of Doris's patience disappears. "*I* blow everything up? I'm sorry, young lady, but you're the one who churns through people at an alarming rate."

"Maybe. Or maybe we both do that? Because I understand that you want your place to yourself again. That's fine, Doris. Whatever. What I hate is how you're telling me. It hurts.

It's like you're saying we mean nothing to you," she says, her voice wobbling.

Doris blinks for a good minute, completely turned around and confused, her mind running off in random directions: Raymond. Her father. The Farm. Jane. Jane. Jane.

Do I blow everything up? No, she decides. *Astra's wrong.*

The boy's eyes are open now and he's watching Doris closely. Having to listen to all this. He shouldn't have to bear it. Children should be kept from such dramas. Why had she brought this up with him present? What was she thinking?

"Come on. Let's get out of here, Hugo. Let's go outside," Doris says, talking only to him now.

"Okay. Can we work on the bikes?" he asks, shyly.

"Yes, but only until Jesse gets back with your lunch. Fifteen minutes."

"Yay!" he says, slipping from Astra's lap and dashing towards the front door.

Doris pauses briefly before leaving the room, but when she sees the devastated look on Astra's face, she understands it's too soon to bother making amends. She sighs and steps out into the hall.

Whenever Astra works at the health food store, Doris watches Hugo and she doesn't find him much trouble at all. Because kids are kids are kids. Together, they eat rice cakes smeared with goat cheese, and apples with cinnamon sprinkled on top. They walk slowly around the neighbourhood, careful never to step on the cracks in the sidewalk. They poke sticks into holes in trees and collect chestnuts. They reread the same books: Seuss, Lobel, Sendak, and Brown. They build forts on the couch. They nap in the La-Z-Boy. But their favourite thing to do is work in the garage with the radio tuned to the classic rock station.

The only bike that's insured is Doris's Yamaha. It has a blood red frame and black leather saddle. She's preparing to sell the others: the Ducati, which will be sold for parts; the Honda with the clubman handlebars and ridged pegs; and the Suzuki with the passenger pillion. There was a period after Jane left when Doris still hoped to find someone to fill that seat again; unfortunately, that never turned out to be.

Doris gets her hearing protection from the workbench, shrinks the band to boy-size, and snaps the ears over Hugo's head, which makes him look like a turtle. The boy grabs a rag from his toolbox and takes it to the Yamaha. Because of him, whenever Doris goes out for groceries or for a ride around town, the bike shines, prompting kind, bearded men to chat with her in parking lots or on the side of the road. But she doesn't mind this type of conversation. About something material and practical. About models, makes, fuel efficiency, and the best summer highways. It's easy. Clean. Uncomplicated.

With more than normal effort, Doris throws her leg over the Suzuki and settles into the worn seat. A man is coming to look at this one tomorrow. It has a tendency to sputter and she needs to know if it will start smoothly. The engine coughs, stops, coughs again, then it catches: low, chugging. Good enough. But the vibration of the motor brings the exhaustion of mowing back, and when she tries to turn the key, her hand is almost too weak for the job. She releases the handlebars and lays her palms on her thighs. The pain in her knuckles is both dull and acute at once. Lately, she's been wondering if she should go see a doctor. Ask what the problem could be. Because she knows, deep down, that Astra can't be the only cause.

She watches Hugo rub the chrome around the speedometer. Remembering the raw expression on Astra's face, and feeling a little bad, she says, "Don't be so mad at your mother, Hugo. She doesn't deserve it."

The boy turns and peers at Doris quizzically. He pulls the ear protection off one side. "What?"

"Don't be so mad about your mother's hair," she says.

"She didn't ask me if I wanted her to cut it."

"You think she should've asked?"

"Yes. Don't you?"

"No. No, I don't, Hugo. You know you're not her boss, right? She shouldn't let you tell her what to do so much."

This idea is too complicated for the boy to comprehend so he returns his attention to the bike, rubbing his soft rag around the hinges on the brake handles. For a moment, Doris lets herself consider how he'll cope with the move.

Oh, stop, he'll be fine.

Then she wonders if Astra will forgive her for whatever it is she seems to think she's done. Realizing that Hugo is sniffling, she calls him over. "Oh, don't cry, you silly thing. Your mother is right. Her hair will grow back."

Hugo drops his rag on the floor and rushes to Doris, fully sobbing now. Throwing himself into her arms, he dries his face on her shirt. "How long will it take?" he asks, voice muffled in the cotton.

"A while. But in a day or two you'll be used to her like this and life will go on. You won't mind how she looks then. She'll be your same old mom. I promise."

Once Hugo stops his crying, they head back to the house for lunch. Squatting under the coat pegs, struggling to help Hugo out of his shoes, she overhears Jesse and Astra in the kitchen.

"I can't, Jesse. No way. She just fucking told me to move out. I'm not going to ask her to babysit now."

"Come on. She would do anything for you and that kid."

"That's why it's so weird," Astra says. "I'm worried about her. Maybe I did something? I mean, she's terrible at talking about her feelings. So I'll probably never figure out what's really going on."

Hugo stares at Doris like a big, stupid puppy as she tugs the second shoe from his foot. "Go. Get out of here. Go eat your lunch, and be nice to your mother," she says, ruffling his hair.

As Doris stands, Jesse is saying something she can't make out, but she hears Astra clearly. "No. If you want me to come to the party, we're bringing him. She doesn't deserve to be around him after acting like that."

Well, there we go. What's done is done, Doris thinks as she slips down the hall to her room. In bed, she pulls the blankets over her head and promptly falls asleep.

When Doris wakes up later that evening, the house is silent, and the clock reads 8:34. They must be out already. *Better get used to it and enjoy having the house to myself*. She goes to the fridge, finds a beer, and throws the cap into the recycling bin under the sink. Without turning on the kitchen lights, she stands at the window and contemplates the boats that are lit up in False Creek. Looking around, she can tell it was Jesse

who cleaned up after lunch; Astra is terrible at wiping counters and always leaves the job half done. Even the floor is spot-
less, with not a strand of hair left on the tile.

Then there it is: that extra silence that descends following
so much noise. She takes a deep breath and tries to empty her
mind, but she can't seem to control where her thoughts turn.
She replays the earlier argument with Astra, and then recalls
what she said about Doris not deserving to be around Hugo.
She wishes she'd offered to take care of him, instead of retreat-
ing to bed like a big ol' baby. Because what was Astra's plan for
the evening? Was she going to put Hugo to sleep at the party?
She checks her watch: it's past his bedtime now. He'll be up
late, which will only make for a difficult day tomorrow. More
tantrums. More arguments. More tears.

Doesn't matter, she reminds herself.

Once she tires of standing, she takes her beer to the living
room, turns on a lamp, and slumps into her La-Z-Boy. Across
the room, above the empty couch, hangs one of Clodagh's
photographs, one of Doris and Raymond taken the sixth
year at the Farm. They are still young, standing in the dull,
February-brown fields, just west of the greenhouse. It's a
black-and-white photo, the sky churning and stormy overhead. Unless someone pointed it out, you wouldn't know that
there was another person with them, tied to Raymond's back,
because all you can see is her moccasin-bound foot poking
out an inch above his hip: two-month-old Astra is there.
Doris has often considered taking the photo down, unsure if
it's healthy to see Raymond every time she sits in her chair.
But Hugo adores the photo. He likes to stand on the couch
and kiss his mother's secret toes, and in that spot the glass is
smeared from his lips.

In all the years Astra and Hugo have lived with her, Doris has only taken them up to Celestial once. Astra hadn't been home since moving out at seventeen, but that's how she chose to celebrate Hugo's first birthday. She figured it was time for her father to meet his grandson. When Astra introduced Raymond to Hugo, he didn't show much interest. Eventually, though, she shoved the chubby boy into his lap and began to talk about him. About how much he liked being read to, and how he loved potatoes and fruit just as she had as a child. It didn't take too long for Raymond to relax and start playing with the baby's toes, pinching one, and then another, and then the next, and making him laugh.

After lunch, Astra let Raymond take Hugo down to the gardens to show him around, but she didn't join the women at the old communal dining table; instead, claiming to be exhausted, she napped in the car until it was time to drive home. Clodagh and Doris spent the remainder of the visit catching up over tea. Sativa had recently moved out, and Clodagh, who wasn't accustomed to living on her own, was lonely and had a lot to say.

Back on the road that evening, Astra appeared deep in thought. Once they'd been driving for a while, Doris asked how she was feeling about the visit.

"Raymond hasn't changed at all. I was hoping he would have been a little more excited to see us, but whatever. I've done my part. I took my son to visit him. I can die with a clear conscience," she said, with a blank expression. That look concerned Doris at the time: Astra was so guarded and reticent. It was the same look she wore earlier today.

It was later on that drive, about halfway back to Vancouver, that Astra admitted out of the blue that it had been harder than she'd expected to face Clodagh—which was why she'd avoided her all afternoon. Doris, surprised, pried further. Because it seemed strange. Clodagh and Astra spoke on the phone often enough, and Clodagh had always been kind to her.

Astra was sitting in the back at this point, trying to nurse Hugo to sleep. "She's his grandmother," she said after a while. "I didn't think it meant much, not really. I never had grandparents, and Raymond barely cares. But when I saw her . . . This is the kind of thing that matters to someone like her."

Doris swallowed and gripped the steering wheel. "You're telling me—"

"Yeah. Freedom is Hugo's dad," Astra said.

At that point, Doris turned on her hazards and pulled over to the side of the dark highway. Looking back between the seats at the young mother and the baby, she said, "Please tell me that he knows, Astra."

"I haven't told him yet. We'd decided not to stay in touch anymore the last time he came to Calgary, and then I found out I was pregnant. What was I supposed to do?"

"You can't keep something like this to yourself! Here I thought you'd gotten involved with someone awful, but you haven't even given him a chance!" Doris found herself nearly shouting.

"Freedom doesn't want to be a father. I've heard him say those very words about a hundred times," Astra said, jiggling the boy on her lap.

"You can't know that for sure."

"Well, I'm *going* to tell him. Obviously. I'm just not sure when or how."

"If you don't—and soon—I will. I won't be a part of any cover-up. Not even for you," Doris muttered, pulling back onto the highway.

What she hadn't expected was that Astra had been completely right. Once she told Freedom, and he came out for a brief visit, Doris found him hands-off and clearly uncomfortable. He did everything he could to avoid holding the child. Then Clodagh was a disappointment too. At first, she was more involved, calling and visiting Astra often. But once Sativa had a child of her own the following year, Clodagh devoted herself to that grandchild instead, putting Astra and Hugo out of her mind altogether.

Raymond had failed her. Clodagh had failed her. Freedom had too. *Really*, Doris thinks, *I'm all they have left.*

She puts the beer down on the side table. The carbonation on an empty stomach is making her feel worse. She rubs her knuckles tenderly. *Oh, why oh why am I still thinking about these people? Stop it. Stop it. There's no need to anymore.* She pulls herself up off the recliner, turns out the lamp, and after taking a quick peek into Astra and Hugo's room—even though she knows perfectly well she will find it empty—she returns to bed.

Through sleep Doris hears an alarm. But by the time she's awake enough to realize it's only the phone, it stops. She closes her eyes, happy to have missed it. Then the ringing starts up again. *Maybe Astra will answer.* But there are no footsteps running down the hall to get it. *Right.* Doris groans and drags herself up.

When she reaches the couch, the ringing stops once more. She sits down, completely awake.

The next time the phone rings, her hand shoots to the receiver and she recognizes Jesse's voice right away. "Everything is okay. Don't panic. Astra just told me to call you."

"Why?" Her hands are tingling all over and she can barely feel the phone in her fist. "What's going on, Jesse?"

"Hugo was in the hot tub, and then he went under."

"He can't swim. Astra refuses to put him in lessons," Doris finds herself saying, though this certainly isn't information that needs to be communicated right at this moment. "I don't understand. What hot tub? Where are you?"

"The hot tub here. At my friend's house."

"He's okay, though?"

"I don't know, I think so. They're on their way now."

"Who's on the way?"

"The paramedics."

At this, Doris stands. "The paramedics," she repeats, so light-headed she isn't even sure this is real. She puts her hand on the back of the La-Z-Boy to steady her feet. "It's that serious? Who was supposed to be watching him?" she says, while her eyes swim.

"Me, I guess. Astra went to use the bathroom, but when Hugo realized she was gone he freaked out—you saw how he's been acting up all day. He tried to chase after her, and that's when he slipped. It was really scary. But I think he'll be fine. I pulled him out really fast, gave him mouth-to-mouth. And he puked right away. There was a lot of water in him, though, that's for sure. The thing is, Astra really wants you here."

When Doris hangs up, the picture of Raymond stops her in her tracks. Her breathing laboured, her throat constricted, she glares at him.

"Fuck you," she says.

Because it's then that she realizes he's the one she's really mad at—not his daughter, not the boy. She's been mad at Raymond for years. Since the day Astra was born. Since the day he left her behind on the Farm with his pregnant girl-friend, who suffered unnecessarily and tragically because—unbeknownst to them all—the baby's placenta was partially obstructing her cervix. But she let Raymond get away with all that, didn't she? Because they were friends. Because he'd been good to her and accepted her before anyone else had. Yet he failed them all in the end. He put himself first. He thought it was okay to act however he wanted, because he was a man. A man with a stupid dream that trumped everyone else's.

In the garage, Doris gets on her oldest bike. The Yamaha. The one she won't sell. The one that shimmers under her shop lights because of the boy's care. Though the rattle of the motor hurts her hands, once she's on the road, the bike runs smoother and the feeling fades. In the rush she hadn't put on a jacket. She's in boxers and a T-shirt. The cool air rushes up her sleeves and ruffles the fabric across her heart. She's for-gotten her helmet too, and this, for a minute, makes her feel young; she hasn't ridden at night in ages. And why hasn't she? Well, she supposes she stopped bothering once Astra and Hugo moved in. When there was less reason to escape her empty apartment.

Earlier, when Doris heard Jesse talking about her, saying that she'd do anything for Astra and Hugo, it made her angry, but only because it was completely true. She wants to give Hugo what Astra never had: Security. Love. A home. She wants to give him what every child deserves.

Whenever Doris babysits the boy at night, her favourite part is reading him stories before bed, how his breath slows.

He has this obsession with touching her stomach after they turn out the lights. He lifts her T-shirt and cups the bulge of her belly in his hands, kneading the rolls there. Apparently, he does this to Astra as well. But at some point, he always whispers that he likes the feeling of Doris's belly better than his mother's. "She's as bony as a carrot," he once explained. And now he says this the same way whenever they cuddle, because the first time it made Doris laugh so hard she snorted.

In the dark they talk about superheroes, the best colours, and name the grossest food combinations they can imagine: kiwis dipped in milk, mushroom-flavoured ice cream, or beans mixed in strawberry yogurt. Eventually they stop talking, and in a blink he's asleep. And every time she gets to do this, she worries it will be her last chance. Soon he'll grow up and be embarrassed by her, or once Astra moves out she'll be too busy to bring him around anymore. Most nights, once he's dreaming, Doris can't resist surrendering to the sounds of him and soon she's asleep too. When Astra finds them in bed together, she lets them be and spends the night on the couch.

Halfway across town, Doris realizes she's been so caught up in thought she can't remember the last few blocks, and she's swept with panic. Is she only sleepwalking? Had there even *been* a phone call? What is she doing? She pulls over and sits on the idling bike under an old chestnut tree. Falling forward, she lies across the handlebars, head in her arms, and sobs.

When she manages to pull herself upright, she notices the curtain of a ground-floor apartment across the sidewalk fall back into place. Someone was watching her, pulled over on the side of the road in her underwear, a fool. She wipes her eyes with her palm and sees it: the address is written right there on the back of her hand. Doris starts the bike and pushes off again.

There are two ambulances and a fire truck parked in front of the house when she gets there. Firefighters mill around on the front porch and Doris nods at them as she pushes past. The suite is dim, the walls in the hallway poster-covered, and the kitchen is a mess of half-eaten salads and empty beer bottles. She is surprised that such a dump has a hot tub.

From the kitchen, the back door yawns open to the yard. She walks out onto the stoop and stops under a clothesline that crosses over the lawn and is bolted into a hydro pole in the alley. The first thing Doris notices is that this party is all women. She freezes. Like a birdwatcher who's spotted a flock of rare creatures in a marsh, she wants to keep looking, but she doesn't want to startle them. The women are all shapes and sizes and ages. Beautiful. Plain. Some of them are sitting in their damp underwear on patio furniture. Some are naked, barely managing to hold towels around themselves. Some are overly dressed, in sweatshirts and jeans. Some are hugging, their arms wrapped around one another as they watch Astra taking care of Hugo on the gurney. The world is vastly different now than it was when Doris was young. She's lucky just to lay eyes on it. It's enough.

As the paramedics tend to the boy, Doris pulls at her T-shirt and clasps her hands over her stomach, embarrassed that she rushed out the door as she is. She feels ridiculous, standing there. Astra and Hugo have so many people to help them. Why had Jesse even called? What can she do?

"Are you Grandma?" a paramedic asks from the bottom step.

Doris looks down at her underwear and at her baggy shirt, loose over her hanging breasts. *Grandma? What in God's name is he talking about?*

"Is Hugo okay?" she asks, ignoring the question.

"It seems so. We have to take him in though, to rule out secondary drowning. It's very common in toddlers. But I'm sorry, the boy's mother said she wants us to wait for his grandmother. Is that you? We can't put this off. It's a busy night."

Across the lawn, Astra is standing beside her son as a paramedic adjusts the straps around his middle. Another is instructing her to hold an oxygen mask over his face. Despite looking terrified, Hugo spots Doris and waves at her from under all the wires and tubes.

Grandma?

Astra glances up and their eyes meet. Her lips start moving. "Thank you for coming," she mouths.

With these few words, whatever has been eating at Doris's bones all day abates for the moment. She is no longer tired. She is no longer sore. Because she could be at home right now, wandering her apartment, staring pointlessly out the window, alone. Or she could be here. She could be the one they call on when they need help.

She isn't alone. Or she doesn't have to be. No, she doesn't want them out of her house. She wants all their troubles and all their issues and all their tantrums. Because maybe that's what family is: it's the people you wake up every morning worrying about.

"Sorry," Doris says. "Grandma. That's exactly who I am."

LAUREN

OVER THE AUGUST long weekend Lauren holds six inter-
views, yet in the end none of the potential caregivers seem
suitable. Two applicants have spotty resumés, and she isn't
satisfied with their references. One fairly adequate woman is
willing to live in the downstairs suite that Lauren and Brett are
offering in lieu of some pay, and yes, she can do the required
picking up and dropping off at school; but she has a boyfriend
out of town, and so she'll want a week off each month to visit
him—which will never work with their schedules.

Lauren finds the rest of the perfectly capable candidates
harder to explain away. At first, she attempts to dismiss them
by telling her husband they simply didn't give her a good
"feeling," but Brett knows her better than anyone; of course
he does—they've been married fourteen years. Her concerns
are textbook. The women are too young or attractive to live
in their basement while Brett works from home and Lauren
is at the office, unable to supervise. Lauren is terrible with

women. She finds it hard to trust them. And although Brett has never given her a substantiated reason to be jealous, she doesn't care. Emotions don't require facts to back them up.

Last week, Brett started full-time editorial work again after being at home with Charlie for the past eight years, and so their whole system has been thrown into chaos. They'd hoped to have found help already, but the search is taking longer than Lauren expected due to what Brett likes to describe as her "extreme pickiness," and what she would argue is purely her desire to find someone "perfect."

The last applicant arrives at Charlie's bedtime, and immediately upon seeing her shimmering, corn-coloured hair, Lauren eliminates her as an option and keeps the interview brief.

After closing the door, Lauren turns to find Brett watching her from the bottom stair in the hall.

"Well?" he asks.

"Sorry. She's terribly inexperienced."

"Doesn't she work at a daycare?"

"A low-rated one. I did my research. It only has three stars."

"I have a suggestion then," Brett says. He tells her he knows someone—a woman he met at the park across the street. She has a son Charlie's age and the boys get on well. "She's been looking for an affordable place in the school catchment, but as a single parent, she says finding a decent apartment is next to impossible," he explains.

"I don't trust people who complain about the bind they're in to total strangers," Lauren says, burning with the familiar flame she gets whenever her husband mentions a woman she doesn't know.

"She isn't exactly a stranger. She's become a friend," Brett continues, carefully.

"A *mom* friend," Lauren corrects.

"What's the difference?"

She rolls her eyes.

Brett is a "good" man. This is a mantra she chants under her breath all the time, especially when he's driving her mad. *A good man. A good man.* But just because he's good doesn't mean he's easy to live with.

"Lauren, please," he says. "I think you'll like her."

"Fine. But I'm not hiring her outright. I need to meet her first."

It takes a week for the woman to find time to come by for an interview. Apparently, she works a few days a week at a local grocery store, and she's been busy helping a family friend who's ill. Lauren believes they should view this wishy-washiness as a red flag. But Brett is patient and even offers to watch both Charlie and this woman's child during the interview.

They arrange to meet at 4 p.m. on Saturday, though that morning Brett wakes with a cold and won't get off the couch so Lauren is forced to bring Charlie along. She emails the woman about the change of plan, and requests they meet at the park instead. When the time comes, Charlie runs ahead towards the playground on the far side of the field, where he greets a child Lauren assumes is Hugo and then they scurry up a primary-coloured climbing wall.

Since he was small, Charlie has hidden behind Brett's legs when other children approach, content with his dad's full attention and not really eager to make friends. But he and this boy are already playing with such animation. They are beaming, and her son is clearly smitten.

As Lauren walks towards them, she feels a little ashamed of the fit of jealousy she had when Brett first mentioned having met this woman. Of course it's quite possible he suggested bringing this family into their lives only with Charlie's best interests in mind, and by the time she reaches the playground, she's fully convinced herself to be open-minded. "Very good to meet you," she says, shaking the woman's hand.

Astra is younger than Lauren, yet not terribly so. It's obvious she had her son in her early twenties—but isn't that the case with most single mothers? She has a plain, unkempt beauty. Dark where Lauren is blond. Slim where Lauren is round. A faint scar cuts through her lips, along her jaw, and into her stringy hair. The line splits her face asymmetrically, like in a Picasso, making it hard to get a complete picture of who she is. Her faded tank top hangs over her sharp sternum and small chest, and she has a bushel of keys clipped to the belt loop of her ripped jeans. Clearly, she is not dressed for a job interview, but there are worse failings.

Lauren places her work satchel on the ground, suddenly feeling silly for bringing such a thing to a park. "It's hot out," she says, searching for a way to begin.

"Yeah," Astra replies lazily.

As their feet shuffle in the overrun grass, eyes chasing their children, Astra quickly delves into her rental troubles, and Lauren commiserates by describing her and Brett's renovation horror stories and the nightmare contractors they've dealt with over the years. They worry together over Grade Three, fingers crossed their sons will luck into teachers who understand their quirks, and they wonder if the boys might end up in the same class at some point. Astra speaks casually and slowly—not with the clip that Lauren is used to from the women at her law office, and she finds herself trying to imitate Astra's intonation. Lauren may come across as confident, but it's never been easy for her to meet new people.

After what Lauren is surprised to learn is almost an hour of chatter—nothing about references, or the job, or the basement suite—the boys run up and complain they're thirsty, sweat sticking their hair to their brows. It's only then that she realizes they are the same height and build, both missing a few teeth. She starts to dig in her satchel for Charlie's water bottle, but before she finds it Astra tells the boys to go back across the park and see if the fountain is working. The women watch them, arms outstretched like airplanes, sprinting below the huge maples, trying to outdo one another with their imitation of machine-gun fire. And again, Lauren is struck with emotion. The truth is, she doesn't make it to the park very often. She doesn't have much time to spend with Charlie. And there he is, her only child, and he's so quick on his feet now.

Everyone says that Lauren and her son are the spitting image of one another—same blond curls, same freckles and lips—though she is aware her looks suit him better. Brett finds their likeness charming and has hung pictures from her childhood beside photographs of Charlie on the staircase wall to show it off. But their fairness and broad smiles are where the similarities end. Every year, Lauren and Charlie have a harder and harder time relating. When he tells her a new joke, she doesn't find it funny. When he asks her to play Lego, she only manages to pretend to be interested for a few minutes. On Saturdays, when they drive to swimming, she finds they have little to say to each other at all. She often wonders if this distance is due to the fact she jumped at the opportunity to return to the office when Charlie was just four months old; that when Brett took over the parenting, he adapted and grew accustomed to his father's kind of love. That this is all her fault. Then again, mothers are always being guilted into regretting their decisions. And sometimes all it takes is catching a glimpse of Madonna on the front cover of *Us Weekly*, striding along the sidewalk in sunglasses and torn jeans, her nanny carrying her child and scurrying to keep up, to make Lauren remember that she's not alone. Some women stay home. Some women work. She only wishes she had a better relationship with her son.

Now the boys are taking turns at the fountain, filling their mouths and spitting water at one another.

"It's better to be this far away, because that almost looks cute from here even though it's clearly disgusting," Astra says, laughing.

They watch as Hugo bends over the faucet again, then his head jolts back and he is screaming.

When Astra takes off across the field, Lauren picks up her satchel, clutches it to her chest, and jogs along awkwardly behind. Nearing the fountain, she sees blood running down Hugo's chin. He keeps crying: "Look at all the blood! Look at the blood!"

Astra drops to the ground, pulls him into her lap, and lets him drip all over her shirt, apparently unbothered by the stains that will be left behind. The boy clings to his mother as she whispers in his ear, but it's impossible to catch what she says.

Throughout this, Charlie busies himself by twisting the toe of his sneaker in the grass while peering at his friend with scientific interest. Lauren can't help but find this behaviour embarrassing. Why isn't he showing any sympathy? Is this normal? Watching Astra and Hugo again, she tries not to count back to when Charlie last clung to her this way, with his cheek buried in her neck; she tries not to ponder the link between her inadequacies as a mother and the lack of compassion her son is displaying.

"Hugo's tooth cut his lip. That's all," Astra explains to Charlie after a brief examination. "Mouths insist on being dramatic. They always bleed more than they should."

Lauren likes the way Astra reassures her son, as if the blood is as hard for him as it is for Hugo. She smiles, reaches out, and pats Charlie's shoulder. All she wants is to touch him, to comfort him too, but he shifts away. Lauren exhales. Well, at least Astra doesn't seem to think her son is a fledgling psychopath.

Once the blood stops and Hugo wipes his eyes, the boys return to the slide, and Lauren points to their grand, sky blue Victorian. "We live right there."

"Yeah. We've been over once," Astra says.

Lauren feels her skin flame. "Oh, Brett didn't mention that."

"Hugo needed to go number two. He won't use public washrooms. It's a thing."

"Oh dear." Lauren laughs, when really she doesn't know how to feel. She'd begun to like this woman, liked how she handled the boys. She'd begun to think Brett was right all along, but here is that fear again. *I must see them together*, she decides. *I must see how Brett looks at this woman, and then I'll know what to do.*

Lauren smiles. "The boys are having such a good time, and we still haven't talked about the job! Why don't you come over so they can keep playing? I'll cook everyone dinner."

———

They're rarely inspired to have people over these days, so Brett is clearly stunned when Lauren brings Astra through the door. He staggers from the couch, where he was lying in pajama bottoms, a roll of toilet paper on his furry chest, watching TV.

"Hey Brett," Astra says, as he quickly gathers his dirty tissues from the cushions.

Brett is not without his own vanities regarding his appearance, and Lauren can tell that bringing Astra over without warning has embarrassed him, but part of her is glad for it. Out in the wild, Lauren's husband has a magical effect on people—women especially. You wouldn't think the world still works this way, yet unfortunately it does. Brett is tall, broad-shouldered, dark and bearded, and all his attractiveness and manliness is multiplied by a thousand with Charlie in tow. For years, women have adored him for being a stay-at-home dad. When Charlie was still exclusively on breast milk and Brett fed him on a park bench, women clustered around him clucking like hens, disparaging their husbands who never mastered the knack of bottle-feeding. Then, because he was a regular at the neighbourhood baby groups too, these women treated him like any other stay-at-home parent, and the stories and gossip he brought home made Lauren constantly suspicious of her husband: was it possible he was having a series of emotional affairs? She pictured their ponytailed heads resting on his strong shoulder as they cried, got his postpartum sympathy, and left tear stains on his jacket. Lauren thought these dramas would end once Charlie started school, but the pattern has only intensified. Because Brett stayed for family reading, and he insisted on joining the PAC, and he built sets for the school concerts every year, women eat him up now more than ever before. This is possibly the best thing about Brett returning to work: no longer will he get to parade around, being the schoolyard slut.

As the boys start building a marble run in the living room, Brett wraps a quilt around his shoulders, excuses himself, and heads upstairs.

"I'll make dinner," Lauren calls after him. "Just get some rest."

As she proceeds to the kitchen to pour her guest a glass of wine, she feels in control for the first time in weeks. So far, she's seen no reason to worry: Brett left the room with barely a glance at Astra at all. And Lauren can tell Astra is impressed by their home, by the long island in the middle of the light-filled kitchen and the buffed concrete floors. The envy in her eyes allows Lauren to appreciate her surroundings in a way she hasn't managed to do in a long while.

Once again, Lauren finds she has no trouble talking to Astra. Their conversation is light and easy. She becomes so energized and distracted by her guest, she burns the sausages and overcooks the carrots, yet she's able to shrug this failure off easily.

"So you know about the suite downstairs, right?"

"Yeah, Brett mentioned it."

"It's only one room really, but it's garden level and it has fabulous light during the day," Lauren says, surprised to find more wine in her hand. So she's a bit tipsy, who cares? She's the exact amount of drunk she likes. "Would you be interested in living down there if you end up helping us out with Charlie? It's only before- and after-school care, really."

"Totally. As I was saying earlier, I've been having trouble finding a place."

"May I ask then, what *is* going on with your living situation? Why do you have to move so suddenly? Is this a tenant/landlord dispute?"

"Oh, no, no, no. Not at all." Astra explains that currently she and Hugo are living with a family friend—a woman she's known all her life—who was diagnosed with lymphoma three years ago. "She was in remission, but now it's back. The last time she was in treatment, she caught one of Hugo's colds and it was a disaster. She ended up in the hospital for nearly a month," she says. "Doris wants us to stay close, to just move into another suite in her building, but I'm worried that, without some distance, Hugo will run up to her apartment every afternoon. And with him in school and all the germs, it's not safe. I'm going to continue helping her out, it's just better if we aren't right under her nose." Astra gazes into her wine and continues: "Hugo was too young to understand that he caused her to get so sick last time, but now it's going to be hard to protect him from all this. I just can't face him watching her get sicker and sicker every day. They are very close, and he can get really down on himself sometimes . . ." Astra stops and glances at Lauren eagerly. "Do you find seven an emotional age too?"

And it's this, how Astra talks about her son, that makes Lauren decide, yes, she too wants this woman in her life. She mustn't worry about Brett—he's a good man. She wants Hugo for Charlie. She wants Astra for herself.

At first, the two families adhere to clear boundaries. They phone to arrange plans, use front doors, knock. Because that's the arrangement: Astra gets a free place to live in exchange for taking care of Charlie before and after school. Technically, she's their hired help. Lauren insists on this distinction, even though she and Astra grow closer each day.

By the second month, Astra cooks dinner four or five nights a week in the kitchen upstairs, and the families no longer use the exterior entrances to get from suite to suite; instead they tread noisily through the adjoining laundry room. Most of the time the doors are left wide open, and the boys move freely upstairs and down—"like brothers," they all joke.

When Brett works into the night, Lauren sneaks downstairs to drink wine with Astra. They sit at her gold-flecked Formica table, the surface of which is cluttered with candles and neglected potted plants. It's a studio apartment, but Hugo is a sound sleeper, a soft lump on the pullout that he and his mother share and fold up out of the way each morning. Incense burns on the windowsill. Sandalwood. Cedar. Pine. Scents Astra claims remind her of Celestial, the commune where she grew up. The smoke stings Lauren's eyes and makes her nose run, but she finds she doesn't entirely dislike the musty smell and she's happy to stay downstairs late.

Lauren has stopped imitating Astra's slow, halting speech; instead she models clarity and strength—both qualities Astra agrees she lacks—and pushes her to start thinking seriously about her future. She's been working at the same grocery store for six years, and it's time for her to find a real job. Lauren convinces her to apply for a grant for single parents, and then to enrol in a legal admin certification course at a local college. She writes a letter of reference for Astra's application package, and culls her closet for business attire that will fit her. Of course, it will be impossible for Astra to succeed in a career to the degree Lauren has (it's much too late for that), but she enjoys the process of teasing out her friend's potential.

Lauren has always thrived in the position of role model. In high school, she was school president, assistant volleyball coach, the editor of the yearbook. During summer breaks from university, she worked on Ontario lakes, leading canoeing expeditions for inner-city girls. And now, every September, she picks out the two smartest yet least-confident articling students at her firm to take under her wing. She thought having a child would give her a similar satisfaction and purpose, but this hasn't been the case. Charlie idolizes his father. He isn't interested in Lauren's approval at all.

Since Astra moved in downstairs, Lauren takes longer to get ready in the mornings and she chooses her outfits with even greater care. On her lunch breaks, she buys new skirts and increasingly expensive sweaters in daring colours like burnt orange or aquamarine. When she gets home she doesn't change into yoga pants anymore, and instead rushes to the bathroom to add another coat of deodorant and touch up her face. It's thrilling to have someone around to impress.

On occasion, Brett calls them his "sister-wives," and Lauren punches his shoulder, pretending to hate the joke. When, really, it's true, their lives are richer as five. She dreads Sundays and Wednesdays and Fridays, when Astra takes Hugo to visit Doris. She dreads the hours she is left at home, alone, with only her husband and son.

When Astra begins night classes, Lauren offers to stay downstairs and watch Hugo while he sleeps. She enrols both boys in swim lessons, and she drags Astra to Tae Bo on Thursday evenings while Brett pitches balls to the kids in the park. The five of them spend movie nights hip to hip on the couch upstairs. On the fridge front there are photos of the boys at their joint eighth birthday party in October, opening presents together on Christmas morning, and having one of their epic backyard water fights. The summer before Grade Four, they take Astra and Hugo on a trip to St. Mary Lake on Salt Spring Island. Lauren is surprised at how quickly a year passes by.

Brett and Lauren have begun having their old friends over again, something they'd stopped doing when Charlie was young. But with Brett now back at work, and Astra living beneath them—almost with them—they've found the inspiration to entertain.

In August, they hold a dinner party for a few couples Brett knows from his university days. And as usual, over dessert he asks Astra to tell them about her childhood—a proven showstopper. When their friends start to *ooh* and *ahh*, Lauren can barely keep herself from groaning, while Astra, blushing, lights up like a firefly with the attention.

"Go on, tell them all about it," Brett pushes. "She didn't even have power or a flushing toilet," he then explains.

"It was all normal to me," Astra says softly, staring into her bowl of homemade ice cream.

Lauren watches their friends pour one another generous glasses of wine, as Brett teases Astra about being forced to drink mud, and how she'd never seen a TV until the age of seventeen—how she still hasn't watched *Star Wars* or *E.T.* "She's a complete cultural pariah, and it's adorable, isn't it, Lauren?" he says, laughing.

As Astra answers a barrage of questions, Lauren clears the plates and goes to the kitchen, while thinking how pathetic it is that this is the only story Astra ever tells. Lauren knows perfectly well that Celestial wasn't all that wonderful. Astra's told Lauren how neglectful Raymond was at times, how he barely educated her, and how he didn't even notice when his friends sexualized her at an extremely young age. And yet here they are, glorifying all that for the entertainment of others? Why does Brett insist on making her do this? Can't he see how *sad* it is that Astra believes her childhood is her only claim to fame, and surviving it her only real accomplishment?

After the guests leave, and Astra and Hugo return downstairs, Brett and Lauren load the dishwasher.

"You were rude tonight, you know," he says, wringing out the cloth and starting on the counters.

"What?" She slams the dishwasher closed. "I wasn't rude."

Brett goes on to say that she'd corrected or interrupted Astra too often over the course of the evening. Then, when Astra finally had a chance to talk to their friends and tell them a bit about herself, Lauren made a display of stomping off to the kitchen. "Is it that you're jealous of her?" he asks, looking at his wife as if this were a serious question.

"Oh, come on," she snaps. "I'm not 'jealous' of her."

"It wouldn't be the first time."

"Do you really expect me to hear her talk about Celestial *again*? What's actually embarrassing is how much you baby her. She's never going to learn to take up space if you're always making 'room' for her, acting like she can't kick off a conversation all on her own. Maybe there's something else she wants to talk about?"

He scratches his brow. "You've been drinking. Let's talk about this tomorrow."

Lauren laughs. "No, no, no. *We've* been drinking. And there's nothing to talk about at all."

Now, Lauren is aware that her interest in helping other women can get complicated and darken over time. And while she tries to keep her external dialogue constructive, sometimes her thoughts can meander towards the overtly critical. After a bad day at the office or a loss in court, she is prone to inspecting the thighs or wrists of any woman she sits near on the SkyTrain. She judges the length of the skirts worn by other lawyers, and the meals her colleagues order when they're out for lunch. But this is only something she does to boost her confidence when she's down, and as long as she keeps it all to herself, what's the harm?

Because the truth is that Astra isn't perfect. There are always dishes piled in her sink. She leaves the laundry in the washer overnight so it stinks of mildew. And she's always overemphasizing how tired she is, when really she can't be any more fatigued than the next person with a family and a job. In some ways, Lauren thinks Astra is a little greedy as well. She hasn't offered Lauren and Brett even a token amount of rent or a portion of the utilities, even though the housework and childcare they have her do is minimal. Yet, if you add it all up, Lauren has probably helped Astra more than the other way around.

It's also true that Astra doesn't make her son bathe when he doesn't want to, and she often calls in sick to work and keeps him home from school just so they can have more time together—when don't they have enough? Even though Lauren knows she isn't an ideal mother herself, she finds their intimacy a bit revolting. How much they talk. How often Hugo sits in Astra's lap. The thought of touching someone that much makes her claustrophobic.

When Lauren has occasionally inventoried Astra's short-comings to Brett in bed, she only wants him to agree with her. To reassure her. To say he still thinks that she is the bet-ter woman. But he doesn't. He takes off his reading glasses, shakes his head, and turns off the light.

A couple of weeks later, following a day of back-to-school shopping, Lauren brings two bottles of wine downstairs and thumps them on Astra's table.

"Shall we drink that day away?" she asks, with a forced laugh.

It certainly had been a difficult one. Twice, when Lauren told Charlie he had to try on clothes he didn't particularly like, he stormed out of the store—once even calling her "evil." Then, when Astra attempted to step in, Lauren snapped at her, telling her to stop shoving her nose in their family's business. But the worst part of the whole day came when Astra gave Charlie a look of absolute pity in the car on the drive home. It felt like a knife in the back. Because Astra has no clue how difficult it's become to have authority over Charlie when they barely have any time together alone. The house is always full of people now, and he barely acknowledges her when she gets home from work. He might listen to Astra and Brett without complaint, but he fights Lauren on everything. And so in the spirit of setting the record straight, to prove their relationship hasn't always been this tense, Lauren decides it's time to bring up her labour story. She wants Astra to *know* just how close they used to be.

Lauren loves to recount the story of this day. Brett made her a CD: Sade, the Be Good Tanyas, Sarah Harmer—all her favourite female singers. They rented a birth pool, hired a doula, and lucked into having the best midwife from their team on call when the contractions started. After only eight hours in a candlelit room, Charlie was born. He latched perfectly on the first try, while Lauren ploughed through a plate of the forbidden unpasteurized cheeses that she'd longed for while pregnant, and drank a full glass of Fonseca as he nursed.

Lauren barely left bed for two weeks, soaking up as much of her baby as she could. She traced every square inch of him: the pruned skin on his feet and fingers, the blotchy red of his bowed chicken legs, the sweet arch of his barely there hairline. Those weeks they'd been so close, inseparable, like he was still part of her.

She watches Astra closely as she goes into detail about Charlie's birth, aware that this is *the* story all mothers wish for. Whenever an acquaintance or a colleague mentions they tried for a home birth, failed, and ended up with a caesarian, Lauren secretly feels vindicated. Even if she and her son are like oil and water now, at least she can say she got the first act right. "Did you have a home birth?" Lauren finally asks.

"Yeah, in my apartment."

"Good for you," Lauren says, hiding her surprise. "Did you have midwives and a doula?"

"No. Hugo came pretty fast. I ended up having him alone."

"What do you mean, 'alone'?" This comes out harsher than Lauren intended.

"I didn't plan it. I probably should have called my doctor or just gone to the hospital, but it was like I was taken over—you must remember that sensation—as if for the first time you could handle anything?"

"So you had a doctor, not a midwife? Given your upbringing, I'd have thought having a natural birth would have been important to you," she points out, perfectly aware that this is dangerous territory—Astra had once mentioned that her mother died in childbirth for goodness' sake.

Astra's face tightens and her eyes fall submissively to her lap. It gives Lauren a shiver of pleasure to see this woman put in her place again.

Vindicated, she switches gears and says, "I'm sorry, Astra. That does sound horrible. Where was Hugo's dad during all this?"

"He wasn't there. They've only met once," Astra answers, still looking down.

"Really? That's unfortunate."

"It's okay. It's better for everyone," she adds, before taking a long drink.

After climbing the stairs and finding Brett in bed, Lauren shares what Astra told her. About how Family Services had intervened, and how they'd kept Astra and Hugo at the hospital for two weeks while they did a psychological assessment.

"Why? It's not illegal to have a baby at home."

"True. But her friend Chris got worried about her, so he turned up at her apartment. She was living alone, and she hadn't returned his calls in a few days. He found her lying on the cold floor with the baby. No blankets or anything. The cord still attached. She'd had him right on the ground! Anyways, he was the one who called an ambulance, and then when the paramedics arrived they were concerned enough with the situation that they got social services involved."

"That's horrible."

"Or maybe it was exactly what they should've done? I understand that having Charlie at home was perfectly fine for us, but that's us, Brett! Astra took zero precautions. How could she be so stupid?"

Lauren turns onto her side and faces her husband, watching him as he mulls over this new information. For the first time since Astra moved in, he isn't jumping to her defence, and Lauren sees a window in. "Do you want to hear what makes me most upset?" she adds, running a finger over his furrowed brow. She knows he appreciates it when she touches him; he wishes she were more affectionate.

"What?"

"Astra didn't tell Hugo's father about the baby for over a year. And so now, understandably, he doesn't want to be involved. But she said this like it was *his* fault!"

Brett is quiet for a while. When the air conditioner kicks in, he says, "We only have part of the story though, Lauren. It's possible that he wasn't a good guy and she's too embarrassed to tell us."

"No, no. She said she just doesn't 'care' if he's involved. But she *should* be putting Hugo first in this situation. She *should* be doing the work to make amends, don't you agree? I thought I knew everything about her, so to find out she kept this from us? This is huge, Brett. She's selfish. This is pertinent information, and we should have known about it all along. And I can't help but think about you and Charlie, what you mean to each other. Imagine if I got in the way of that? Imagine if I tried to keep him from you if we ever broke up."

"We're not going to break up."

"I know. I know. But you understand what I'm saying."

Astra's life has gotten much easier since moving in with them. Now that she's in college, she doesn't work at the grocery store anymore. And so, besides helping Doris a few times a week, she gets to study all day in her free apartment until she has to pick the boys up from school. Lately, Lauren has started to worry about this. Because of course Brett is in the house too, working upstairs in the cramped linen closet where he's installed a small table for his computer and papers. She has considered offering him her rarely used office, with the large oak desk below the dormer, but for some reason she hasn't. Sometimes she wonders if she isn't a little mean to her husband. And if this is so, has Astra noticed? Has he ever complained about this to her? Do they meet in the kitchen for coffee on occasion? Or for lunch? Are they growing closer when she isn't around? Lauren has been confident that she and Astra are the better friends, but how can she be so sure?

Lauren's worst fears are confirmed in January, when she comes home unusually early on a Friday. Taking off her coat, she hears the boys jumping off the bed upstairs, but Brett and Astra aren't in the kitchen preparing dinner. She finds them in the living room, propped against opposing arms of the couch, facing one another, toes undeniably overlapping in the crack that divides the cushions. This small touch. How they are looking at one another. Their shock as they turn and see her in the doorway. The moment lasts only a few seconds, yet that's all it takes for Lauren to learn all she needs to know.

Astra pats the spot where her feet have quickly pulled out from under Brett's, and Lauren sits where she's told.

As her husband asks her about her day, she barely hears him. *This is just another emotional affair,* she thinks calmly. Because this time she isn't angry with him. What other option did he have? He's probably lonely. He's probably scared of her. He probably has to hide most of his true feelings. So, she can forgive him. But Astra? No. Whatever she was to her—nanny, friend, enemy—it's over.

The evening drones onward. The boys want a sleepover, so they drag all the throw pillows upstairs and build a fort in Charlie's room. Astra isn't in a hurry to go down to her suite, and everyone seems oblivious to Lauren's discomfort. They keep the conversation alive and swirling like a blizzard, while Lauren barely pays attention. Then, amid the storm of their voices, she hears Astra ask why they never had another baby.

Lauren speaks for the first time all evening: "Because I'm not a natural mother."

Brett chuckles. "That's certainly a fact. Of my two wives, Astra is definitely the maternal one."

Lauren knows she's expected to laugh, but she can't bring herself to do so.

"Well." Astra sighs dramatically. "The professionals don't necessarily agree."

"Stop, Astra. You're always so tough on yourself," he says softly.

Astra shifts on the cushions. "Do you guys think I'm a good mother? I know it's a weird question, but your opinion means a lot to me."

"Of course we do," Brett replies. Astra smiles. She clearly knew that this is what he would say.

Lauren feels empty. And when Brett glances at her, urging her to add to the conversation, she only scowls at the carpet.

"Lauren? What do you think?" Astra asks.

How dare she? How dare she ask me such a thing?

"Lauren," Brett cautions. He can sense what's coming.

"I don't know. Maybe? Maybe not? It isn't up to me to judge. Do you think *you* are a good mother, Astra?"

As Lauren says this, Astra unfurls her mantis body from the cushions and stands up. She is tall, bony, withered. Is it actually possible that Brett finds her attractive? Maybe he likes her build and her voice? Maybe he likes her scars? It's certainly obvious he loves her backstory. He loves to pity her.

When Astra stomps off through the kitchen and down the creaking stairs, Lauren can almost feel her husband's wish to follow her. "That woman is unstable. I don't want Charlie around her anymore," she says, wringing her hands.

"Lauren," he pleads. "Don't do this. Our lives are finally good." He slumps back into the couch and pulls a pillow over his face.

"Don't you think it's messed up that they still sleep in the same bed?" she whispers. "They're weird."

"There's no room for two beds downstairs. And you wanted her to live there!" he exclaims through the pillow.

Lauren eases it from his face. "Is it that you're in love with her, Brett? Or is this just another one of your 'crushes'? I need to know how far this has gone. Because she's crazy. You understand that, don't you?"

"Get a hold of yourself, Lauren. You're the one who's losing it," he says, getting up and leaving her alone on the couch.

———

The next morning, after sending Hugo downstairs to his mother, Lauren locks the door at the top of the laundry room stairs. She sends Astra an email to say they've all come down with a bug, that Charlie won't be going to school on Monday, and that they won't need her help for some time.

While Brett works and Charlie is playing in his room, Lauren looks for the perfect place to eavesdrop on the suite. She finds it beneath the kitchen table, where either a vent travels under the concrete or the insulation is thinner. First, she tries Charlie's toy stethoscope, then a paper Dixie Cup from his last birthday party, a tomato soup can, and a champagne flute, before discovering that a simple pint glass works best to siphon the acoustics from below. When Astra and Hugo walk around their apartment—Lauren listens. When Astra's phone rings—Lauren listens. When Astra showers, reads her son a story, dices vegetables—Lauren listens to it all. Really, she shouldn't care. Astra is only their old nanny for goodness' sake, the one who in the end didn't work out. Yet Lauren thinks about Astra almost constantly, and she can't shake this impulse to monitor her every move.

The days keep passing. The two families don't speak. When Brett begs Lauren to chill out, she refuses. She tells him that if she catches him speaking to Astra, she'll leave and take Charlie with her. It's such a vicious threat that Brett doesn't bother fighting back. Astra stops trying to make contact. Stops knocking on their door, emailing, and phoning too. She borrows Doris's car and keeps it across the street by the park. After her night classes, Astra untangles Hugo from the rusted hatchback and carries his limp body to bed while Lauren watches them from the upstairs window.

One week following their fracture, Lauren realizes that even Astra's presence downstairs is not good for her mental health. She must get rid of her. And she must make peace with her family. She must learn to love them as they are.

On her way back from work she stops at Brett's favourite Thai place. Walking the remaining blocks home, she bumps the takeout containers with her knee and spills the sauces into the corners of the plastic shopping bag. She hopes the spring rolls aren't contaminated. That the dinner be perfect is suddenly integral. Opening the door, she finds the house quiet and empty. She heads to the kitchen, puts the food on the counter, and pours herself a glass of wine by the green glow of the stove's digital clock.

When she can't take the suspense any longer, she gets a pint glass from the cupboard, lowers herself onto all fours, and crawls under the table, the toes of her nylons snagging on the rough bits of the concrete floor. Glass: rim to the stone. Ear: to the cool base. Silence. Scrambling from under the furniture, Lauren slips and smashes the pint glass under her hand. It hurts, but she chooses to draw her knees over the shards, welcoming the pain.

She leaves the broken glass where it is, unlocks the door at the top of the stairs, and tiptoes down to the laundry room. Because they could of course still be down there. Hiding from her. And if she finds them, she's already prepared what she'll say. This will be their final act. She'll tell Astra just what she thinks: She isn't a suitable nanny. She isn't a stable person. She isn't a good influence. She's unfit to care for Charlie. Lauren will lie and say Brett agrees with her—that he wants her gone as well. She will lie and say they never cared about her at all.

Lauren knocks on the door, her heart beating in her chest. There's no answer. She tries the knob next and finds it unlocked. She lets herself in and turns on the light. The table is gone. So are the chairs and their small shelf of books. The plants and the photos on the wall. All the magazines too. The kitchen is a mess, boxes and paper strewn across the floor. All that remains is their smell: incense, mildewed laundry, and burnt butter.

Back upstairs: Thai food on platters. Bottle from the wine fridge. Serving spoons. Chopsticks. A pitcher of cold, cold tap water. Spring rolls. Shrimp. Lay it all out there. When her family gets home, they will find her here. A happy woman at the dining room table, sitting under the chandelier. Lauren waits. Five minutes. Ten. The food is getting sticky and cold, but she refuses to start without them.

When Brett finally enters, an amused expression crosses his face. The blood has glued the nylons to her knees. The fabric tugs at her skin as she gets up from her seat and crosses the room.

Standing at his side, she spreads a smile across her face. She sweeps her hand over the food like an auto show model. "I got dinner," she says. Because she must hold it together. She must prove that she can be a bigger person than she is.

Brett kisses her forehead. His beard is scratchy and smells faintly of cheese. She puts an arm around his middle. Hugs him close.

"That feels nice," he says. Then he takes her other hand, notices the slashes through her palm, and frowns. "What happened?" The blood has dried, but as he uncurls her fingers to examine the wound, the cut reopens and more pools in her cupped hand.

"Bodies bleed. It doesn't matter," Lauren replies. Then there is Charlie. He pauses in the doorway. "I got our favourite," she tells him, as kindly as is humanly possible.

"I don't care. I'm not hungry," he says, before dashing up the stairs to his room.

"It's been a hard day for him," Brett explains.

"He knows they've gone?"

"We helped load the truck. The boys were sad. But it's okay. They'll see each other at school. Everyone will be fine."

"Yes, I agree." Lauren nods, trying to look serious, and pretty, and womanly, and natural, and not scared or worried about their future at all—when all she is, is terrified. Because does she even love this "good man"? It's so hard to tell anymore. "I was thinking that you should have my desk. You need the space more than I do. Please. Take the whole office," she says, even though it hurts very badly. As if some glass splinters had flown down her throat and caught there, cutting her up from the inside.

"Really?" Brett says. "You'd do that for me?"

"Of course. I don't even know why I held on to it for so long."

NICK

"ARE YOU REALLY okay with sitting in the car for a whole hour while I'm in there?" Astra asks, rummaging through her canvas bag for her phone. She puts it on silent and then shoves it in the pocket of her red wool coat. Her hair is still damp from the shower, tied in a loose knot on top, and her lips are slightly chapped. When she's anxious, like she is now, she bites the upper one where there's a scar.

"I don't mind. I have my book. Just have a good time," Nick says, making sure to sound cheerful. It's critical that he buoys her for what lies ahead.

Astra smooths her scarf over her chest and prepares to make a run for it. It's a downright nasty day, nearly dark already although it's only mid-afternoon, puddles along the curb and crows huddled together on the power lines overhead. "I don't think I'm supposed to have a good time, do you?"

Nick chuckles. "Or productive? You know what I mean."

Astra squints, considering this, and then she agrees. "Sure. Productive. I'll do my very best."

Nick watches his wife rush through the heavy rain to the gate, and then take the gravel path around the side of the house. Once she's out of sight, he uses the lever and pushes the driver's seat back as far as it will go to make room for his legs. Next, he props his novel open against the steering wheel, but finds he's not in the mood to read.

The therapist's house doesn't have a sign indicating that she works there, and he wonders what the neighbours think of people going in and out all day. The house is early twentieth century with a heritage designation plaque affixed to the porch, intricate woodwork siding on the top two floors, and a mansard roof. It's hard to tell from the outside, but from what he's seen online, these houses are often renovated to be fairly modern inside, with new marble kitchens, gas inserts in the fireplaces, and the mouldings overpainted a warm paper-white. Lately, during the slower moments at work, Nick's been obsessing over the daily listings his agent sends him. Although Astra says she doesn't want him to take on another mortgage, this time on their behalf, he believes finding a bigger place is paramount. Right now, the three of them are crammed into his tiny, open-concept loft, and Astra's son doesn't even have his own bedroom. When he's not asleep on the couch, the kid, desperate for privacy, hides in the bathroom. When Nick asked Astra what Hugo did in there for so long every day, she said she thought he sat on the toilet seat and worked on his Spider-Man drawings. Though mother and son claim that this is fine, that they can live anywhere, Nick finds this living arrangement untenable. He wants the boy to have his own door with a lock, a rec room in the basement where he can hang out with his friends, and a basketball hoop in the driveway. Nick's goal is to find them a suitable home by summer.

He leans across the passenger seat and rubs some fog away from the window so he can peer out. He figures Astra is settled inside by now, her damp coat hanging by the door. He pictures her on a comfortable armchair. Leather. Deep brown. Like an old-school psychoanalyst would have. And, because she's always fiddling with her hair, it's likely she's redoing her bun. Part of him wishes he was in there with her—although he's aware that this is a strange thing to want. No. This will suffice. It's good of him to be here, to be dedicating his Saturday afternoon to this: to getting his new wife to a place she needs to be.

Nick and Astra knew one another for only a few weeks before getting married, but it had taken him forty-two years to meet someone he wanted to settle down with. Prior to Astra, he wasn't the kind of guy who required a relationship to complete him. He had friends. Books. His apartment. He'd been perfectly happy alone, until the afternoon Astra walked into the Supreme Court library and handed him a crumpled list of cases she needed copied. Right away he knew she was "the one." He asked another librarian to watch the desk and then he spent the remainder of the day helping Astra, pulling books from shelves, thumbing through indexes, and marking pages, while she idly tagged along, teasing him and complaining about work. Astra was unconventionally intelligent and obviously a little rough around the edges with her bitten nails, staticky pencil skirt, and the subtle scars around her mouth, but that's exactly what Nick had been waiting for: a complicated woman.

The rain is falling heavier now, and his view is again obscured by condensation. He clears another spot to see out: the house is dark and it appears empty—even though he knows it's not. He looks at his watch: 3:23 p.m. Thirty-seven more minutes to go. He wonders if she's gotten into anything pertinent yet with the therapist. Astra is more or less emotionally astute, though she has a tendency to circle around a problem, nibbling at the edges timidly, and it can take a lot of encouragement and effort to convince her to really bite in.

"I'm so nervous," she told him on the drive over. "What if I sit there, frozen, too embarrassed to say anything at all?" Noticing that she needed some guidance, Nick said he believed she should bring up Doris's death. Her grief seemed like an obvious place to begin. Astra nodded solemnly. "Yes," she agreed. "That's what I'll do."

It was only a few days after their small wedding ceremony in Queen Elizabeth Park that Doris's health took a turn, and Astra began spending most of her time in the hospice ward at St. Paul's. Nick hadn't been prepared for this, nor could he keep up with his wife's unpredictable waves of grief: sometimes she expressed relief that Doris was finally free from pain; sometimes she sobbed and hid under the covers; sometimes she claimed it didn't matter, they weren't even real family. When, in actuality, Doris *had* been a mother figure to Astra, but getting her to actually acknowledge this has been difficult. Nick likens talking with Astra about her past to unrolling a spool of barbed wire fencing—at every point there are tangles and sharp bits where they snag and stall. Astra claimed this resistance to discussing her feelings was because she'd never really "let go" or "dug deep" with anyone before, and so Nick suggested she find a therapist. Because he wants his wife to heal. For her. For him. For their united front. And now, thankfully, here they are.

He jumps, startled, when Astra finally opens the door.

"Hi," she says, grinning and wiping the water from her brow. "This rain is intense! I don't think I've ever seen anything like it. It must be worse here, up by the mountains."

"It's sort of fabulous, isn't it," he agrees, starting the car and cranking the defrost dial. There it is—that rush when he sees her. His heart quick and erratic, like a toddler playing drums.

"So, how did it go? I want to hear all about it," he says. The wipers are screeching away, yet fairly ineffectual against the rain.

"It was pretty good. I feel pruny and soft. Like I've been submerged in salt water for about twenty-four hours. But I think that goes with the territory, don't you?"

Nick takes this as a favourable response. "Absolutely," he says. "And how was she? Did you guys connect?"

Astra stops organizing her belongings and dumps her bag at her feet. "Actually, Nick," she continues, assuming a careful, singsong affectation that's foreign to him, one clearly intended to soften the blow of what's coming, "I don't really want to talk about it, if that's okay."

"Oh, sure," he says, surprised.

During the weeks leading up to this, her first appointment, Astra spoke endlessly about the different therapists she found online, finally asking him to weigh in and help her choose. Together they analyzed photos, read reviews, googled, and googled, and googled. He knows that, left to her own devices, she would tell him everything that they discussed, and that the therapist must have recommended their sessions remain private. *Actually*, he repeats to himself, mimicking his wife's silly tone. *Actually, Niiick.*

He switches on the blinker, eases into the next lane, then dares a brief look at her. Her eyes are puffy and the tip of her nose is pink. She's been crying, poor girl.

He clears his throat. "I totally respect your privacy. This is your therapy, Astra. I just want to know if we've found the right person. I've become a little invested."

She takes off her scarf and then dials down the heat, which is blasting at them like a hot gale. "I know. But please don't worry. She's perfect."

"She has techniques that will help? She won't be too easy on you?" he adds.

"Oh, I see! So that's what you think? That I need some tough love?" she asks, swatting him lightly on the forearm.

He laughs freely now, and thinks: *Precisely*. "I just want you to get the most out of the experience. That's all I'm saying."

"I get it," Astra says, relaxing into her seat. "But no. To answer your question, I don't think she'll be too easy on me."

"And she understands what it is you want help with?"

Astra folds her hands in her lap. "I *said* she was great, Nick. Please stop."

Since it's apparent that this is all the information he's going to extract from her, he rests a hand on her thigh—a habit when they're in the car together. This is one of the ways they demonstrate their affection, their dedication to being on the same team. Normally, she'd take his hand and give it a squeeze, yet today she doesn't. She sits extraordinarily still, eyes fixed straight ahead almost robotically. *That's okay too*, he decides, pulling his hand away. *She's had quite the day.*

———

A month later, Nick retrieves plates from the cupboard, selects glasses from his liquor caddy, and carefully sets two places at the tiny table in his loft's micro kitchen. He glances at the clock above the fridge and frowns. All day he's been looking forward to Astra walking in the door, kicking off her shoes, and throwing herself into his arms before accepting a glass of wine and marvelling at the meal he's prepared. She was fairly deprived as a child. She never had a birthday party or presents, she never stayed in a hotel or took a trip, and she definitely didn't have someone at home cooking her favourite meals, so now he showers her with these modest pleasures at every opportunity. Unfortunately, Astra is late and dinner will be both cold and overdone.

His wife only ever cooks the basics. Soups, stir-fries, salads. And she works over the stove like someone brought up in Communist Russia, first digging deep in the fridge to find the most wilted and sad vegetables, then planning an entire meal around them as if they can't afford better. Her dinners aren't terrible, they're simply functional, whereas Nick approaches the kitchen with considerable flair.

Tonight, Hugo is staying over at Brett and Charlie's apartment, and Nick is preparing halibut and risotto. With this particular dish, timing is everything, so he checks the clock again. They usually sit down at seven, but it's already ten minutes past. He opens the oven and pokes at the fish. It's rubbery and blackening at the edges. He removes the baking sheet, places it on the stovetop, and covers everything in foil.

Though they hadn't explicitly confirmed their plans for the evening, this morning Astra mentioned she'd be home right after her meeting with Doris's lawyer. Nick's very eager to hear about this appointment, regardless of the fact that Astra keeps insisting it's just a formality, and that the most she'll get is Doris's old car. His hunch is that whatever the lawyer says, it will at least provide her with some closure. Secretly, he hopes it will also encourage her to open up. Because so far, despite four therapy sessions already, Astra hasn't started confiding in him in the way he expected.

When his wife finally puts her key in the door, thirty minutes late, the nagging feeling of annoyance with her tardiness falls away. Nick puts on a smile and begins scooping the risotto onto their plates. But once she is standing in the doorway of the kitchen, it becomes clear that they won't be sitting down right away. Astra is out of sorts. Her hair is even messier than normal, and her coat has a long brown stain down the front.

"Hi," he says, setting down their plates. "What happened to you?"

"Coffee. I spilled it on the bus," she answers, dabbing at the coat madly with fistfuls of wet paper towel.

Nick gave this coat to Astra a few weeks after they were married. When he handed her the huge box with the elaborate bow, her eyes filled.

"Well, are you going to open it? There's a gift inside, you know," he said, teasing, and pleased by her reaction.

"I don't even care. I love the box!" She'd never been given something so practical, so beautiful, and for no reason, with no strings attached. "Why do you love me so much? I don't get it," she cried.

"How could I not? You're incredible," he said as he watched her twirl in front of the dark living room windows, the city sparkling in the background.

Now Nick takes Astra by the forearms and holds her firmly before him. She is tall, but he still towers over her. He bends his knees and meets her gaze straight on. "Are you okay?" he asks. "You seem stormy. What's going on? Is it the coat or did the meeting go badly?"

Her eyes drop to the floor. "I don't want to talk about it."

"Okay. I figured you'd be upset, but we should discuss these things, don't you think?"

"Please, give me a minute to get in the door at least, Nick. I need to get out of these clothes," she says, pulling away without a glance in the direction of their waiting dinner.

This walking away is pretty much the only change he's noticed since Astra started therapy. She claims she's "setting boundaries," but Nick would argue the behaviour could just as easily be labelled "withdrawing." The reason he wanted Astra to find a professional to talk to was so she'd become *more* willing to communicate and work through her issues with him, not the opposite. And so it's frustrating when she leaves the room like this. But maybe he shouldn't expect her to transform overnight. Pendulums must swing in one direction before they build the momentum to go the other way.

Finding himself unable to shake his annoyance, he sits in front of his plate. Then, right as he's about to start without her, she calls down from the loft: "I'm sorry if I'm acting weird."

"It's okay. But you *are* being a little strange," he adds, with a short laugh, forgiving her easily.

"It's just that I have to phone Raymond. And you know how I hate that."

"Raymond? Why?" he asks, looking up at the railing of their bedroom.

She pokes her head over. "I promise I'll tell you every-thing. I only want to get this over with before I lose the courage," she says. "Okay? Can you wait for me?"

He puts down his fork. "Of course," he says, all the while thinking: *Oh boy. Here we go.*

Nick has met Raymond only once, on the day of their wedding, which, even though it was late fall, Astra had insisted on holding in the park. She had been fairly confident he wouldn't even show, but then there her father was, almost on time, pulling up in his beat-up truck and parking illegally at a yellow curb. When she saw him, Astra asked everyone to wait five more minutes, before running over to greet him.

That day, Astra's near-black hair was parted to the side and fell down her back like streams of chocolate. She was a rare beauty on a cool afternoon, in a spring dress the colour of morning sun. As she stood beside her father, Nick couldn't help but notice their uncanny resemblance. They were both willowy yet strong, and their faces were the same: triangular and sharp, with those chiselled, prom-inent cheekbones and those magnetic dark eyes. They had the same lazy way of walking too. Whenever Astra and Nick went anywhere, she moved at a frustratingly slow pace, and he often had to link his arm in hers and drag her along to keep them at a decent clip.

There wasn't an opportunity for Nick to be formally intro-duced to the man until after the ceremony, once the guests were back at the crowded loft drinking wine. And then he was disappointed when Raymond only shook his hand briefly before commenting on the grapes. "How many miles and in how many trucks have these travelled?" he asked, a little patronizingly, while greedily loading his plate.

Astra had mentioned her father only a few times; even still, Nick understood that he was a character, an enigma. He'd been prepared for some sort of heart-to-heart where they would size one another up, after which Raymond would concede that Nick was the right man for his daughter. Yet Raymond didn't ask him anything. Not what he did for a living, or how he met Astra, or if he was an axe murderer. He simply left Nick without a second glance, walked over to where Doris was sitting by the window in her wheelchair, and started shovelling grapes into his mouth.

That's when any remaining possibility of Nick ever liking the man fell by the wayside. Because even though Astra had appeared pleased when Raymond got out of his truck, Nick knew how excruciating the days leading up to the wedding had been, worry furrowing her brow as she baked for the reception and stitched up a tear in the waist of her dress. Astra kept insisting that she could "sense" it: he wasn't going to come. And she felt stupid for even inviting him in the first place when it was only going to lead to disappointment. But it wasn't until he left Nick standing there to go eat his grapes that Nick allowed himself to get angry. And in that moment it became categorically important to him that Astra recognize the kind of man her father really was. He was selfish. Disrespectful. He didn't deserve her love. Despite this and all of Nick's efforts, to this day she still digs in her heels whenever he brings Raymond up.

After emerging from the bathroom, where she went to place the call in private, Astra sits across from Nick at the table, her clammy fingers clouding her wine glass.

"Are you ready to tell me what's going on?" he asks, keeping his voice level to encourage her. He is prepared for a long conversation. For tears. It will be a dramatic night, he can tell.

"She left me everything," Astra explains flatly.

"Sorry?" Nick adjusts his seat. "What do you mean? Like her house?"

"The house. Her savings. Her investments. All of it. She has an educational fund for Hugo too. She even left him her motorbike." Astra takes a large gulp of her wine, then wipes her mouth with the back of her hand. "Oh God, I hope he never rides that thing."

Shaken, Nick sits there for a minute, staring at his wife. He never got to know Doris well, and he'd assumed she had other family—maybe a nephew or niece on the other side of the country. "Wow," he eventually says. "That's intense. Are you okay?"

"I was kind of freaking out. But now I'm better. I just needed to talk to Raymond. I thought he would be mad at me or something?"

"Why would he be mad?"

"Because she left me Celestial too. I always thought it belonged to him. But, no. The Farm has been hers since the beginning. He's just living there."

Like a parasite, Nick thinks but doesn't say to his wife.

"I have all the information in my bag. The Farm never made money, not once in forty years. Doris mailed a cheque up every month. Anything Raymond needed, she gave him." Astra is sobbing now. "In the winter, when the Farm was low on food, she paid for our groceries, Nick. For my clothes and shoes too. And she never bothered to tell me!" Her face is flushed, her hands flying everywhere: rubbing her eyes, fixing her hair again.

He places a box of tissues on the table, and takes her hand in his. As he waits for her to calm, he fiddles with her wedding ring. It's simple: thin, gold, a perfect understatement to pair with this modest woman of his.

She leans forward and they share a damp kiss. Then, when she sits back, she sighs softly. "The part I'm struggling with is, why didn't she leave *him* the Farm? That's what I want to know."

"What was Raymond's reaction?"

Astra's eyes fill again. "He got kind of quiet. And I *do* feel bad for him. God, he's so alone up there."

"What do you have to feel bad for? You should kick him off. Sell it if that's what you want to do."

She pulls her hand away and picks up her wine glass. "Why would I want that? You're always twisting my words whenever I talk about him. Do you hate him, is that it?"

I might, he thinks. Instead he says, "Of course I don't hate him. I'm only saying that he's a grown man. You don't have to baby him."

Astra pushes her chair back. "Maybe I need a walk."

"What? You just got home, and you haven't even told me what he said."

Astra sighs again, this time with irritation. "He said I was free to do whatever I want. He said, 'Astra. You're the star of the cosmos, ruler of the skies.'"

Nick laughs, even though he knows it makes him appear insensitive. "That's ludicrous. What does that even mean?"

Astra grabs her coat from where she'd thrown it over a spare stool. "It doesn't *mean* anything. It's just what he says when he's in over his head."

"Wait. Don't go yet. I want to hear how the conversation ended."

Her shoulders slump. "I told him I'd never take his home away. I told him I'd help him out." Nick frowns. "See! I knew you'd disapprove. This is why I didn't want to tell you anything. I knew you'd try to convince me to do something different."

"All I wish is that we'd discussed this first. We're supposed to be a team, Astra. We're supposed to make plans *together*."

"Fine." She shuts her eyes briefly, and when she opens them again, she speaks in that new, ridiculous tone she's become so fond of since starting therapy. "I'm sorry, Nick. Next time I'll talk to you first." She pulls on her coat. The stain is nasty. He'll take it to the dry-cleaner for her tomorrow. That's what he'll do.

"Thank you," he says, though nothing feels resolved at all. "I accept your apology. We can talk when you get back. I love you, Astra."

Her back is to him now, but he hears her sigh one more time. "I love you too."

Astra won't say where she's taking them, yet Nick is pretty sure he knows where they're going the whole drive. Every evening this week she's been at Doris's apartment, sorting through her things, boxing items up for donation, cleaning, and getting the place ready.

"Ready for what?" he asked a couple of times.

"I don't know," she replied. "I'm still trying to figure that part out."

When they arrive at the estate and get out of the car, Nick is momentarily hopeful. The house is in an outstanding neighbourhood, relatively close to the new SkyTrain line, and a short walk to some great grocery stores and his favourite butcher. The house is stone and large, and the grounds—though overgrown—are green and dappled with mature fruit trees. It's only once they're inside and climbing the stairs that he recognizes it for what it really is: a monstrosity. The place has been haphazardly broken up into apartments, their entrances shabby—boots and umbrellas left drying on the worn, dirty carpet. Immediately his allergies flare up and he has to suppress a sneeze. He's further disappointed when they step into the top-floor apartment, which he expected to find nearly empty, boxes stacked here and there. Instead it's set up as if Doris were still alive. Hugo, who was listening to his headphones the entire ride over, makes himself at home right away, rushing past in the tight hall and throwing himself on the couch without removing his shoes.

"Well?" Astra is grinning, her arms spread wide. "What do you think?"

"I'm not sure?" Nick mutters, checking back over his shoulder to make sure the door is still there.

"Come see the rest of the place," she says, taking his hand and pulling him in deeper.

There are dusty fireplaces in each room, fabric lamps, and the hallways are dreadfully dark. When Astra switches on the bathroom light, he sees them: dinosaur-sized silverfish scurrying under the claw-foot tub. The kitchen is slightly better, though it's narrow like a train car with chipped maroon cabinets. He notices that the small window over the sink has a large crack in the glass.

When they return to the living room, Astra sits in a sagging recliner as he leans against a mantle cluttered with photos of various people from the hippy days. Hair long, babies propped on hips, goats nipping at their heels. "How much does this place take in a month?" he asks.

"Quite a bit, actually. The accountant says six thousand after expenses and taxes and everything. Which is surprising since most of the tenants have been here since the eighties and Doris never bothered with rent increases."

"That's not a lot, as far as I'm concerned," Nick says as he studies the ceiling and the water-stained patches on the plaster. "This land is probably worth a fortune though," he adds.

Astra frowns and then glances at Hugo on the couch. The boy is still wearing his headphones, moving his feet to the music, and his eyes are closed. Regardless, Astra drops her voice to a whisper. "I'm not selling it, Nick. Doris wanted me to *have* this place. Not get rich off it."

"Or she wanted you to be financially secure. Maybe she actually believed in you, thought you were perfectly capable of making decisions for yourself."

"She wanted me and Hugo to be secure, yes. That's obvious now. But I keep thinking: what if we move in here instead of buying something new? Wouldn't that be easier?"

"Live here? It's too small."

"It's two bedrooms, plenty of space for us."

The lighting is so poor, it's hard to identify Astra's expression, but Nick can feel her passion radiating from across the room. Honestly, he doesn't know what to say to this. Especially since earlier today he finally found the perfect place for them. He can't help but be annoyed. He's the one who applied for their mortgage, the one who wasted hours wading through new listings, and now she's throwing this curveball into their plan?

"Well, what are you thinking?" she asks.

"It's an idea," he says, trying his best to keep the irritation out of his voice. "Though I must admit I was hoping to leave apartment living behind. To have a detached house for the first time. With a yard and all that."

"There's a yard here. We'd share it, but it's huge."

Nick scratches the back of his neck. He is sweating, but he doesn't want to take off his jacket. He wants to flee this disappointing room. This sad apartment. This teardown of a house. "I'm uncomfortable with the idea of being a landlord too," he goes on. "I don't want to have power over other people like that."

Astra shoves her hands in her pockets. "I would be the landlord. That's what I'm saying. That would be *my* job. You'd be living with me. I have an opportunity here, Nick. If I'm careful with what Doris left me, Hugo and I will be fine for a long, long time. I could be the new Doris. I could just mow the lawn and occasionally call a plumber. I can picture myself living that way. I could finally quit my job."

"You have a great job."

"No, I don't. I hate it. Lauren is the only reason I started working there."

Nick shrugs. "I know. It's just . . ."

"What? Please do tell me." Astra is using that tone again.

Now he groans. "I'm so hungry, I can't think clearly. How about we go get some dinner and talk more then?"

"Sure," she says, though it's obvious she's disappointed. She gets up from the chair, crosses the room, and kisses her son on the forehead.

Hugo pulls his headphones off. "What's the problem?"

"Nick's hungry. Let's go eat."

"You said we were going to order food in."

"New plan," she explains, ruffling his hair. "Come on."

"Astra, so you've asked Nick to join us," the therapist is saying, before Nick has even gotten through the door. He supposes time is of the essence when you're on the clock. He strides over to the couch and takes a seat beside his wife.

"Yes, I have," Astra says, tucking her hair behind her ears. She is wearing it down today, which is a welcome change.

Astra's hand is between them, so he takes it and then smiles at the therapist. "It's a pleasure to meet you."

The therapist is watching him guardedly, conveying little about her impression of him so far. He leans back and breathes deeply through his nose, reminds himself that she is Astra's therapist; it's only right that she be wary of "the husband" at first. *I'll win you over in five minutes*, he thinks.

"I'm unsure where to start," Astra says, her eyes darting to Nick and then returning to the therapist. "I know I say this every time, but it's always true."

Nick jumps in. "She said the same thing when I drove her to her first session. She was like, 'Why am I even going? What am I going to say?'" He chuckles at the memory.

"And how did you respond when she said that?" the therapist asks, focusing on him now. She is a handsome woman, in her late fifties. Her grey hair slicked back neatly, exposing long beaded earrings. Although it's her hands that are most striking, heavily ringed in amber, turquoise, and jade, and rough as if she works with them, when obviously she doesn't.

Unsure of how to answer this, Nick turns to Astra for assistance. "I don't really remember? I must have told you to talk about Doris?"

"Yeah," she agrees.

"I'm sure I mentioned your father too."

"Most likely."

"Okay," the therapist says. "And I'm sorry, Nick. You said you drove Astra here for her first session?"

"Yes."

At this, Astra's gaze falls to her lap.

"And did you pick her up afterwards?"

"No, I waited in the car. I had my book," he explains. He shifts his weight on the stiff couch cushions.

"I'm sorry, you were right outside?"

Nick looks over at his wife, hoping she'll jump in and corroborate his story, yet she leaves him to deal with this line of questioning on his own. "It was raining. I didn't want her to take the bus all the way home. We live downtown. Near the Main Street terminal."

The therapist nods sharply. "I get a sense of pride, as you talk. Would you say that's true? Did you feel good about bringing Astra here?"

Jesus, he thinks, *what does that prove?* "Of course I felt 'good' about it. She's my wife. I gave her a ride, it's not a big deal."

"Yes. Okay," the therapist says. She leans forward and puts her elbows on her knees. "I wonder why you didn't mention he was waiting outside that day, Astra?"

His wife is still focused on her lap. "I don't know."

"How was it, having him out there?"

"It was nice, I suppose. I felt supported. And . . ." She stops.

The therapist pries further. "And what? Go on."

"It was a bit strange, because I swear I could feel him thinking about me. It sounds stupid, but it's true."

Nick pulls his head back with a grimace. "I wasn't thinking about you, Astra. I was reading."

The therapist uses the arm of her chair as a table, and jots a note in a slim black book. Then she closes it again.

Astra goes on. "I guess it was a bit distracting too. Like I was *aware* of him the whole time. I kept wondering what he would think if he could hear me." She briefly peeks at him as she says this, then she adds, "I've taken the bus ever since."

Nick grits his teeth. If they were alone he'd argue this point with his wife: *It's impossible to feel someone thinking about you.* He's reminded of the superstition that if your ears are ringing, then someone must be talking about you. It's exactly the kind of nonsense that Astra would believe.

The room is not what Nick pictured that first day while sitting in the car. Although he was right to assume the house had been gutted, the reno is more severe than he imagined. Everything is painted a brilliant, bluish-white, the lighting is harsh, and the furniture appalling: knockoff modern from a big box. There is only one oil painting, on the far wall, above the therapist's head, swirls of black and grey—a representation of clouds looming over a mountain, he supposes. The only colour, a scattering of flecks at the bottom: yellow, red, orange, gold. Or it's possible the clouds aren't even clouds, perhaps they represent a mood or trauma. The light bits of paint: hope lurking under all that darkness. He presumes every item in a shrink's office must be symbolic. The lighting. The art. Even the therapist's rings must have *meaning*.

"Nick," the therapist is saying. "I'm curious, why do you think Astra brought you here today? Did she mention her reason to you?"

"No. She asked me to come, and so of course I said yes." He is managing to put sentences together, but in truth he's finding it hard to pivot away from Astra's earlier comment. It was *nice* of him to have given her a ride. And he didn't think about her the *whole* time; he had other pressing issues on his mind. Work. The house. Other concerns he can't recall at this exact moment. The therapist is watching him, waiting for more. "Astra's remarkably firm about not discussing her sessions," he adds. "So I never press her for information."

The therapist scratches her temple with the tip of her finger. Her nails are clipped painfully short. "Okay. Well, why do you *think* Astra asked you to come?"

"She wants me to support her. To help her."

"All right. And do you think she needs help?"

"Sure, I do."

"Why is that?"

Uncomfortable, Nick chuckles. All these questions are tedious. She's talking to him like he's a second-grader. But both Astra and the therapist are staring at him as if this tactic weren't obviously performative. And incredibly annoying.

Astra is biting her lip. The hair around her brow is a tad greasy, and she has bags under her eyes. She seems tired, older. Why would a therapist use LED bulbs? Everybody in this room looks the worse for wear.

"I'm sure Astra has already told you. A lot has happened in the last six months." Nick is mindful of his tone and is careful to keep it bright. "She took care of a dying friend. Now she's grieving. It's enough to make anyone need someone to talk to."

"And you guys got married," the therapist adds.

"Yes. I married her as quickly as possible," he says with a grin. He's aware that people find this fact about them charming.

The therapist doesn't smile. "Why the rush?" she asks.

He shrugs and finally lets go of Astra's hand. He wipes his palm dry on his jeans.

"Did that feel like the only way to keep her?"

Nick laughs again, yet only for a second before he abruptly falls silent. He wishes he could stop this nervous habit. "Sure, though I wouldn't use the word *keep*. That's a bit much. And our marriage is outstanding. If I mentioned everything amazing about Astra, we'd be here for hours."

"My point is only that it can be tricky at the beginning."

"Maybe. I suppose we still have a few things to learn about one another." Nick glances over at his wife. She's untucked her hair from behind her ear, and now it's falling forward so he can't see her expression. *Ah*, he thinks, *this is why she wore it down—so she'd have somewhere to hide if things got awkward.*

The therapist crosses her legs with a swish of pant fabric. "All right. Before we hand this over to Astra, Nick, maybe you can tell me a little about any challenges you perceive in your relationship so far?"

"Hmm... I suppose most of our problems surround Doris, and Astra's grief. Her childhood too. She has a bit of trouble opening up and trusting people."

"Okay, but that's Astra's stuff. Right now, I'm interested in you. How do you struggle? What do you find difficult in your relationship?"

Nick thought he'd been prepared for this session; now he's not so sure. He checks his watch: time is crawling. "Well, my apartment is a problem," he says slowly, careful again. This must be how soldiers feel in Iraq: tiptoeing through the desert, worried about IEDs buried beneath the brush and sand. Don't make any sudden moves!

"What's the problem with the apartment exactly?" she asks.

"Well, we *were* searching for a new place. Unfortunately, now I can't quite figure out what Astra's plans are."

Astra cuts in. "You *know* what my plans are." She directs her next statement to the both of them. "I want us to move into Doris's apartment. I took Nick there last week. But you didn't like it, did you?"

"The apartment was fine," he retorts, though of course it was just the opposite. There's no way he'd ever live there.

"I love it," Astra is saying. "Some of the best years of my life were when I lived there with Doris. Hugo feels the same way."

"She loves the place so much she's been sleeping there," Nick adds, regretting it as soon as the words are out of his mouth.

"We slept there *last* night. One night. Doris didn't want a memorial and Hugo wanted to spend more time there, as a way to remember her. He's been really messed up about all this," Astra says, turning to glare at Nick. "And we invited you to come with us, but you refused."

"I wouldn't say I refused."

"Yes, you did. I asked you twice. Hugo even asked you. And you said no each time. It's like you're punishing me for wanting to talk about our options. Or you're horrified that I might want something different from what you've decided for us."

"Is that true, Nick? Would you rather she didn't want to move in there?"

"It's possible. Maybe," he says, then he tries to explain. The dust. The size. The cost of replacing single-pane windows. Then somehow Astra takes over the conversation again, and he can't even listen to her anymore. He's completely lost. He wants to buy them a house! How is that a problem?

After Astra finishes her point, the three of them sit in silence, the silver clock on the table ticking steadily.

The therapist claps her thighs lightly. "Why don't we change direction?"

Nick stops her. "Hold on. You asked what I find difficult in our relationship. I didn't get a chance to finish."

Now he really dives in. First, he talks about Astra's new habit of leaving the room whenever he inquires about anything personal, how she calls it "setting boundaries." Then, he moves on to Raymond. How frustrating it is that Astra won't admit that she has major issues there. He even uses the word *parasite* when describing him, because ever since he discovered the financial facts concerning Celestial, that's the only way he can think about the man.

Astra, addressing the therapist, interrupts again. "This is what I was telling you last week."

The therapist is focused on Astra in a manner that conveys absolute understanding.

"What were you telling her?" Nick asks, glancing from one woman to the other. God, he definitely had this wrong. This is a trap of sorts. *Yes*, Nick thinks, *this is an ambush*.

"See how he's always talking about me and my family? About my childhood? Picking it apart and thinking he knows better about . . . well, about everything! He's been talking about me ever since we walked into this room. I know you've noticed."

Astra takes a wary glance at Nick, and then she continues ranting to the therapist, accusing him of "shutting her down" or "silencing her." When really all of this is absurd.

He's supported this woman since the day she walked into his library, when he helped her do *her* job. Because that's who he is, he's a guy who takes care of people. He was raised by a single mother, so he understands exactly how hard it can be. And beyond that, he's a good, moral person. He believes in all types of non-traditional family structures, he's an advocate for wage equality, and he's almost certain he's sequestered the need to propagate his own genes by dedicating himself to being a spectacular stepfather instead. He's dedicated to supporting and raising and empowering his partner and her son. He does not "shut her down." He advocates *for* her. He's always trying to *understand* her. But, no, no, no. Apparently, he's some monster.

"I used to invite this sort of thing," Astra is saying. "I wanted people to take over my thoughts, to meddle, to take care of me, but I hate the feeling now. I don't want it in my marriage."

Nick can't keep himself from scoffing at the word *meddle*. But his wife isn't paying attention to him anymore, she's just going on and on and on, about how whenever they argue, he wins. About how he's always telling her that she's making poor decisions. About how he never really listens. He pretends to, but he's just waiting to get a word in. To tell her what's what.

Nick wishes he could simply throw his hands up in the air and storm out of the room, but he isn't stupid. He's aware that the therapist is watching for his reaction. She's judging the tone of his voice and his body language, so he must stay in control, choreograph his movements to perfection.

"Let's stop for one second," the therapist says. She pivots her body to Nick and gives him a small smile that is not exactly warm. "Earlier, you said that you told Astra what to talk about the first time you brought her here. Is that an accurate description of what happened? Did you 'tell' Astra what to talk about?"

"I wouldn't say I *told* her. She asked me what she should talk about."

Astra rolls her eyes. "I didn't ask you. I said that I didn't *know* what to talk about."

"That's the same thing."

"No it's not. Not at all." Astra makes a small sound, maybe a groan. "This is *my* life. I want to be the one to talk about it, for once. I want to be the one identifying my problems."

"Well, great! That's exactly what I'm trying to get you to do." Nick rubs his brow with his sleeve.

"Yes, my point exactly. You're trying to get me to do what *you* want. And Nick, I'm sorry. I'm not going to. I'm not the same as you."

"That's true. You're not. You have zero life skills."

At this comment, Astra puts her head in her hands, but he doesn't care anymore. He's been patient long enough.

The therapist, who doesn't appear fazed at all by how much this conversation has gone off the rails, who doesn't care that they're in a worse place now than when they first walked in the door, says, "What do you mean she has no life skills, Nick?"

There is a long pause. Should he say it? *Fuck it*, he decides. "Well, one example is her dice."

"Sorry." The therapist holds up her hand. "This is an interesting point."

"Thank you," he says, rudely.

The therapist flips back a few pages in her book and runs a finger over her notes until she finds what she's searching for. "Is this the same dice you mentioned during your first session, Astra? I marked it down, although we haven't had a chance to explore further."

Now Astra starts talking to the therapist intimately, almost as if he weren't in the same room. And it's a terrifying sensation. Like he doesn't know her from Adam. And for the first time in their short relationship, he wonders what he's gotten himself into.

The therapist is nodding again, leaning forward with her elbows on her knees, fully tuned in as Astra tells her about where the dice came from and the years she lost it. How it kept managing to find its way back into her life. How it's always helped her when she's stuck. How, really, it's all she has.

All you have? Nick thinks. *Thanks a lot.*

He remembers the day he asked Astra to marry him, how she used the dice then. Picked it up and rolled it on the bed before saying yes. Since then he's managed to convince himself it didn't matter, that she would have married him regardless of the roll, but at the time he wasn't so sure.

"What's going on inside you right now, Astra?" the therapist is asking. "I'm noticing your hands, how they're gripped in your lap."

Nick returns his attention to his wife. It's true. Her hands are two tight fists. She opens the right one and flexes it. The tips of her fingers have gone completely white and there are lines in her palm from her nails.

"Were you holding it, Astra?" the therapist inquires.

"Yeah, I guess. I swear I could feel it there."

"She still uses it," Nick adds, but he's talking softer now too. And he's relieved to find himself wanting to touch her, to comfort her. This entire session has been unnerving, really. A rollercoaster. *A fucking mess. A real fucking mess.* He's certainly going to tell Astra he thinks this therapist is garbage. She isn't helping anyone; she's a relationship wrecking ball.

"Do you wish she didn't use the dice?" the therapist asks, turning to him.

"Of course. It's a toy. It's not something to depend on."

"What should she depend on instead?"

"Me!" he says. "Obviously."

"Okay. But why does she have to depend on you? I'm becoming aware of a bit of a pattern already. How quickly you jumped into this relationship. How you asked Astra to marry you after only two weeks. How when you drove her here that first day, you told her what to talk about. Was that so you could maintain some control? And Nick, please don't take this the wrong way. I'm not trying to be overly critical."

Nick looks away from the therapist and up at the painting again. He searches for the bright stipples under the cloud. Now he sees umber, burgundy, rust, and brown. The tones are both darker and more intense than they were when he first walked into the room. There's barely any light left in the painting at all.

Back in the car, Nick rolls down the window. He was asked to leave the session for the remaining fifteen minutes, so that Astra could conclude her hour with the therapist alone. The sun is sinking behind the far mountains, and there are bright new leaves on the trees. He tries his best to understand what just happened, to find a nugget of hope after all that, to find the light underneath the darkness. And then he pictures Astra's face: that crooked, perfectly damaged smile. She is his complicated woman, that's for sure. So what if the therapist was right that they still have a few things to learn about one another? Isn't that the point of marriage? To learn everything there is to know about your spouse? To grow together. To eventually become one.

Right at the beginning of the session, when they talked about the apartment, he'd been honest and told Astra that he didn't want to live there. He explained that the house wasn't his style, and that he didn't want to inhabit her past; he wanted them to move forward. And Astra told him that was fine. "I don't care if we end up at Doris's or not," she said. "That's not the point. The point is that we're together. That we talk things through, and that I can suggest things without you getting angry with me. All I want is a say in my own life."

In the moment he was too riled up to actually hear this for what it was, which happens to him on occasion, but now he can register her words clearly. She'd taken his hand again as she spoke, and tucked her hair behind her ear and furrowed her brow in the way he adores.

Really, all that's happened to them this afternoon is they tried something new only to discover that therapy isn't what they need. *We'll be fine without it*, he decides, peering back through the golden hour to the house that is holding his wife hostage inside. He glances at his watch again. *She just has a few more minutes to go. Then it will be just the two of us again. Exactly as it should be.*

DOM

EVERY MORNING, RAIN or shine, when Dom steps out of his building to go to work, he spots the older gentleman with the slight stoop and neat hair walking his chestnut dachshund. The dog's eyes are watery and loose in their sockets, and the pair often pause to sniff the bottoms of flyer boxes, the bases of street signs, and the soil around the ornamental maples that border the busy street. The man is well-dressed, always in a crisp button-up shirt, and appears—as far as Dom can tell—happy, content, at peace with this life where he walks his dog through the city alone. His face is not pinched or sour, and as they move slowly from one point of interest to another, his gravelly voice can be heard giving encouragements like "Good boy," "There, there, let's go now," "Good, let's go." Dom, who has come to admire the gentleman, sometimes feels as if he's observing a future version of himself.

Occasionally, he encounters the gentleman on the weekends when he's out for a run, or in the evenings on his way home from work, and each time Dom is sure to say hello—regardless of the fact that the gentleman hasn't once acknowledged him in return. And so, on this particular late summer afternoon, after popping into St. Lawrence Market for some cheese and meats, his reusable bag straining with craft beer, Dom is surprised to find the man ahead, halfway down the block, talking with a teenage boy. And he can't help but be a little put off by the warmth between them.

Why the hell doesn't the man ever say hello to me?

Upstairs in his apartment, Dom changes out of his work clothes and then arranges the beer bottles in the fridge in straight rows, labels facing forward. While he's normally very observant about what he eats, when he doesn't have other plans, he allows himself this treat at the end of a busy week: ripe Brie, a baguette, and a few beers.

He's removing the cheese from its butcher paper when his condo buzzer sounds.

"Is this Freedom?" asks a faint, male voice, nearly drowned out by traffic.

"Yes? If you have a package, the doorman will sign for it. Just ring the desk."

Dom hears rustling on the other end, then a weak cough. "It's Hugo. You know, your son?"

"Oh," he says, almost inaudibly.

"Can I come up?"

"Yes, yes, of course."

Dom drops his finger from the intercom and leans against the wall. *Maybe this is just a scam. Maybe I'll open the door and be robbed*, he thinks hopefully. Then, after what feels like only a second, he hears a timid knock and finds himself peering through the peephole at the same boy he saw outside.

"Hello. If you don't mind, could you take off your shoes?" Dom says, stepping back to allow the stranger in. "Sorry. I can be annoyingly particular," he adds.

Hugo shrugs, kicks off his grungy sneakers, and then— without shaking Dom's hand or giving him a hug or engaging in any of the formalities one would normally perform when meeting a long-lost relative—he heads towards the living room, pausing briefly at the bike rack which is installed at the end of the hall. Hugo gives the bike's back tire a spin, and the condo fills with the ticking of spokes. "Doesn't your building have a locker for these?" he asks, stopping the wheel in his palm. His backpack is still slung over one shoulder.

"It does, but my spots are full. I do some buying and selling in my spare time," Dom explains, while thinking: *Really? Our first conversation ever is going to be about bikes?*

Hugo walks to the living room window and peers out at the eighteenth-floor view. "This place is pretty swanky. I'm sure you don't need a side hustle to get by."

"It's just a hobby. Something to help fill the weekends," Dom says, as he reaches the boy's side. In the coming dusk, the giant lake stretches out before them like a black mirror.

Hugo is quite tall, his hair long, and his sweatshirt is missing the hood string. *This is my son*, Dom thinks. A kid he met only once when he was a baby, a kid he's only heard about through emails from Astra every few years. Someone, if he's honest, he'd given himself permission not to think about all that often.

Hugo turns away from the window to scan the room. "What do you do again? Astra never told me."

"I manage a robo-adviser. Do you know what that is?" Dom asks.

"Nope. Not a clue."

"It's not a bank, it's more like an independent financial management company. We use computer algorithms to trade stocks so we can keep our fees low. And we work almost exclusively online. We have clients of all ages and income levels. We help with short-term goals, like buying a house or a car, and with retirement plans too. Are you familiar with investing at all?" This is his standard elevator pitch, and he's only falling back on it now because it's easy and all other subjects feel off-limits. While he talks, he's careful to avoid looking directly at his son. He doesn't want Hugo to detect something in his face—possibly horror or fear—that he's incapable of hiding. Because what is this, anyway? Who should take the lead here? He decides it's Hugo's job—he's the one who showed up without warning.

The boy leaves the window, drops his backpack on the couch, and sits down heavily, exactly as Dom imagines he must do in his mother's living room, with his feet up on the coffee table, exposing the holes in his socks. Astra wouldn't blink at this, but Dom is experiencing chills that run from the top of his head and down his spine. And his gut is in knots, wrecked by some feeling he can't identify. He wishes he could claim it was excitement, but that's not it at all.

Hugo pulls his phone out and, while he scrolls, Dom allows himself a closer inspection. The kid has Astra's deep brown eyes, and Dom's square jaw and dimpled chin. The same nose too. The same lips. Really, it's his own face, only younger, reflected back at him. But there's something distressing about the boy. He's jittery, and Dom has to fight the urge to retrieve his wallet, which is sitting in full view by the cheese on the counter.

When Hugo finally puts his phone away, Dom tries to get their conversation going again. "So, how did you get here?" he asks.

"Airplane. Bus. Taxi. You know, all the normal ways."

"Right, of course. I meant, how did you find me? Not that I was hiding from you, obviously, I'm just a little confused. Here you are, out of the blue. Have you ever been to Toronto before?" *God, I sound like a customs agent,* he thinks. *Calm down.*

It's clear that someone is trying to reach Hugo urgently, because the phone keeps dinging repeatedly in his pocket. "I've never been anywhere," Hugo says, ignoring the texts. "Just Vancouver, obviously, and to some of the islands. That was my first plane ride."

"Wow. Okay." Dom dries his sweaty hands off on his pants. "So this is a big deal. And are you visiting someone here? Or is this a work trip?"

Hugo laughs dryly, the sound like wind tearing through the pages of an open book. "I don't have that kind of job. I work part-time at a comic book store. I'm here to see you, Freedom. That's the big deal."

Insecurity is an affliction that occasionally plagues Dom; and although tonight's particular bout began earlier, when he saw Hugo talking to the gentleman with the dog, it's this direct comment—*I'm here to see you, Freedom*—that strips him of any remaining self-assurance. He lets his hands hang uselessly at his sides; there's no longer any blood left in them. "A comic book store? That's cool," he says, swallowing lumps. They keep coming and coming. "I should tell you though, no one calls me Freedom anymore."

"Why? What do they call you?"

"Dom."

"Huh. Okay." Hugo's phone is going again. *Zzzzt. Zzzzt. Zzzzt.* A call this time, though the kid remains intent on ignoring it.

"I changed my name when I was around twenty. Just a bit older than you are now." Dom is talking fast again. "I'm not all that surprised Astra never mentioned it to you though. She never remembered even when we were dating."

Hugo's eyes are darting around the condo, never staying on any object for long. *He's probably just as nervous as I am,* Dom reassures himself.

"Clodagh gave me your address when Astra got married," Hugo explains. "I think I wanted to write to you or something, maybe invite you to the wedding? Astra said I could ask whoever I wanted, but I never bothered. I found that slip of paper in my drawer the other week, the one with your address, so I just decided to come. Flights are cheap right now for some reason," he adds. And then, as if realizing he's said too much, he shakes his shaggy bangs over his forehead.

"I forgot Astra got married," Dom says, though he hadn't forgotten at all. Now he wonders if the tight sensation in his gut could be guilt. Or the sense that he should feel guilt. But why would that be? He and Astra came to an arrangement about Hugo long ago. There wasn't a legal document saying so, but Astra wanted it this way. Dom wasn't required to be a part of their life. But what if Astra has told Hugo a different story? Like that Dom left them? Or that he wasn't interested? He's never considered this before.

"So where are you staying?" he asks, as a way to change the subject, though immediately he regrets this, because he knows the answer.

"Here? I don't have anywhere else to go."

"Okay, when's your flight home?"

"In a week. Next Friday."

"Okay," Dom says again, even though he's not sure if any of this is okay; he's stuck on the word like a loop.

This time, when his phone starts up, Hugo turns it off and tosses it onto the coffee table with a clatter. Then he glowers at Dom. His eyes are brown, yes, but they are most like Astra's in their intensity.

"One more thing," he says. "You can't tell her I'm here, all right?"

"And why is that?"

"We aren't getting along right now. And if you call her, she'll probably jump on a plane and try to bring me home. It's the least you can do. I've never asked you for anything before. All I want is to hang out for few days, and I want you to keep this between us."

Dom's mind races. He wonders what Hugo told the gentleman with the dog. *I'm trying to find my father. He was never a part of my life. By any chance do you know him?* He blinks hard to rid himself of the image.

"Can you promise me?" Hugo asks again. "Come on, man. I need this. I just need a break from my life and from her."

Dom studies this kid, this young man who is still basically a stranger. "Sure. If it's that important to you, I won't call her," he says awkwardly. "And *mi casa su casa*, and all of that. Of course you can stay."

After he makes up the couch in his den for Hugo, Dom sits at the white marble counter with his laptop. He emails Harish, his closest friend and business partner, and explains the situation. Tells him that he'll need to take the following week off work. Then he tiptoes to the fridge and gets another beer. He's never had to do this in his own place before: be quiet, worry about waking someone up. It occurs to him that this is something parents all over the world are doing right at this moment. He wishes he could ask one of them, any of them: What should you do if a kid wants you to keep a secret? Do you do the opposite? Or: How old does a child have to be before they can be treated like they're fully grown? Or: How do you get to know someone you should already know better than anyone in the world?

He checks the folder on his computer where he files his exchanges with Astra—eighteen or so years of their sporadic communication. Their last correspondence was a little more than a year ago. The subject reads: *Hugo's graduation*. Dom opens her initial email. It's an invite, ending with that same signature she always uses: *xx, Astra*. Next, he reads his reply, comprising two short sentences: work was his excuse. But that was allowed, wasn't it? Isn't that exactly what she wanted him to say?

When they were young, when they were both new to being out in the world on their own—Astra in Calgary, and Dom in Toronto for his first real job at the bank—they spent hours talking on the phone, or not talking at all, but holding tight to the receiver and listening to one another breathe. Dom flew out to Calgary on his vacations so they could be together, and with each promotion and raise he increased the frequency of those trips—getting a flight every long weekend if he could manage it. That phase lasted for about six years, and even though they ended things time after time, they always went back on their word and got together again. Their final breakup wasn't until his visit one winter, when he admitted he was getting tired of leaving his friends so often. And although, at the time, they were in agreement about no longer seeing each other, even then he wasn't so sure they'd be able to end things for good.

Trying his best, Dom managed to refrain from calling Astra for three weeks, and when he finally picked up the phone, he found her number no longer worked. He hung up, tried again, and listened to the robotic message once more: *Sorry, the number you have dialled is not in service.* Though he was stung that Astra had gone this far to sever him from her life—they'd promised each other they would at least stay friends—the larger feeling was one of relief. They couldn't go back on their word this time. The breakup was official. And moving on didn't turn out to be as hard as he expected. It was so easy in fact that, a year later, when Clodagh mentioned that Astra was living with someone new, and that they'd had a baby, he remembers distinctly thinking that he'd dodged a bullet.

Dom didn't hear from Astra for almost two years, until the day she called him from Vancouver with the news he hadn't seen coming. At first, she apologized, said she felt terrible for keeping the pregnancy and the fact that he had a son secret, and then she invited him to come out. "I want you to meet him, Freedom. And it's probably better if we talk about all of this in person."

In shock, Dom went to Vancouver the following weekend. During the flight, he ruminated over the entirety of their history: the stories Clodagh had told him from when they were little; the week they'd spent together as teenagers at Celestial; the years they were together off and on, when he thought he might have been in love with her. Was it possible that when he saw her he'd feel that spark again? Would having a son change him? Change everything? Would the pieces of his life suddenly click into place? He didn't know what to expect. Especially since he'd never once pictured himself as a father.

And yet, when he stepped into Doris's dark little apartment and saw Astra again, none of the old feelings came back, especially not with his howling fourteen-month-old baby suddenly in his arms. Hugo was much denser than he'd imagined a baby would be, and so squirmy he was hard to hold on to. Noticing his awkwardness, Astra and Doris kept peppering him with suggestions—"Bounce him a little," "Talk to him," "Try holding him over your shoulder"—but the screaming alone was too much for him to handle. Not two minutes later, he gave up and handed the baby right back to Astra, in whose arms Hugo instantly became content. The rest of the weekend Dom kept his distance, trying his best to be invisible, because every time Hugo caught sight of him he began crying all over again.

Before his flight home, Dom sat on an armchair in Astra and Hugo's messy bedroom. Astra was lying beside their son, who was silent for the time being, deep asleep, his round cheeks flushed and his feet twitching in dream.

"Don't we have to come up with a plan?" Dom whispered. "Like, for what we're doing here?"

"Have you figured out what you want?" she asked, as she stroked Hugo's fine hair.

"I just wasn't really prepared for any of this. So I still don't know. What do you want?"

"I don't know either," Astra said, sighing. "But if you don't want to move out here, I get it. That's okay. We're going to be fine."

"Or I *could* move. If you want me to," he suggested, half-heartedly.

"I'm not trying to get back together with you, Freedom."

"No, I understand that. Me neither."

"And you've got a lot going on with work and stuff, don't you? Because you should know, Hugo and I have been pretty good on our own. I like our life. And we have Doris. All I really wanted was to make sure everything was all right between us," she said. "And it looks like it is, isn't it? You're fine going back to how things were?"

"Yeah, sure. I'm fine with it, if you are."

"Totally," she said.

At home again, whenever he found himself thinking about Astra or Hugo, he likened the whole situation to a mathematical equation. Pluses, and minuses, and genes. He focused on work. He met Harish, and together they launched a thriving company. He bought a new and ludicrously expensive condo. He rarely dated, and when he did, he picked people he didn't really like all that much, so things didn't end up getting too messy or emotional. He hated messy. He hated emotional. And whenever he felt forced to mention to friends or co-workers or to women he was seeing that he had a son back in Vancouver, he explained the situation exactly like it was: he was basically the kid's sperm donor. He and Astra had been friends. Childhood friends. Then a little more, before it ended fairly amicably. All parties involved believed this arrangement was best.

But was it? he wonders now, as he peels the label off his empty beer. He wishes he hadn't agreed to keep Hugo's visit from Astra. He would like to talk to her. To hear her say that they made the right decision. He'd like her to absolve him of responsibility all over again. But he won't call. He's not about to break the one promise he's ever made to his son.

He turns out the light and puts the bottle in the sink, making too much noise with every turn he takes. As he gets into bed, he decides to stop dwelling on the past, and to come up with a suitable plan for the next week. His son wants to get to know him. Fine. All he has to do is tread carefully. Stay away from heavy subjects. Keep their conversations light. He will treat Hugo like a tourist and he will play tour guide. And this shouldn't be too hard. If Dom "gets" anything it's men in their early twenties—his office is full of them. They like their phones, succulents, craft beer, Ping-Pong, and their chemist-style pour-over coffees. He will get through this week unscathed.

Satisfied, he puts in his earplugs and pulls down his face mask, but he does not sleep.

As the weekend passes, Hugo barely utters another word. He doesn't seem interested in the city or in leaving the apartment. He barely even looks out the window. When Dom tries to engage him in conversation, Hugo keeps his answers short and returns to the den at the first opportunity. Really, all Dom has learned about his son is what his feet sound like as he crosses the floor. Dom checks the calendar on his phone often, counting ahead to Friday, wishing time would move faster, because his plan isn't working at all. Nor has his belly recovered. And he can't figure out why he sticks around all day, when it's apparent Hugo has zero interest in spending time with him.

On the third afternoon of Hugo's visit, Dom works at the kitchen counter, waiting for his son to emerge. Hugo has been awake for hours already; Dom has heard him shuffling around behind the door, as well as a cough and the computer turning on.

Dom starts a new note on his laptop:

THINGS TO DO DURING HUGO'S VISIT
• zoo?
• shopping?
• buy the boy some socks? And a new sweatshirt? Jeans?
• bike to the Beaches?
• subway ride?
• office tour?

He closes his computer when Hugo finally opens the door, rubbing sleep from his eyes as he makes his way down the hall to the bathroom. A minute later he comes out again, texting. He sits beside Dom, still staring at his phone.

"Want to go out for lunch?" Dom asks.

"No. Too early," Hugo says.

"It's not early at all. It's nearly one."

"I just woke up."

"Okay. Fine. Who are you texting?"

"My girlfriend."

"I didn't know you had a girlfriend."

"Well, I do." Hugo pauses, his jaw working. "Miranda. She's basically the only reason I'm here."

"Oh really? It was her idea for you to come? That's awesome."

"Yeah. I was going through some stuff and she thought I should meet you."

"Hugo, we *have* met before."

His son lifts his gaze for an instant, then lets it fall back to his screen. "No, we haven't. I was a baby. That doesn't count." Dom decides not to argue with this, because the boy is not wrong. "Anyways, Miranda thought it would be 'cleansing.' She said it'd give me some perspective to spend time with you."

"Perspective on what?"

"Do you actually want me to say?"

"I think so."

"Perspective on you. On my mom. On why she is the way she is. Why she can't handle the idea of living on her own. Why she drives me up the wall. All of it."

Dom gets up—a defensive reflex, and the wrong thing to do. He feels Hugo watching him as he opens a cupboard and buries his head inside. "I don't have much food left in the house. We've kind of cleaned the place out. I might be able to pull together a sandwich?"

"I'm fine."

"Or cereal?" he offers.

"Sure."

Dom pours his son a bowl and pushes it across the counter. He doesn't want to picture Astra, but as much as he tries to separate the two of them, he can't. Every time he catches a glimpse of Hugo, he finds himself thinking about her in parallel. The way she used to bring her face so close to his that he could hear the flap of her lashes as she blinked. How she smelled like vanilla extract and neem toothpaste; sweet, boozy, and fresh. How she laughed nearly constantly—she probably still does. She was always so determined to find humour in the incredibly hard stuff. She insisted that if she joked with him about her past, about her dad, or even her mom, none of it could hurt her. "Our parents were so delusional! Did either of us even have a 'childhood'? Were we ever allowed to just be *kids*? No, I don't think so. And you're the only one I can talk to about any of this. You're the only one who *gets* it," she often said, as they lay together on her flat futon in her crap apartment in Calgary, her clothes strewn recklessly on the hardwood. "Clodagh especially. She's too much." But Hugo isn't like his mother in this way. He doesn't seem to find anything funny at all.

Dom sits down again. "I'm not sure I know why Astra is the way she is, as you put it. She is her own person. Really, we didn't know each other *that* well."

"No?" Hugo is stirring the cereal round and round with his spoon. "Are you sure?" he says, in a tone that is an accusation of sorts.

"What's going on, Hugo? I don't get it. Is she okay? Is she having marriage troubles?"

"She's fine, but she got a divorce ages ago."

"Oh really? I didn't know."

"Doesn't matter. They tried living apart for a while, but then they broke up pretty quick after that. He was a bit of an asshole. Pretentious too." Hugo begins eating, hungrily, then he stops and puts his spoon down. "Wait. You didn't call her, did you?"

"No. And I'm sorry to hear about the husband. That's too bad."

"His name was Nick."

"Right, Nick." Dom takes a sip of his coffee. "Well, if you're here for some perspective, maybe you should ask me some questions? We're not going to understand each other better if we don't talk."

"No, thanks. I like it like this."

"You like this? All I do is sit here, waiting for you to get up, only to have you go right back into your room."

"Exactly. It's the perfect set-up. Astra's always bugging me and worrying about me. So please don't be like that too. You're doing exactly what you're good at."

"And what's that?"

"Doing nothing," Hugo says.

Dom cannot untangle his rage from sorrow at this statement. He wishes he could ask Hugo what exactly Astra has told him.

Hugo is studying him carefully. "Are we done?" he asks, getting up. "If you don't have any other plans, I'm going to go have a nap."

Dom did have plans, more plans than he could count, and he isn't stupid, no naps are going to happen. "No, no. Whatever. Do what you want, Hugo."

When Dom calls Sativa, his sister is sitting in the passenger seat of her minivan, riding along as her middle child practises for her driver's test in a quiet parking lot. Dom fills her in on the Hugo situation quickly, while she occasionally interrupts him to shout, "Brake, brake!" or "Turn left!" and then apologizes.

She and Chris have five children, and she's usually busy with at least one of them whenever he calls. She's always distracted. Always with family stuff on her mind. Sometimes he swears he can hear her making mental grocery lists while they talk, even though he's certain they have help for that.

Finally she says, "I'm listening now, Dom. Sophie is parking. Here, I'll even get out of the car."

"So why do you think he's hiding in the den?" he asks.

"I don't know. I mean, maybe it's normal? Teenagers *do* hide. How old is he now?"

"Almost nineteen," he says. "But we've barely talked at all. I feel like I'm running a B&B. Like I'm some weird dude renting out my den for extra cash."

"Well, have you tried engaging with him? Don't let him dictate your relationship just because you're scared of him."

"I'm not scared of him," Dom retorts, though of course he is. "And I've *been* trying. I've asked him why he's here. I've asked him out for lunch."

"Yes, but have you asked him any real questions?"

Dom thinks back. "He works in a comic store and he has a girlfriend. That's all he's told me—he doesn't want to talk."

"Come on. He flew all the way out there. He doesn't *want* to sit in another room even if it seems that way. This is where you come in. This is where you need to stand up for yourself."

"He told me to leave him alone." Dom clears his throat. "I'm being respectful."

"I don't know then. You should probably hang up and call Astra instead. Because what if there's something wrong? What if he's in crisis? What if he has mental health issues—these days you need to be very careful. If you're not comfortable asking him yourself, you should call her and get to the bottom of it."

He considers Hugo's greasy hair, his disinterest in the outdoors, and how he's been drinking all his beer. "He's on his phone a lot. And I think he might be playing multiplayer video games online," Dom admits.

This is actually exactly what he's been doing. Dom discovered the truth last night at around eleven, when he went to the den and knocked. When there was no answer, he peeked in. Hugo was at the desk, hunched over his computer, sound-reducing headset on, rapidly tapping on the computer's cursor keys. "Fuck yes," Hugo said quietly. Then he rubbed his hands together and clapped. "Ready for some more?"

"Do you think that's a sign of something?" Dom asks.

"It's so hard to say."

"Well, I can't call Astra. Hugo doesn't want her to know he's here with me."

"Or he might."

"What do you mean? None of this makes any sense."

"All I'm saying is you don't know what he wants, do you? And honestly, don't act so surprised. This was bound to happen at some point. You weren't going to get to hide from him forever, Dom."

"What are you talking about? I was basically the kid's sperm donor. We were all okay with this until now."

"You were *not* his sperm donor. Why do you always say that? It breaks my heart that you still think of yourself that way!"

Dom's ears grow hot and he clears his throat again. It hadn't occurred to him that his family might not agree with his version of events—with his version of who Hugo is. He looks out the window. Sky. Water. Construction cranes gleaming and turning. The same view he sees each day. He misses his old, simple life, when he could just gaze out the window and not worry about anything.

Sativa sighs. "Are you still there? I don't like to upset you, but we've all seen this coming for years. And if you want my advice, you should try harder. That's probably all Hugo wants from you. He needs to feel you try. And go call Astra. Tell her that her son is there and that he's safe."

———

Dom manages to sleep in, and when he wakes he turns on his phone to find an email from Astra in his inbox. He closes his eyes. Considers pressing delete before even opening it. Considers throwing his phone out the window, yet he doesn't. He sits up and adjusts a pillow behind his back.

Subject: Hugo
Hi Freedom,

I don't mean to alarm you. It's probably too soon to be as worked up as I am, but I thought you should know that Hugo is missing. Or maybe missing. There's a chance he's with his girlfriend, but I don't have her number. I know he's basically an adult, so I shouldn't be so alarmed. It's just he's not responding to any of my texts or calls and this isn't normal behaviour for him. I felt it was my responsibility to tell you. I've always tried to keep you informed about the big stuff. I'll be in touch when I know more.

Hope you're doing well.
xx, Astra

Dom drops the phone and tosses his duvet aside. He gets up and opens the blinds. The morning is perfect. Joggers are out in droves by the shore, tiny sparks of colour along the pavement. And sailboats are flickering in the lake, disappearing behind waves and re-emerging in a flutter.

I am part of the big stuff now, he thinks.

In the kitchen, Dom makes a coffee and then takes a seat in front of his computer. He emails Janet and Harish, reviews the agenda, and then videos in for the morning meeting. Janet describes the first draft of the "Joke A Day" essay they commissioned a Seattle comedian to write for their financial blog. They discuss the rollout of their new high-interest savings account, and then Dom signs off. He spends the next few minutes staring at Hugo's closed door, trying to empty his mind completely. Then this thought again: *Astra*. It might be true that they made an arrangement, but he's starting to wonder if it was the best one. His stomach rolls.

Later, over their now-customary bowl of cereal at one o'clock, Dom finds out that Hugo doesn't want to go to the zoo. He doesn't want to go for a bike ride or check out the Beaches, and he detests shopping. When Dom suggests they go to the office so he can meet his team and play Ping-Pong, Hugo snorts, then explains that he isn't into that sort of shit. His foot is bouncing rapidly on the floor, the stool creaking beneath him.

"What shit aren't you into? Work or me?" Dom asks, trying to loosen him up.

"I'm not into 'workplace atmosphere,'" Hugo replies, making air quotes around the words.

"All right," Dom says.

Needing a distraction, he goes downstairs to the building's gym. He stretches, lifts some weights, and afterwards he heads outside for a run. Halfway down the block, he passes the gentleman with the dog. He makes sure to say hello, though the man turns the other way as usual.

"Whatever," Dom mutters to himself.

Back at home again, he showers and dresses to go out. At seven, he knocks on Hugo's door and suggests a vegetarian restaurant nearby that specializes in grilled avocado, but Hugo wants to order in vegan pizza instead. When their dinner arrives they eat in silence, Hugo texting constantly.

After they finish, Hugo goes back into the den to play more video games, and Dom reads the comedian's essay in the kitchen. The piece is a mess: the writing feels forced and the humour paid for—which it is. Regardless, he stamps his approval and sends it back to Harish.

He decides to go to bed early, but after half an hour of trying to sleep, he sits up and turns his phone back on.

"Astra?" he says when she picks up.

"Yes?"

"It's Dom. And he's here. Hugo is here with me."

He can hear her gasp, a sharp intake of air. "Oh, thank God," she says.

He is very nervous having her on the line now, their connection tinny, their son just down the hall. "I'm not going to tell him that I called you, okay? He made me promise I wouldn't," he says, hurriedly. "It was your email. I couldn't stop thinking about it. I didn't want you worried like that."

Astra still hasn't said anything more, and her silence is achingly long. Finally she swallows. "Thank you, Freedom. I won't tell him we talked either. I don't want to undermine whatever it is he's doing."

"Sativa told me I should call you."

"I appreciate it. Thank you. So, how are you guys getting along?" she asks quietly.

Dom rubs his brow. "It's so hard for me to say. He won't talk to me. I don't know if this is how he always is, but he basically locks himself in my den to play video games. And he's been drinking all my beer."

"You shouldn't let him drink," she says. Then she explains that when he's not doing well, when things become too much emotionally, he shuts himself away and tunnels into his computer like this. He needs to be eased back into the world gently. "Is he smoking weed?"

"No. I don't have any of that."

"Well, it's better for him than beer. Alcohol only aggravates his issues," she says. "He has pretty severe anxiety. To be honest, we've nearly exhausted our options at this point. He stopped taking all his medications a while ago, and now we're trying a natural approach. Meditation. Exercise. All that. But it's a fight to get him to commit. He told me he wants to move in with his girlfriend because I'm so annoying about it, but I don't think he should. I don't think he's ready. And Miranda doesn't get it at all. I don't trust her." Astra makes a small sound, a groan. "I'm trying my best with all of this," she adds carefully.

Dom lies back on his bed and fixes his gaze on the light fixture above.

"I think it's great he went to see you. It's surprising really," she continues. "Just the fact that he got on a plane is impressive. He's making a statement. He's trying to tell me something. Because he's right, if he'd asked me, I would have told him he couldn't handle the trip. So there you go. I would have been wrong. But it turns out I'm often wrong when it comes to Hugo." She laughs, ever so slightly, and then she lets out one of her long, breezy sighs. The sound is familiar, even after so many years, that suddenly it's as if they are both in their twenties again. Two struggling people, breathing on the phone together, hoping that's all it will take to heal.

"Did he want me to come to his graduation?" Dom asks finally. "I looked back in my emails. That's the last time you wrote."

"Oh yes. He definitely wanted you to come, but he knew talking about things like that was really hard for us. When I told him you couldn't make it, he just said it was fine. That he didn't care. But really, he's never understood why we didn't try to be more of a family. I always gave him these pathetic little excuses. Like that you couldn't leave Toronto because of your job. Or that I wanted it this way, that I loved it being just the two of us. And he always believed everything I said. He told me it was okay. But I don't think any of it was okay with him at all. And who knows why we did what we did. All I can be sure of is that I thought I was protecting him, but I guess he doesn't want that anymore."

"I bet he does."

"No. He doesn't. He's telling me he wants something different now, and he wants you to be a part of whatever that is. And I can't believe I'm saying this, but I'm kind of relieved. It's been a lot lately. Actually, for years now. It's been a lot."

Dom lowers his voice to a near whisper. "This is too much for me too though, Astra. I'm not so sure you're right about him wanting me. He doesn't even seem to like me."

"Sure, it's hard. And we should have talked about what we'd do when he finally demanded to know you. Honestly, he's been hinting at it for years. I just kept putting it off, and putting it off. I wish I'd reached out earlier. I suppose I still felt guilty for how I handled everything with you—you know, waiting as long as I did to tell you about him. I'm still embarrassed about keeping him a secret. Who does that?"

"We were so young."

"Yes. True. But now here I am, with Hugo so mad at me he flew across the country without telling me. I *hate* it when he gets mad at me. I always have. And what if this time it's permanent?"

Dom closes his eyes. "It seems like he's angry with me too."

"Oh, of course he is. He has a right to be incredibly angry with both of us, don't you think?"

At this, Dom has to put the phone against his chest. All he wants to do is crawl under the covers and sleep until Friday. He wants his quiet, simple life back. The life that he created, that was calm and controlled and didn't ever hurt him. But that isn't possible anymore, is it? It's probably not even something he *should* wish for. He's been running and hiding for years already, and now Hugo is begging him to stop. Dom dries his cheeks with the back of his hand, takes a deep breath, and returns the phone to his ear. "Do you have any advice for me?" he asks. "Like for the coming days?"

"Oh God, I don't know. Just take it slow," she says. "Start over from the beginning. Feed him, he loves to eat. And be patient. You'll figure it out."

"Okay," Dom says, so softly he isn't even sure she hears it.

"And let's just cross our fingers that he forgives us eventually. And I do appreciate you calling, Freedom. It's good to hear your voice again. But I'm going to hang up before I say any more. Hugo wants me to step back, so I'm going to respect that," she says, and then the phone beeps and falls silent before Dom can say anything in return.

Dom's mother was the one who taught him how to run. He can't even count the number of houses they fled from when he was a kid. There was a tent for a time, a yurt and a teepee, and then a rooming house where a boy named Dave tried to suffocate him by pinning a stuffed elephant over his face. There were tiny flats, mouldy trailers, and then a stormy winter when they lived in a caboose in some guy's yard, which they abandoned in a hurry after he came knocking on the door in the middle of the night for "visits" with Clodagh one too many times. As a boy, Dom slept under blankets that smelled of damp basement, of cat, of mouse shit, of patchouli. Some of these rooms had ceiling tiles swollen and drooping with water, some were decorated with billowing saris, one was sponge-painted in purples and speckled with silver stars. But Clodagh's van was always there, their escape vehicle, ready to chariot them along to the "next place" on the map once things got bad enough. That was all before Dale and high school in Nelson. Long before that fateful week when he was seventeen, when he followed his mother up to Celestial Farm and he met Astra again.

In some ways, Astra seemed older than she was—probably because she'd lived with adults most of her life—but at other times she seemed worryingly young. While she taught him to pinch off the new growth on tomatoes, how to water the roots without getting the plant's leaves wet, and how to mist the peppers, she also padded after him like a puppy, looking for any possible reason to touch him. At first, he tried to keep everything between them moving slow. Astra was only fourteen and he was leaving for university in a few days—but these were just a couple of the reasons why he shouldn't have been staying in her cabin or spending every moment of the day with her. Still, he longed to be near her. Because as soon as he noticed her through the windshield of his car, standing in the Encampment beside her father, he saw himself for the first time.

Astra had a favourite spot, a watering hole further up the river, away from prying eyes. While Freedom cannonballed off the grassy bank into the cool water, Astra, a timid swimmer, sunbathed at the water's edge. He'd dive to the river bottom to grab a handful of pebbles, then, treading water, lob the small rocks at her, one at a time, while she pretended not to notice. She just kept staring up at the sky, as pebbles flew overhead with the sparrows.

It was there that he confided in her about Dale's temper, and he told her about all the moves and all the terrible places he and his mother had lived. He admitted that his earliest memory was of watching Clodagh tie furniture to the roof of her van. But what he found even more surprising than his ability to be honest with Astra was that she understood. "We're the same," she told him. "Because we come from the same sort of place."

"And what place is that?" he asked.

"A place that isn't even real, that only exists as an idea. A place filled with irresponsible dreamers like them, and left-over kids like us."

In the late afternoons, they took long, aimless drives in his car, Astra slouched beside him with her dirty feet on the dash above the glove compartment, her legs slim and awkward like a foal's. He didn't bother telling her that normally girls her age shaved, because he didn't mind. The hair on her legs was soft, bleached white by the sun, glistening like spiderwebs against her tan. Freedom drove with one hand on her knee, while her tangled hair whipped out her open window. She told him she hadn't cut it since the nurses shaved it all off at the hospital. Its length measured the amount of time that had passed since the cougar attack, since he was last at Celestial too. He'd only been a little kid then, but he remembers that day vividly, how he wished there was something he could do to scare the animal away, something other than scream and scream and scream. So whenever Astra turned her dark eyes on him and smiled, and he saw the scars that rippled over her lip and down her jaw, the memory of being so helpless squeezed his heart like it was a rag being wrung dry.

On what turned out to be his last night at Celestial, Clodagh asked them to take care of Sativa for a little while. Down at the river, Freedom waded in up to his knees to skip stones, as Astra and his sister admired him from their spot on the slate. The night sky was dark blue, bats looping across it like calligraphy. With Astra and Sativa nearby, he recognized that something had changed in him over the course of the week. Before he arrived at Celestial, he'd been so certain and focused on his future. He had a dorm room number and a full scholarship for school, but now he was wondering if he should even go. His mother didn't want him to leave—she kept saying so. She needed him. His sister needed him. And now he had Astra to worry about too.

When Sativa started yawning, Astra heaved her onto her back, and he followed them up the path towards the Encampment.

"Don't you sometimes wish she was our daughter?" Astra asked over her shoulder.

"No. That's really weird. She's my sister."

"Well, I love kids. Imagine having someone to be with all the time? Imagine if this was our Farm? If no one else was here but us? It'd be so different if we were in charge."

"Sorry, Astra. But I'll never have kids," he said firmly, and he left it at that, even though he saw her disappointment in him cross her face. Maybe they weren't entirely the same after all.

The following day, everything happened so fast. First, he and Astra went for a long drive after breakfast, but she wasn't in the mood to talk. She just glowered out the window the whole time. He was convinced her silence was because he'd upset her the evening before, but she kept insisting that wasn't it. Then, when they returned home, and Astra stormed off to her cabin to be alone, there was Clodagh with her hands on her hips, telling him that it was time for him to leave for Vancouver, that she was finally ready to let him go—although when she hugged him it was with such ferocity that she must have believed she was never going to see him again.

He still didn't know what he wanted, or who he should listen to, or which path was the right one for him to take. And he remembers trying to explain this to Clodagh, but she didn't hear him. She only reminded him that he was young. She told him there was no reason to feel bad for leaving. There was no reason to feel responsible for any of them anymore. And although he was relieved to hear this, after he pulled his keys from his pocket and threw his bags into the backseat, he paused, hoping Astra would open her cabin door and tell him the same thing. That she'd be okay without him. That he was free now, that he could have the life he always wanted—but she didn't. Not until later. Not until Hugo arrived.

When Dom's alarm goes off the next day, he pads down the hall and presses his ear to the den door. The room is quiet, so he carefully looks in: Hugo is sleeping soundly on the couch under the comforter. His face slack and peaceful. His chest rising and falling steadily. The sound is intimate and innocent—something he should already know.

He returns to the kitchen and makes a peanut butter and spinach smoothie in his Vitamix. He drinks it while surveying his condo in the summer morning light. Most weekdays he's in the office, and he's never spent so many consecutive daylight hours at home before. It suddenly seems incredibly bare. *Maybe I should get a pet, or a plant, or a rug*, he thinks.

The morning passes the same way as the one before. At around one in the afternoon, Hugo emerges, and eats his cereal without saying much. After he retreats to his room again, Dom packs his pannier and rides out to the Beaches. He changes into a wetsuit in the public washrooms and then heads over the hot sand to the water, where he swims laps along the shore until his whole body is exhausted. Once he's home again, he showers, dresses to go out, and then at seven he knocks on Hugo's door.

Today he suggests the sushi place right across the street, promising it will be quick. Before Hugo can say no, Dom beckons him to the window, and points at the pink awning below. "We'll be home before you know it, and then you can keep doing your thing."

Hugo backs away. "Can't you pick up our order?"

"No. They don't do that. They're trying to be carbon-neutral or something."

Dom is surprised when this story works, and Hugo grabs his sweatshirt. "Fine," he says. "Let's go."

They sit in the small, fluorescent-lit storefront as customers file in and pick up their dinner. "I thought you said they didn't do takeout?" Hugo says, eyeing Dom with suspicion.

"I lied." Dom smiles. "Sorry, I wanted to get you out of the apartment for once."

Hugo laughs for the second time all week, and then takes another mouthful of gomae.

Dom is definitely a little uncomfortable being out in the real world with his son for the first time, but he's not going to let that ruin everything. "So," he says, trying his best to sound casual. "Tell me about your girlfriend."

"Seriously?"

"Yes, seriously. I want to hear all about her."

Hugo sits up straighter. "Okay," he says, slowly. He frowns. "We've been together for almost five years."

"That's amazing. I've never dated anyone that long. Very admirable."

"She has black hair and it's super long. It goes down to about here," he says, chopping his hands at his lower torso. "And she's short. The top of her head doesn't even reach my shoulders."

Dom wonders if this is what Sativa or Astra meant by asking real questions. Was a conversation about his girlfriend's hair length enough? Because, in truth, Dom finds himself growing increasingly curious. He wishes he could see a picture of Miranda, but he's unsure of how to inquire about such a thing. He leans forward, resting his chin in his hand to illustrate his interest—a tip he picked up in a workshop at a financial convention.

Hugo keeps his eyes on his meal as he talks. "She wants me to move in with her, but my mom doesn't think I should."

"And what do you want?"

"I don't know. Astra thinks we're moving too fast. I suffer from a bit of anxiety. It's usually no big deal, and it's sort of under control these days. I guess her point is that stress can make it worse. She's worried about that. She doesn't like Miranda all that much either. They're very different. Miranda has goals and stuff—I think you'd appreciate her actually. She's kind of conservative like you," he says. Those magnificent brown eyes are locked on Dom again, but they are softer in their focus now.

Okay, Dom thinks. *This might actually be working.* "Thanks for telling me about her. I appreciate it."

"Sure. It's fine."

"I hope I can meet her one day."

"Yeah. Maybe we can both come out next time," Hugo says, cautiously.

"I'd like that. And I'm sorry about your anxiety. Does it make it hard to go out?" Dom asks.

"Yeah, it can."

"I think I got a sense of it right from the beginning, with how you were acting. But let's be honest, this is a fairly intense situation we're in, Hugo. I had no idea what you needed when you walked in my door."

"I'm fine now, actually. I don't feel so bad. And I made it here, which is a huge deal for me. I wasn't sure if I'd freak out up in the air and demand they land the plane in Saskatchewan or something stupid like that."

Dom, forgetting to restrain himself, lets out a small laugh. "You should be proud then. And I won't push you, but while you're here, can we try to do a few things together? Even small stuff. I want to hang out more over the couple of days we have left, if you don't mind," he says. "I hope you understand that you showing up was tough for me too. In a way it forced me to re-examine the last twenty or so years, and all the ways I might have blown it when you were a kid."

Hugo doesn't speak for a minute, focusing on his hands as he rips a chopstick wrapper into tiny pieces. "You don't have to say you blew it," he says. "I'm sure it was complicated."

"It was," Dom agrees.

Hugo shrugs. "But yeah, that's cool. I'd like to check out Toronto with you. I could be into that."

"Fantastic," Dom says, then he sits back and watches his son finish his dinner.

The following day, they leave the apartment together at noon. Outside, near the corner, they catch sight of the older gentleman. Hugo marches right over to pet the dog, who is straining on the leash and panting laboriously in the heat.

"Thanks for your help the other day," Hugo says, when he stands. Then he turns to Dom. "This is Gregor. I thought I was totally lost when I was looking for your building. He calmed me down and assured me I was in the right spot."

"I don't think I was much help. But it's a pleasure to meet you," the gentleman says, putting out a hand. His skin is spotted and papery, yet his grip is firm. "Have you lived in the neighbourhood long, Dom?" he asks.

"Yes, about ten years," he answers. He can't believe he's finally speaking to this man who he's been observing for so long. "Thank you for helping my son."

"Oh, all I did was tell him I thought he was on the right track. I'm basically blind these days. I can't see three feet in front of me. It's this dog who is taking me on my walk, not the other way around. So around and around we go. We never even cross the street."

"Oh, I'm sorry. I had no idea," Dom says, noticing the gentleman's eyes now. They are almost completely clouded over.

Gregor, fully smiling, continues: "I have four children myself."

"Do you?" Dom is surprised at this information too. He always assumed the man was a bachelor.

"My two that I had with the first wife, we have some troubles. We work on it, but it's never easy with us. It's my younger ones who I visit with most, they both live in the city. We eat together once a week. They bring groceries, this and that. But all of my kids are wonderful kids. I tell them that often, even when they don't want to hear it."

"That's nice," Dom says. He glances at Hugo and an understanding passes between them: they are a pair in this instant, amused by an old man telling his life story in the noon-day heat.

"These walks with my dog are my only respite. My only chance for some quiet. I'm lucky the wife hates the chore or she'd be out here with me."

Dom is so overcome by this, that he has to take a step back. "You live with your wife?" he says. Here he'd thought that the gentleman lived alone, that they were the same in this way. *I've felt more over these last few days than I've allowed myself to feel in years and years and years.*

"Where else would I put her?" The man smiles again, then turns his attention to Hugo. "You're a good kid too. So take care of your old man, will you?"

"Sure thing," Hugo says.

On the streetcar, Hugo doesn't say much, but the silence between them is much easier now. Why had Dom pictured them talking non-stop? Did he really think they would suddenly tell each other their deepest secrets? Or come to some understanding about what they should mean to one another right away? It's going to take some time—forever, maybe.

When they step off the streetcar onto the sidewalk, Hugo thanks the driver.

"Yeah, thanks!" Dom calls comically over his shoulder—he never does this normally, he's just copying his son. Who, as it turns out, is an incredibly kind person. *A good kid*, as Gregor said.

They stand on the hot pavement, squinting against the light, swarms of people pressing in from all sides. Hugo pulls off his sweatshirt and shoves it in his backpack.

"Are you okay? Is this too much?" Dom asks.

"I'm great," Hugo says. "Should we walk?"

After a few blocks, Dom leads Hugo into a coffee shop, where they buy pastries that they take to a bench in the park. There are young people lying on blankets in the shade, and some others are throwing a football back and forth in the grass. With the sun hot on the back of his neck like this, Dom finds himself returned again to that last summer at Celestial Farm when he was seventeen years old. Skipping pebbles at the river. Astra's head popping out from the water, head slick like a seal. Long drives on the gravel roads. Her hand in his. Oh, music. Oh, an open window. If only there was a script for life. If he could have read ahead and seen just how elemental Astra was going to be. Because now it's apparent. That week at Celestial was fundamental. It laid the groundwork for this. For him being here, on this bench, with his son.

They drink their coffee slowly, as Hugo drums his fingers on his cup. Pigeons flap around a woman on the neighbouring bench as she tosses handfuls of crumbs at her feet. A family bikes past, the kids toddling on their training wheels.

Hugo takes another sip, and then he says, "Can I ask you a question?"

"Yes, please do."

"Do you think I should move in with Miranda? Would you say I'm ready for that? I figured out how to get all the way out here, how to find you. And I think I'm managing okay, don't you?" His foot is going again. Jiggle, jiggle.

Dom leans back against the bench and pats Hugo's thigh, then he leaves his hand there and the foot slowly stops. "I can't answer that. You're the only one who knows if you're ready."

"You think so?"

"I'm sure of it."

He's aware that his son is staring at him but he keeps his eyes locked on the football as it arcs and spins through the air. If he moves at all, he will start to cry. Because it's all coming at him, like a bus hitting his chest. He concentrates on the paper cup in one hand. The other on his son's leg. The cars honking behind them in the heat, and pop music playing from some radio, wafting over in the breeze. Everything is bright. Everything is beautiful. He breathes in and out and in and out, until suddenly Hugo is no longer at his side on the bench. He is standing in front of him, saying: "Come on, Dad. Let's keep going."

HUGO

AS THE BUS pulls up at the stop, Hugo hears a series of text alerts come through his earphones. He ignores them, scans his pass, and thanks the driver from under the hood of his damp jacket. After he weaves through the crowd of passengers, all swaying on their feet and clinging to their phones as if for balance, he takes a seat in the back row, vacant except for a litter of colorful flyers left on the chair. He rolls the papers into a tube, which he drums on his thigh. The phone chimes in his ear again.

Are you on the bus yet?

Please don't be late.

This evening means a lot to your mom, the least we can do is be on time.

Hugo? Where are you?

Text me back please.

The bus continues on at a crawl through the city, stopping every two blocks, lowering for strollers and wheelchairs, before nosing back out into the rush-hour traffic—Miranda would be furious to know he wasn't on the express. Pressing his forehead against the window, Hugo looks up at the dusky sky, which is low with moody brown thunderclouds. It's the kind of accumulation that could drench them in a downpour, or the wind could just as easily pick up, launching the clouds over the mountains, granting the city a spectacular moment of late afternoon sun. Across town, his mother has most likely noticed this tumultuous sky too. He can imagine her peering out at False Creek from her kitchen window, her hands in the dishwater, her hair a neglected tangle down her back, as she searches for meaning in the weather. When he was a kid, she was constantly pointing out the signs that lurked all around them: in red skies, rabbits, black cats, tea leaves, broken dishes, knuckles rapped on wood—even in the roll of a dice.

When Hugo finally reaches the tall concrete building where he and Miranda have lived since they moved in together, he finds his wife as he expected: already dressed up to go out. She's wearing her good dress and a cashmere sweater, because she insists on making even the ordinary an occasion. He and Miranda are completely opposite in most ways—he couldn't care less about appearances, punctuality, or good benefit packages, while to her these things are sovereign—but this is part of their charm as a couple, the reason they work so well. He is messy, late, and disorganized, while she is perfect. When she nags him, he acts befuddled, and this is the way they flirt. They joke that they're already in their seventies and that they've been married for fifty years instead of only a week.

Miranda thrusts the baby into his arms. "I tried you at the store and I texted you," she says quickly.

Hugo kisses his daughter's furrowed brow, and her cloudy-grey eyes blink up at him. "Oh yeah, I heard that when I got on the bus. I forgot to read my phone."

"Please check your texts more. What if it's something important?" Miranda says, squatting down in the entrance-way to pack the baby's oversized diaper bag.

"I was already on my way home," he points out.

Miranda raises her eyebrows at him.

"But sure. It's no problem. I'll get better at checking in."

Hugo goes to the living room, flops down on the couch, and lays Eloise on his lap for inspection, to measure how much she's changed over his day at work. She was born five weeks early and weighing only four pounds. Now, at almost a month old, she's nearing nine pounds and growing like a weed.

Miranda groans at him from the doorway. "What are you doing?" she asks.

"I just got in, I want to say hello."

"Then you'll change? We're already late."

"I don't need to change," he says, without looking up from the baby.

Although they live only a thirty-minute drive from one another, Hugo hasn't visited his mother in nearly five years. He emails her on occasion. On her birthday, on Mother's Day, at Christmas. Sometimes she sends him virtual cards, which open in an explosion of animated confetti. She used this method to send them a gift certificate and a note of con-gratulations after Eloise was born. His mother's digital signa-ture inside read: *xx, Astra*.

Miranda was the one who'd included Astra on their group email announcement, and she'd been waiting for Hugo to pick up the phone and arrange a time for Astra to meet her granddaughter, but he kept putting it off. So, after getting Astra's card, Miranda called his mother behind his back and the two of them made this plan for a family dinner. Tonight, she would finally meet Eloise. Tonight, there would be a coming together, for better or for worse. And he doesn't know how to feel about this exactly. He was a kid the last time they saw each other. Now he is a father and a married man, an entirely different person, and he has no idea how this reunion will go.

Eloise kicks her skinny bowed legs, and she makes a soft, wet sound with her tongue. "Hello, little bug," he says. "We don't want to go out, do we? But you have to meet your nana. Your mother is correct, as usual. I'd truly be the biggest ass-hole if we waited even one more day."

It was on the airplane home from Toronto, after meeting his father for the first time, that Hugo was revisited by his child-hood awe of the universe and his place in it. How could the Earth be so big, and yet so small when you put it up against the rest of space: the stars, comets, suns, black holes, and fuck knows what else. Thoughts like this kept him up all the time when he was little, and he'd have to roll over and shake his mother awake:

Are you sure I even exist, Mama?

You exist.

How do you know?

I know, because I'm here too. Because I see you. Because I feel you in my arms.

But how do I know you exist? How do I know you're not lying? What if I made you up?

I don't know, Hugo. Just stop thinking about this stuff, would you? You're only stressing yourself out. You're stressing me out!

He didn't reply to any of Astra's texts or calls during his visit to Toronto, not until he was at the airport and about to board his flight home. Then, sheepishly, he sent her a message telling her where he was, before asking if she would pick him up when he landed. His phone indicated that she'd read his texts, and so he assumed she'd call him right away. Waiting by his gate, he stared at the screen impatiently, willing the thing to ring. He knew he'd have to explain himself, explain why he'd worried her so unnecessarily, and he wanted to do it now rather than in person.

It was only as the flight attendant requested they turn off their devices that he received a short reply: *I'll be there, xx.*

Once they were at altitude, Hugo squeezed his eyes closed against the hum of the engine and concentrated on the Sprite bubbling in the flimsy plastic cup he held in his hand. They were so high up. Too high up. *Fuck.* He was overcome by the familiar fear of being too small. And then came the fear of his own breathing, or of not breathing. It was the fear of fear of fear, intensifying by the second and quickening his pulse.

Luckily, he must have fallen asleep, because soon they were landing, and there was the fresh hit of salt in the ocean air as he disembarked, and he was riding down an escalator and he had everything with him: jacket, shoes, phone, backpack—how had he managed to pull himself together? Then someone bumped him with their rolling luggage, right near the bottom step, and he stumbled into the crowd. There were too many people, and there was too much rushing, so he stepped aside to gather his bearings.

When the crowd finally thinned, he became aware of her eyes on him. She was leaning against a pillar at the far end of the arrivals area, trying to act nonchalant, something she always did when she was upset. She was good at hiding her feelings from other people, but she never bothered to do so with him. She lifted her hand and waggled her fingertips at him, but she didn't smile.

Head down, he marched over, fully prepared for her to make a scene. Just like she had on her wedding day, when he abandoned her during the reception in Nick's crowded apartment and didn't return until most of the guests had gone; or when she was called into his high school to discuss his shoddy attendance record with his homeroom teacher. This time she'd probably tell him he was cruel for making her worry, before engulfing him with one of her stifling hugs and crying out, "Did you want me to die of fright?" Instead, when he reached her, all she said was "You're wearing new clothes. You look different."

"Yup," he answered, keeping his gaze fixed on the window behind her.

"And how was your flight?"

"Great."

"Good," she replied, shoving her hands in the back pockets of her jeans.

He'd been expecting a million questions and accusations, and plenty of tears, yet she did none of this. She wasn't being herself, and he couldn't make sense of it.

They were silent while they exited the building, and it was only when they were waiting to cross the street to enter the parkade that Astra asked breezily, "And how is Freedom?" As if he flew across the country to visit his father every weekend.

"He's fine."

"Was it a good visit?"

"It was better than good, it was fantastic."

She stiffened ever so slightly, and then made her way over the crosswalk without him, leaving him to stand there alone. Why did he insist on being such a dick? Sure, it was hard not to take her for granted, and to remember that she was the only person who gave a shit about him besides Miranda. Still, he couldn't dump on her again and again and again, and expect there never to be a consequence.

He trailed behind her as she marched up the concrete stairs to the car. Normally, they would be arm in arm, or bumping shoulders and elbows, unsure where one started and the other ended, personal boundaries non-existent between them. They were always in each other's space, even when they weren't getting along. But now, after one short week apart, they were the wrong poles of two magnets. He stood at a distance while she searched for parking change, and then he slumped into the passenger seat of her dirty car, pulling the hood of the new sweatshirt that Dom had bought him up over his head and closing it over his eyes so he couldn't see anything at all. He didn't want to think about how fragile it all was. His old, all-encompassing love for her. His new, fledgling love for his father. He'd only wanted to mend the some-what-broken part inside him, by finally trying to have both.

In the days that followed, Hugo spent most of his time in his room. He called his boss and explained that he needed another week off work for his mental health. And although he and Miranda had decided to look for an apartment as soon as he got back into town, now they weren't even talking. His first night back, he'd confessed that he was having doubts about moving in together. Upset by this change in plan, she told him they should take a "break" until he knew what he wanted. "Don't call me until you decide. I can't handle all this back and forth anymore," she said through tears before hanging up.

For the first time in his life, Hugo had nowhere to be and no one to answer to. And for a little while, being so alone, so unwatched, felt freeing. But then it was day after day of sinking into the void of his room. When he was a teenager he'd put a lock on his door, a small hook and fastener, which he now kept latched at all times. He promised himself he wouldn't answer when Astra knocked, and yet she never did. She didn't bug him once. She simply carried on as if he wasn't even home. But this was exactly what he wanted, wasn't it? For her to give him some space. For her to stop being so emotionally invested in everything he did. Sure, she was mad at him, but was it possible she'd finally gotten the message?

It wasn't long before the guilt about hurting his mother began to take over. As did his fear that Miranda would eventually run out of patience with him. And he was disappointed in himself too. He'd felt so confident, so different, during those last couple of days in Toronto with Dom, but he'd lost his grasp on that more mature version of himself as soon as he'd come home. He found it hard to think clearly. And so he started taking pills again, just to lighten the load on his mind. He had a shoebox of options under his bed, leftovers he'd saved from a decade of trial-and-error attempts to combat this plaguing anxiety. All afternoon and into the wee hours of the morning, he led raids on World of Warcraft on his computer with his angst dulled to a background murmur. Sometimes, when Astra was out, he'd order in beer, then walk down past the other apartments in his pajama pants to pay the delivery man in cash that he stole from his mother's depressing junk drawer of elastics, frayed cords, leaking pens, dead batteries, and burnt-out bike lights.

Then, bored by his own company, and with the four walls of his childhood bedroom encroaching on him, he took out Doris's motorcycle. It wasn't insured and he didn't have a licence, but he watched enough how-to videos on YouTube to cover the road basics. First, he drove around the neighbourhood. One block, two, three. Then, he went further. To South Vancouver. To Richmond. Even downtown. Without a helmet. Weaving in and out of traffic in an increasingly reckless fashion. Cutting off buses. Slipping into oncoming lanes. Veering in the wrong direction up one-way streets. The wind numbing his bare hands. Beer and pills coursing through his veins, both of which helped him stay upright and moving forward.

He wanted to be daring, for once. To be brave, for once. To be different than he was, or how everyone saw him, or how he felt about himself. He wanted something to hit him. And then something did. A minivan with a father at the wheel somehow drunker than Hugo.

He woke up in a hospital bed. The bright lights bearing down on him. Without his identification he was just John Doe, and he let that linger for a full day, relishing the chance to be non-existent.

Broken ribs. Dislocated shoulder. Severe concussion. An IV in his arm. But what hurt most was the road rash that ran from his forehead to his toes, pussing and sore. It took nearly a week for him to be able to lift his better arm without crying out in pain. His new hoodie hadn't made it, nor had it protected him. Still, he kept it, torn and bloody in a plastic bag hanging off the foot of his bed.

Hugo changed during his stay in the hospital. There, in spite of his condition, he was treated like a fully functioning adult by all the doctors and nurses. He was allowed to speak for himself, to report freely on how he felt both emotionally and physically.

"You're not a very bright boy, are you?" his favourite nurse said each day as she sweetly brushed his hair from his brow, away from the bandages.

"No, I'm not."

"But you're alive. You've been given a second chance. You should eat omegas when you get out. Eggs. Fish. They're good for the brain."

"I'm a vegan."

"And," she added, ignoring him, "remember that life is a blessing."

"A blessing," he repeated.

It helped that no one took his problems *that* seriously either. He was young, a little troubled, but most likely he'd end up all right. It was apparent they'd all seen worse, which was sobering, and in sharp contrast to how Astra used to treat him at home, back when she cared.

Two days after the accident, when he finally called her, he told her that he didn't want visitors. That he needed time alone to figure stuff out. Of course what he *really* wanted was for her to ignore what he said and see *through* his words. He wanted her to jump in her car and drive over. To hold him like she used to do. But she did none of those things. After asking once if he was really, truly okay, she promptly hung up. And this confirmed his fear. He was on his own now. He'd pushed her love to the brink of collapse, and she was too exhausted to keep trying anymore.

By then he was missing Miranda. Missing her desperately. So he called her and told her he was ready, that he loved her, that he hoped she'd have him back.

"Only if you're ready to commit. *And* if you never get on a motorcycle again."

"I can do that," he said without hesitation.

Hugo sits beside his daughter in the back of the car while Miranda drives. They've been out quite a bit since Eloise was born: to Costco for groceries, to a baby shower at Miranda's hospital, to the open house out in Langley the previous weekend. And they visited all the touristy sites with Dom and his family while they were in town. The suspension bridge. The nature playground out in Richmond. The seawall and the beaches. They even visited Science World, though his twin half-brothers, at eighteen months old, were much too young to appreciate any of it.

Hugo's anxiety has been escalating steadily all day, but it's still a relatively "low-state" panic—shallow breaths, numb lips, racing thoughts—and he knows how to manage this now. He can pinpoint these sensations, identify their source, and then breathe through them. But, given the circumstances, he's decided to indulge in some extra help this evening. He digs in his pocket and finds his emergency Xanax. Discreetly, he dips his head so Miranda can't see him in the rear-view, slips the pill between his lips, and tastes the comforting chalky bitterness before he swallows. He leans back, closes his eyes, and waits for the resulting calm to wash over him.

In anticipation of this evening, he's been trying to make sense of his mother after all this time. He wants to understand

her as a whole rather than as a collection of parts, yet thinking about her is like peering through a kaleidoscope. Who is
she really? Is she his first shifting memories of her—always
flailing, always rushing around and in constant motion? Her
short hair sticking up every which way. Torn jeans and grubby
sneakers. A jangle of keys and change in her pocket as she flew
out the door and down Doris's cobblestone driveway to catch
the bus. The grief he felt whenever she was out of sight, terrifying and confusing. As if the elastic that connected them was
being stretched to its breaking point. "Where is she?" he'd ask,
a pain in his chest, his chubby hands pressed to the window,
Doris's firm, callused hand on his shoulder. Then that explosion of energy when she burst back through the door at the
end of the day, with bags and food and often guests tagging
along at her heels. But everything was dumped on the floor
when, even at five, six, seven years old, he was swept up into
her strong arms and placed on her hip, his cheeks wet from a
slurry of her kisses. *Oh, I fucking missed you. Oh, how did you
get so fucking heavy?* She believed in swearing for joy, especially in front of children, and this made him laugh because he
knew they were breaking all the rules. *Shit, shit, shit,* he'd say,
copying her and grinning. *Fuck, fuck, fuck,* he'd whisper in her
ear. And she would pull back and stare at him with astonish-
ment on her face: *Where did this unbelievable kid come from?*

Or is she his co-conspirator in their damp hovel under the
stairs? "We are the mice. We are the servants. We eat their
scraps and know all their dirty secrets," she'd say, as they cud-
dled on their pullout and listened to the family she worked
for treading across the floor upstairs. All he remembers about
that house was that the boy who lived there was his friend and
had a nervous disposition, and that his parents were always

fighting and yelling. The woman especially—at her husband, at her son—her voice driving through the floorboards like a screw through dry wood. Hugo understood then that he was the luckiest kid in the whole wide world, because his mother never yelled like that! When she was angry, she held him tighter. When he made a mistake, broke something, called her a "shithead," she was the one who would cry and apologize. It was smothering to be loved so fiercely, yet wonderful too. She was woollen sweaters, bare summer skin, and sweatshirts slightly sour with her smell: coffee; orange peel; acrid, almond sweat from doing half-hearted push-ups on the kitchen floor. She would say, "I suppose we better go up there and save that poor family before they kill each other." And they'd fling open the laundry room door, laughing, pretending they didn't know what went on up there. They were spies. Saviours. Superheroes.

Or is she this: Tired. Moving slowly through the days. Sometimes it was impossible to drag her up from the couch and she'd just lie there, staring at him blankly.

He remembers her face, weary and sad as she listened to him tell her about the mean boy in his class. Or about being pushed off the playground structure. Or about how his hat, the one he'd saved up for, was stolen. Those pre-adolescent years were quiet and peaceful too. Sure, school was horrible, as was after-school care. But at five-thirty, there was his mother, never late, and it would be time to go home to their small, top-floor apartment with the iron fire escape, where they'd spend their evenings on the alley-rescued, velvet love-seat watching the movies she'd missed out on as a child.

Astra always had a project on the go: a new tin of paint for the living room, a new place for them to live, a new love interest, a new recipe that more often than not failed because they'd forgotten a key ingredient at the store. Like yeast. Or milk. Or tahini. *Fuck.* He never once saw her make a list, or heard her plan for the future. They never took a trip. They never visited his grandfather. They never visited his father. It was just the two of them.

But by the time he was fourteen or fifteen, their story—*her* story—began to fracture ever so slightly. Hugo began to realize that chapters were missing. Paragraphs were redacted. Key sentences read like gibberish. By the time they got to Nick's, everything was haywire. "*Astra,*" he called her now when he was mad. Yet she still tried to pull him into her arms when she was upset and explain why she was the way she was—*Too much information, Astra!* That's when he stopped confiding in her. That's when he started saying less and less and less, but this only drove her to monitor his emotions more closely, asking him if he was "okay" all the time. And so part of him began to wonder if there *was* something a little wrong with him. There must be if he made her so "worried." But what did she know? What was it about him that made her so afraid?

And then there was the day he used Astra's computer to search for a pie recipe after picking apples from the hundred-year-old trees around Doris's house. When he opened her laptop, he found the email from his father, explaining that he couldn't make it to his high school graduation, and his mother's reply: *That's okay. Hugo will understand.* And even though he knew she'd asked Freedom to come, and he had declined, and Hugo had told his mother exactly that—*I understand, that's fine, I don't really care*—this hadn't been true. He *did* care. He searched for Freedom's address in her account, and then he combed through every email they'd ever exchanged about him. He found his mother's descriptions of him, to this man he didn't know, so personal and pathetic, they made him burn with shame:

Hugo is walking! Well, more often, he is falling down. You should see the bumps on his head.

He's talking in full sentences now. He says, "How about dis?" a hundred times a day. I should record him for you.

Hugo broke his arm falling off the monkey bars. They had to put him under to reset it. I was so, so, so terrified when I signed that waiver.

He's been suspended for spitting on a kid for the third time. It's always the same kid. He's not nice, he deserves it, but he's sad too.

I just passed him in the bathroom. I didn't mean to look, but he has pubic hair, Freedom!

Fact after fact after fact. But she never asked: *Would you please come out to see him? Why don't you care? Why don't you love him?* And he decided this must be the reason she looked at him the way she did, because she knew she could have done more. He slammed the computer shut and left the bag of apples on the counter to rot.

So he doesn't know who she was, who she is, or how he should think about her now. But does anyone know how to think about their mother? Does anyone get it right? And how do you apologize for being young? For being angry? How do you say: *I don't know why I blamed you.* Or: *I'm sorry for betraying you.* How do you ask: *Can you tell me which parts were your fault and which were mine?* How do you tell your mother: *I got married. I had a baby. I'm not really your kid anymore.*

There was another question that troubled him now. How could he be sure that when he went home, he wouldn't revert

to the boy he used to be? How could he stay the person he'd
worked so hard to become?

When they park in front of Doris's garage, he looks up at the
top floor of the house and sees his mother's figure move away
from the window. He unbuckles the car seat, pulls Eloise out,
and follows his wife up the creaking stairs, past the cracked
stained-glass windows, past the dusty chandelier. And then
there she is, waiting in the doorway, grinning nervously, her
arms flung open wide. As she pulls Miranda into an embrace,
immediately he sees this: his mother is fine.

Great, even.

Astra's lips are painted a vibrant mandarin orange, and her
hair is cropped at her jaw in a severe bob. She's dressed differently too; she's wearing a tent-shaped linen dress, the textile
printed all over in large black palm leaves. He's never seen her
in anything besides jeans before. Nor has he seen her wear
makeup. Nor had he realized her hair is actually quite black.
Does she dye it? No, he sees a few stray pieces of grey spring-
ing from her middle part.

The apartment is almost unrecognizable. Everything is
new and surprisingly neat. Miranda, a nurse, obsesses over
cleanliness, even reminding Hugo to wash his hands before
each meal, but his mother has never been a tidy woman. As a
child, his clothes rarely made it from the laundry basket to the
drawers, and she left pots to soak for days in greasy water. But
now even her shoes are lined up on the shelf, her jackets are
hanging orderly, and the hallway runner has vacuum tracks.
And he can tell somehow that the house isn't just this way
for their visit; this is how she lives now. On the coffee table

there's a bottle of wine, a small stack of carefully wrapped presents, and the car seat. Astra is there, bent over his daughter and holding her tiny slippered feet, the smile on her face both familiar and strange.

She moves aside and observes Miranda studiously as she undoes the buckles. Then the women sit side by side on the couch, while Hugo takes a seat on Doris's old La-Z-Boy. For some reason, his wife has not entrusted the baby to Astra's care yet, even though his mother is looking at Eloise eagerly.

They discuss the drive and the comic book store, and he half-heartedly explains that it's getting busier again with a new generation becoming obsessed with comics. Miranda mentions her baby shower at work, and while she speaks, Hugo grows more and more embarrassed by his behaviour: he let strangers hold his child before his mother was given a chance.

Astra pours out three glasses of wine.

"Hugo, you'll have to have mine," Miranda says kindly. "Breastfeeding," she explains to Astra. "And driving too."

"Right," Astra says, rolling her eyes at her own foolishness. "I should have asked you first."

Hugo knows he shouldn't drink either after taking that pill, but he feels more unbalanced than he'd imagined he would be, being here, being home. Seeing her.

He picks up the glass. "Thanks, Astra," he says. Then he grimaces. "Thanks, Mom," he corrects, although under his breath.

While the women continue to exchange small talk about the baby, Hugo studies the room. Everything has been altered—except for the recliner he's sitting in and that photo that's always hung over the couch: the one with Doris, his grandfather, and his mother's secret moccasin-shod foot.

Now there's a new framed photo hanging beside it, which also appears to have been taken in the fields at Celestial Farm, possibly by the same person and with the same camera. Only this time his mother is alone in the shot. She looks about two years old. Naked, plump, her hair roughly shaved to stubble. Her freshly bare scalp is a brilliant white, vulnerable and glowing starkly against her summer-tan limbs and round belly. Bandages bind gauze across the left side of her face and over her eye, and a sling is wrapped tightly under her chin, covering part of her mouth. Bruises purple her skin from her eyes to her collarbone, and goosebumps rash her chest. She appears cold and alone, although he knows she can't be; someone is there with her, taking the photo instead of holding her in their arms. The image makes him sick to his stomach.

He turns towards his mother now and examines her wide, orange lips. *She has scars*, he realizes. Of course she does. She always has. Why had he never registered this before? But what happened to her? And why did she hang this photo? Why would she want to be reminded of such a thing every time she walked in the room?

"Is it okay if I change Eloise here on the couch?" Miranda is asking Astra.

"Be my guest," she says. "Hugo, while she does that, why don't you come see what I've done to the kitchen?"

There is new olive green tile on the floor and the walls have been painted a crisp white, where before they were a grease-flecked mustard yellow. Doris's chipped cabinets are gone, and in their place, new teak cupboards and open shelving are anchored to the walls.

"Do you like it?" Astra asks.

"It's nice. And it feels bigger."

His mother reaches above the fridge and gets another bottle of red. "Is it okay to have more? I don't know where you're at these days," she adds.

"Absolutely. I'd love some."

She winks and unscrews the cap, before retrieving two black mugs from the cupboard and pouring a generous splash into each. He doesn't recognize these ceramics; as it turns out, it's all pottery she made herself earlier this year. She tells him about how a few of her long-time tenants converted Doris's garage into a shared artist studio, complete with a kiln and a darkroom, something he would have loved as a teenager. "Are you still drawing?" she asks hopefully.

"Yeah. A bit," he answers, diminishing the truth. Really, he draws whenever it's slow at work. He has his own desk there. A lamp. The perfect set-up. The owner of the store is incredibly supportive.

Standing there in front of his mother, he finds himself overcome by a childish urge to tell her everything. He wants to tell her about the sketches he's been asked to send to Marvel, and the freelance storyboard work he's been doing at a start-up gaming company. And just how scared he was during Miranda's C-section at the hospital only a few weeks before. But he doesn't know how to start. Anything he says will only point to the years they've lost.

"So I guess you're an artist now too?" he asks a little pathetically.

"Oh, no. I'm not sure I'd call myself that," she says. "I just like cups and bowls. I'm nothing much at all."

"You're something," he says, regretting how weak this sounds too.

"Well, that's true. I'm definitely here," she agrees. They clink their mugs together and drink.

Astra drums her fingers on the counter for a moment, then she stops and turns to face him. "Is it all right for me to ask if you're doing okay these days?"

"Sure. Ask away."

There is a pause. "Well, are you?"

"Am I what?"

"Are you okay?"

He laughs. "I am."

Another awkward silence falls over them, but before it becomes unbearable, Astra reaches over and grabs his hand. She squeezes it firmly. The way she used to while walking him to school, or when he was at the dentist having his teeth pulled, or when they sat together watching movies. Her hand is thinner while also the same.

"Let me go get the baby," he says, pulling away. "You haven't had the chance to hold her yet."

Back in the kitchen a few minutes later, he picks up his mug of wine and leans against the new countertop while his mother, who is sitting at the table now, arranges Eloise over her shoulder and begins to rhythmically pat her back. Unsatisfied with the position, she gets to her feet and starts swaying her hips. As the baby settles into her neck, Astra takes a long inhale of her peach-fuzzed head. "I know this is a total cliché, but she smells like family."

Miranda enters the room and thanks Astra for the gift of the slippers and lotion, but as soon as the baby hears her voice, she begins to fuss. "I think she might be hungry," Miranda apologizes.

"By all means," Astra says, returning the baby to her mother, though clearly she's disappointed at having to let go so soon.

Once Eloise is happy on the breast, Miranda asks Astra about the renovated kitchen. Hugo himself can't tell if he loves the change or hates it. Naively, he'd expected to find both his mother and the apartment unchanged from the last time he saw them. It makes him a trifle sad that this house is all new colours, new smells, and fresh paint. And is this visit even going as he'd wished it would? What had he wanted from it exactly? Had he wanted to prove something to Astra by showing her his child? And if that's true, is it working?

"I'll be right back," he says.

Walking down the hall, he peeks into his mother's bedroom, and then into the one that used to be his. It is a simple guest room now, furnished with a rocking chair and a double bed that's covered in a quilt.

Once he's in the La-Z-Boy again, he can no longer hear his family's conversation in the kitchen. He pours another glass of wine and gulps it down. Then he leans back in the chair and looks at the photo of his mother again.

Hugo wakes up to Astra shaking his shoulder. "Get up, sleepyhead," she whispers. Then she steps back as if she's touched something hot. Her face is very familiar now: drawn down with concern. He wipes a stream of drool from his chin, stands too fast, and collapses back into the worn leather chair. *Shit*, he thinks. He is repulsed by this feeling, this *old* feeling. A complete loss of control. Why had he taken that pill? Why did he have to go and drink so much wine? He doesn't need these things anymore. This is not how he wants to be seen after all this time.

"Sorry," he says, hoping that Astra will excuse herself and give him a chance to pull himself together in private, but she doesn't.

"Are you all right?" she asks.

"Yes, yes. I'm fine." He shakes his head clear and smiles. "Let's go eat. I just need some food. I forgot to eat lunch," he lies.

As she follows him back down the hall, she continues to talk. "You know, I remember this phase, Hugo. I imagine you're not getting any sleep these days. It can be so hard. You were a terrible sleeper until you were around four."

"Was I?"

"The worst. I was up with you all night every night for years."

As Miranda scoops out large helpings of each dish onto their plates, Hugo begins to feel more stable, more like himself, and he's determined to stay this way. Astra is sitting now, beaming, pleased to find herself in possession of the baby again. He pulls out one of the kitchen chairs across from her, and has a long sip of water before he puts his glass down. "You know, Mom," he says, careful to keep the emotion from his voice, "I feel like there are a few things I need to tell you. And I guess I've been a bit of a jerk. I should have just invited you, but last week, Miranda and I got married. It was while Dom was here," he stammers in a rush. He hadn't planned on telling her this part, but it feels necessary to keep going with the truth. He is tired of keeping things from her. He rubs the sleeve of his sweatshirt across his brow.

"Oh, I know all that already, Hugo," she says, then she gets up, rounds the table, and stands close at his side. With one hand holding Eloise firm to her shoulder, she runs her fingers through his hair. The act is so intimate and familiar that any remaining tension in his shoulders immediately dissipates. His body loosens into the chair.

"I think it's great that you guys got married," she goes on. "Really. Congratulations to the both of you. I see how good you are for one another. And when I heard, my feelings were not hurt. I don't really like weddings. I had a terrible time at mine. You must remember that," she says. "Having the three of you here, right now, *this* is perfect. *This* is how we can celebrate."

Hugo frowns at Miranda. "I'm sorry. I don't understand, did you tell her?"

Astra is holding the baby with both hands again, but she doesn't leave Hugo's side. "No, no," she continues. "Miranda didn't tell me anything. Freedom and his family came over for dinner before they left town. We actually talk pretty often these days. He's been keeping me updated."

"You talk?" Hugo cannot believe this. He can't for the life of him imagine the two of them in the same room.

"Yes, we sort of reconnected a while back. And now we talk pretty often. I can't believe you have brothers. It's completely wild, isn't it? But at the same time, I'm starting to feel like everything is right these days. I'm happy for your dad. They're cute boys, aren't they?"

"They are."

Astra sniffs Eloise's head once more, and she doesn't even try to conceal her pleasure. "Did I ever tell you about the time I tried to steal a baby?"

"What?" Miranda says, joining in with a laugh.

Astra sways Eloise back and forth as she explains that, when she was a child, she used to visit the house next to the Farm, where a perfect little family had moved in. There was a mom and a dad, a girl around her age, and a baby—all of them as foreign to her as characters in an English novel. She especially loved to spy on the house at night when it was lit up like a cake and easy to see the family moving about inside. The baby must have been colicky, because the mother was constantly rocking her. "She paced and paced in front of the living room windows, holding the baby like this," she says, nodding down at Eloise who is now completely asleep in her arms. "And she would stare out into the night, right at me, but she never saw me standing there in the dark. I was so envious of those kids, having a mother like that. She was very beautiful. She looked like a painting," Astra says, sitting down at the table again. "So I decided I was going to steal the baby. It wasn't a logical idea at all. Still, I tried to convince the sister to come along. I remember telling her that I could take care of them. That I could raise them. I actually believed this, which says a lot about me at that age I guess."

"What happened?" Hugo asks.

"Oh, I don't know. Nothing really. We took the baby from the crib once, I remember that." Astra's expression is lively again, her cheeks flushed with pleasure at her tale. "But the girl stopped opening her window when I knocked. I must have scared her. My plan was a failure."

"I don't think I've heard that story," Hugo says.

"Probably not. I only thought of it now, holding Eloise like this."

"It's kind of sad though, Mom."

"It is, isn't it?" She laughs, her eyes damp but sparkling. And it's now that Hugo is suddenly struck by how much he's always liked her, as a person. He's sorry he let himself forget it. She is an impressive woman, a fact that's easy to see if you spend enough time actually considering her, and all she's done, and all she's lived through. And then there are all the things he doesn't know.

"Now," she says. "Tell me about your new house. I hear you're moving. And Miranda, I hear you have a new job. I'm sorry that I know so much. Poor Freedom was very kind to keep me up to date. I just wanted to give you space. I didn't want to bug you until you were ready to have me back in your life. But Hugo, I need you to understand this; I don't want Freedom's version anymore. It's not enough. I want yours."

"I don't know if there's much to tell," he says, meeting her eyes.

"That's okay too," she says, softly. "How about you tell me just one thing tonight. One thing that's going on and that you're excited about. Let's start again there."

ASTRA

FOR A MONTH now, I've been locked in the same routine. A pattern that helps buoy me upright while I wait, while I straddle two worlds: one foot in my past, the other trying to find purchase in whatever it is that's coming next. In the mornings, I start by waking early. I climb from the camper van and prepare a coffee on the picnic table by the river. Next, I take my mug and begin to walk. I leave the disarray and decrepitude of the Encampment and overgrown gardens of the Farm behind, and head north on the path that runs alongside the riverbank. I keep going until I reach Kim's old house, where I hope to find Justin, the man who lives there now, out in his garden so I can wave hello and say a few words before I turn around and head back to make breakfast. Then I do the same thing before lunch, and again before dinner. The path has become worn underfoot, all the grass brown and lying flat.

Somehow it's already the middle of September, but today the morning is warm. There are hawks gliding overhead and sparrows turning quick circles around my shoulders, chasing the bugs that are startled from the ground by my feet. Once I'm a few minutes down the path, I notice a new log up ahead on the opposite riverbank, which is peculiar, because from what I remember, deadfall only ever washes up in the spring when the water is raging and fast. Curious, I keep my eyes fixed on it in the distance as I carry on. It is black, wet, its bottom half still partly submerged in the water.

Raymond often told me he was going to build a bridge to the other side. Once or twice he even tried, but such a project was far beyond his skill set, and all that remains of his attempts are a few rotten, tar-black pilings on the shore by the fence. The river is nearly sixty feet wide, and in the middle, where it's deep, the current is strong year-round. Even at my bravest, as a teenager, I never tried to swim across. And so when the object moves, my hiking boots become so heavy it's as if they've suddenly filled with lead. I stop in my tracks.

My voice is weak and cracking as it bounces off the bright auburn water: "Raymond? Is that you?"

Now that I'm standing directly across on the opposite shore, I can see it's definitely him and not a log at all. His upper body is clinging to the slate, soaking to the bone, his legs still dragging in the water. Did he fall in? Did he swim? How is it possible that he made it over there?

I watch, helpless, as he slowly heaves himself the rest of the way out. He gathers his work-sinewy arms and legs in a sitting position, shaking with cold or fear as he clutches his knees.

"Raymond!" I call again, though it's no use. It's possible he can't hear me over the sound of the river, but more likely it's that he doesn't remember his own name. Lately he's stopped registering it, especially, it seems, when I'm the one talking. He hasn't even recognized me for who I am since I arrived. For weeks now, he's barely blinked in my direction. He moves around me as fluidly as slow water around a large rock: I don't cause the slightest ripple in his day. While he's out puttering in the gardens, I sneak into his cabin to wash his underthings and bedding. I leave food on his table then return later to take the dishes away. I peer in the one cloudy window to ensure he's safe in bed once it falls dark. That is all.

Is he even aware I'm here? Has he ever been?

Momentarily, I try to convince myself I could make it across to reach him. I imagine leaving my jeans and sweater on the bank. The gasp and the clutch in my chest as I dive under the frigid water. My struggle as I try to tow him back through the river current. Then my failure. The two of us slipping under midway, arms taking one another down. Down to the dark bottom.

I shiver.

No. I don't even want to touch him, I realize.

I pull my feet from the ground and start to run.

Justin has a small inflatable Zodiac that he uses for fishing, and I keep even on the path as he rows steadily upriver towards Raymond. Strangely, I find myself calm. When Justin drags the bow up onto the shore where Raymond sits, I am fine. When Justin wraps a blanket around his shoulders, I am fine. When Raymond swats at him violently, all that passes over me is a mild embarrassment—but that quickly fades. Raymond himself is nearly ninety, after all. When Justin stands and looks across the water, giving me the signal we discussed while launching the boat—one hand up to his ear—I pull out my phone and my hands do not shake as they often do. While I talk to the dispatcher, my mind is tucked safely away in a comforting pattern. I'm calculating which day of the week it is now, wondering where Hugo is, and if my grandchildren are enjoying being back at school. *Maybe I'll phone them this evening,* I decide. Then, looking at Justin again, I wonder what token he would like as a thank you for his trouble: maybe a bottle of wine or a pie? And I almost laugh when I consider what other people might think if they could see me or hear my thoughts. Why is it that I'm not losing my mind with worry? Why am I not wailing in grief at the sky? Why do I feel as if I'm only watching a movie?

Because this is Raymond, I think, answering these questions for myself.

"I've always kind of liked him," Justin says as we follow the ambulance in his tiny, two-seater electric car.

"Everyone *likes* him. He's never had a single worry or responsibility his whole life, so he gets to be charming," I say, paying more attention to the few inches between Justin's shoulder and mine—and recalling the power in his body as he worked the oars—than I am to anything he says or to the fact that Raymond is ahead of us, sedated, strapped down, and being attended to by strangers in masks.

"When I was building my garden, he often stopped by," Justin continues, his eyes on the road, keeping an even distance from the ambulance's bumper.

I smile. "To give advice, I'm guessing?"

He chuckles. "Yes. But it *was* helpful. I'm a city kid, I'll take anything I can get."

Justin's tattoos decorate every inch of his arms, from his fingernails to beneath his T-shirt sleeves. His head is shaved bald, and his large, mostly grey beard hangs over his chest. I've asked around, and so far this is all I know: He moved here five years ago to retire with his partner, but soon after she became sick. They were musicians when they were young, met in a band—she was the lead singer and unfriendly, some say—and he made his living building decks and small pretty sheds. No one can confirm whether they had children or not (I haven't dared ask, nor have I myself mentioned Hugo), and most thought he'd move closer to family after she passed, yet he stayed on. But this is what it's like here now. The region is growing. No one wants to be in the city anymore, with its hot pavement, endless pandemics, and the increasing cost of housing. People want to simplify. To grow their food. To know their neighbours. Most want to just sit outside in the open air and breathe without anxiety buzzing all around them like clouds of blackflies in May. And during the last few weeks here, I've started to wonder if I might be the same. Because what surprised me most was how completely at home I felt the moment I arrived.

I'd avoided coming back to Celestial for over thirty years. And I would have kept avoiding it too if Clodagh hadn't phoned, leaving me with no other choice.

"You're all he has and he needs care. It's time for you to *do* something," she implored in her usual, better-than-thou tone.

Yes. But we all need care, I thought as I hung up. *Why is he my problem?* Yet the following day I called Hugo and Miranda, asked to borrow their small camper van, and then I drove up and over the mountains on my own for the first time. When I pulled through the gates, I found the old driveway to the

Encampment completely thatched over with young trees, and so I took the alternate route towards the gardens. There, I spotted a little A-frame shack by the river that I'd never laid eyes on before.

Hearing the engine, Raymond emerged from his cabin, yelling, accusing me of being a tourist and trespassing, which hurt at first. Because, of course, I've carried on exactly as Doris had for all those years. I pay all of Celestial's bills, and I have a monthly automatic deposit going into the Farm's account; this is in fact *my* land. But then, as I listened to Raymond's attempts to shoo me away, I grasped the severity of the situation. With his long hair thinned to his scalp on top, his beard dreaded under his chin, his bony hands dirt-stained and liver-spotted like a russet potato, he was exactly as Clodagh had described: thinner, diminished, with fewer words and a ranging, unfocused gaze. And he appeared malnourished. When I was a girl, it was this sort of image that kept me up at night. I felt responsible for keeping him alive. Thought that if I didn't feed him, if I didn't track his every move, he'd die and leave me all alone. Apparently, I wasn't that far off. It just took fifty-odd years for my premonition to come true.

I slowly maneuvered the camper past him, and parked it between the greenhouse and his A-frame. Because it was clear: I wasn't going to be leaving Celestial for some time. Not until I figured out what to do with him.

Every day since, I've stuck to my new routine, only occasionally breaking it to take Raymond's old, gas-guzzling truck into town. When I do, I tuck the decahedron in a pocket in the dash. I roll the windows down, turn on the radio, and listen to whatever comes on. I gaze out at the hobby farms dotted along the newly paved road. Goats. Pigs. Rabbit hutches. Vegetable gardens. I slow down to a crawl, and drive widely around the people on the shoulder as they walk their Pyrenees or collies. And when I get into Lunn, people say hello. I'm known there now. I can even say I have acquaintances. And Justin is becoming a friend too. A few times I've almost asked him over for a drink before dinner. At Celestial there's a little platform by the river, with two chairs arranged on it facing westward, where we could sit and chat about nothing much. When I saw the chairs for the first time, I was surprised Raymond had built such a thing after living alone for so long. I wondered who he thought might visit: Gloria? Doris? Was it possible he ever imagined me?

I have been quiet for some time, and now, after Justin takes the exit for the regional hospital, I notice him inspecting me out of the corner of his eye. "What?" I ask, genuinely interested. I might be flirting with him half the time, I'm not quite sure.

"I'm just sorry that you're going through this. It must be hard," he says, in a tone much more serious and considered than I'd like.

"Oh." I bite my upper lip. "Please don't be sorry. I don't think I'm sad."

"No?" He is watching me more closely now.

"No," I say firmly. Because this is true. All I know at the moment is that everything has finally changed, and that this is what I've been waiting for. For Raymond to finally no longer be Raymond. For it to be too late. He won't be able to love me now in the way I've always hoped he would, and that's all right. Because now, I can put this behind me. Because now, in a small way, the future seems brighter than it has in many, many years.

A week after Raymond has been settled into his room, I get a call from Wildwood Assisted Living. "Are you able to come in?" the manager says, his voice all business. "We had to move your father again last night. He needs his stuff unpacked."

"Oh," I answer. I wasn't planning on going in this week, nor do I want to. Not at all.

"Unfortunately," the manager continues, "your father is not adjusting as well as we'd hoped. He keeps barging into people's rooms looking for the exit. We worried that if we didn't put him in the secure wing immediately, he'd find his way out," he says. And I believe it. This is why going to the home is so hard. Raymond spent the last sixty years with his hands in the dirt, and now I've sentenced him to live out his remaining days inside; the story is as tragic as one of an orca confined to a swimming pool.

"All right, I'll come in later this morning," I say.

When I arrive, I'm pleased to see that Kim, who is one of the nursing attendants at the home, is working.

"This is wild," I said when I visited Raymond the first time and found her behind the reception desk. Her hair, which is even blonder now with the mix of white in it, was wavy and cropped at her chin. She was the same. Pretty, with that good, trusting face.

"Not really," Kim answered with a snort. "This town isn't very big, Astra."

"But you moved? I thought your family left? Yet here you are, back!"

It turns out that none of this was true, and I can't for the life of me recall where I got this story. What actually happened was her mother left Kimmy's father, and then she moved her two daughters into a little apartment above the General Store in Lunn, where their life took on a whole other shape. Kim attended school in town, and then she left for a few years of university before coming home again. "Everyone thinks it matters *where* you live, that you'll be more successful if you move on," she explained that day as we got reacquainted. "But I quickly found that what really matters is *who* you live with," she said, and then she proceeded to fill me in and tell me about her family: her wife and their four kids. "This is where I belong," she added. "And I'm glad to see you're back too."

"You are?" I said, surprised.

"Of course. Come have dinner at our place some evening soon."

Now Kim takes me to the on-call doctor's office, where together we review the new, increased rate for Raymond's accommodation, and they have me sign papers concerning yet another medication.

Afterwards, when Kim opens the door to Raymond's new room, we find him slumped before the barred window, naked except for the ratty old sleeping bag that is tucked around his waist. His feet are bare and his shins hairless.

"We can't keep him in his clothes either, which is another problem," Kim explains as she taps her fantastically pink acrylic fingernails on the doorframe.

I begin to laugh, though it makes me look like an asshole.

"It's funny, sort of," Kim says. "But Astra, some of the residents have complained, as have the visitors. So maybe try to convince your dad to put his pants back on, at least."

"Okay, I'll do my best," I say, though I won't bother. It's not like he'll listen to me.

After Kim goes, I move about the room quietly, arranging Raymond's few belongings on the shelves or in drawers while he sleeps, his chin dropped to his bare chest, his ribs jutting out over his small, round belly. Since I arrived at Celestial, he's put on quite a bit of weight, maybe five or ten pounds, and though this is a silly thing to focus on, given everything else, I'm proud that I've returned him to something resembling health.

I dig in my purse and find the package of plastic glow-in-the-dark stars that I bought at the store on my way over. I rip it open with my teeth, then kick off my shoes and climb awkwardly onto the mattress. I ball up little bits of adhesive and stick them on the backs of the stars with my thumb. Reaching up overhead, I press them firmly to the ceiling, exactly as I did in each of Hugo's bedrooms when he was a boy. I don't bother with the Dippers or Orion's Belt like I once did. I put them all over the place. It won't hurt Raymond to puzzle over these new constellations in the sky.

When I climb down, I find him looking at me. "Hi Raymond," I say, standing there, waiting for what I don't know. "It's me, Astra." I coax myself to step closer. I recall the image I had last week, of us pulling one another underwater. How fearful I'd been to touch him. I dare myself to do it now. "Do you know who I am?" I ask, crouching at his knees.

His head dips slightly, and I take his limp hand in mine. The calluses on his palms are starting to peel now. "Don't worry," I say when I let go. "You're a stranger to me too."

The following Saturday, I invite Justin over for a drink after dinner. Before he comes, I light the firepit and dish out the terrible pie that I made earlier on the propane stove. It's a failure, but this doesn't seem like the kind of thing Justin will be fussed about. I'll make another when I have a proper oven and invite him again.

Sitting beside Justin on Raymond's chairs, I can't help but think of how it felt to be with other men in the past. How tense it could be. For years I was desperate to please everyone, and it was exhausting. But with Justin it isn't like that. He simply sits and tells me about his day when I ask. He tells me about a phone call he had with his brother, and he describes the plot of a movie he watched the evening before. But maybe this ease is because we're old now. Maybe it's because he's already had a wife and an entire life. What could he possibly want from me?

I think briefly about my phone in the camper, about all the voicemails Hugo has left over the last few weeks that I haven't answered. I think of the cute videos my granddaughter Eloise has been sending too. Hugo accused me of being a poor communicator in his most recent text, which is true. I send only a word or two in return so he won't worry I've died. I simply can't bring myself to talk to him or tell him why I haven't returned home to Vancouver yet. *Tomorrow*, I think. *Tomorrow I'll call and tell him everything.*

"Did you visit Raymond today?" Justin asks, after refilling both of our wine glasses and placing the bottle at his feet.

"Yes, I had lunch with him actually."

"And did you tell him about your plan?"

"No," I grumble a little sheepishly. "I chickened out."

"But you still *want* to tell him?"

"I think so. It's just that now I've started to worry it's not for the right reasons."

"What are the right reasons?"

"Permission. Blessings."

"And what are the wrong reasons?"

I smile and raise my eyebrows. "To make him mad," I say. Because it's true. I'm still stuck on that image—of how I'm a rock and Raymond is the river. All I've ever wanted is to cause a little ripple in his life, to catch his attention for a moment. And I know that this is partly why I'm going ahead with my plans. Why I've decided to stay. I want to be my own storm. I want to be a hurricane. I want to whip up the water's surface and make waves, even if he never sees it. I want the sun. "Do you think that's sort of childish?" I ask now.

"Maybe? Your dad is old, Astra. He probably won't have a clue what you're talking about, let alone get mad." Justin takes a sip of his wine, then he cups the glass delicately between his large hands. "But I do understand what you're going through, you know," he continues.

"How do you understand?" I say, much too shortly. I am finding myself upset all of a sudden, and I'm worried that whatever he's about to say is going to hit me harder than I'd like.

He runs his fingers through his beard. "I've lost a lot of people in my life," he says. "Too many. But there's one thing that I know for certain. Do you want to hear it?"

I both want and don't want him to continue, but my long silence gives him permission to go on.

"I've found it's much, much harder to lose the people who never gave you enough, than it is to lose the ones who gave you everything," he says.

Well, you're not an idiot, I think as my heart races double-time, a disturbing rate. But I don't tell him that his comment has broken me open. Instead, I look across the water. I look out at the far trees. I take it all in.

Now, after nearly four weeks in his new room, Raymond has begun to adjust. Or, more accurately, it seems he's given up fighting his new life at the home. He puts his clothing back on when he's asked, he no longer looks for the exit, and he spends most of his time in his bed. I go in once or twice a week, and I usually find him asleep. I take his armchair from its place by the window and roll it over beside him, where I sit. Today, I remembered the decahedron from the truck and I've brought it in with me. I twist it in my lap: 1, 2, 3, 4, 5, 6, 7, 8, 9, 10. I can read the numbers by touch, by the etching in the metal; I memorized the map of it years ago. I close my eyes, but then Raymond is talking.

"That's mine, give it to me!" he cries, pointing at my hands.

I hold the dice up, but I do not pass it over. "This?" I say, confused. And for a minute I have to go back in time, question myself: Did I steal it from him? I remember how Clodagh's daughter once took it for a time. But no, it's definitely mine. Raymond gave it to me. He told me that it was Gloria's. He was the one who taught me how to use it.

"That's my mother's. I've been looking for it everywhere," he continues, but now that first bark of anger is gone. He sounds defeated.

"It was *your* mother's?" I say, slowly, trying this new truth out in the open air.

"Yes. Of course it was. How else would I get it? Did you know her? Is she the one who gave it to you?" Raymond asks. His dark eyes are wet, the skin around them soft and the colour of a bruised plum. Outside the window, clouds lie heavily in the sky. Rain begins to patter on the window. It's as if my chair and the ground underneath me have turned to liquid. I am sinking. What about *my* mother? If this is true, what do I have of her?

"No, I'm sorry. I didn't know your mom. What was she like?" I say, acting as calm as I can, when really I'm concentrating on holding my head above water.

"She was strong. That's about it," Raymond says gruffly. "But she was tough too. A nice voice. It's hard to remember."

"Oh. I wish you had a picture of her," I say. "When did you last see her?"

"I was young when she left. Five or six. She left that dice for me. She wanted *me* to have it." He points at my hand again.

"Really?" I say. Then, surprising myself, I pass it to him, and all at once the chair is firm and on solid ground again. I am upright and breathing.

He sits still for a very long time, eyes closed, holding the decahedron against his heart.

"Are you all right?" I ask, once I feel a little more like myself. "Are you asleep?"

Raymond looks at me now. "I'm sure she's dead by now," he says. "I'm sure I won't see her again. But that's how it goes. We are just little specks in this universe. We're just material. Best not try to make more out of it than it really is. But why are you talking about her? Did you know her?" He is alert again, his fist still clutched around the dice. He's clinging to it like it's a life raft. Yet, he gave it to me. He let me have it all this time.

"No, I didn't know her. I wish I had," I say, and this is suddenly very true, although I've never once thought about my grandmother before now. Raymond embodied the philosophy of living in the present so fully, as a child I was convinced he didn't have a past at all.

"My daughter, Astra, is exactly like her," he says, lucid, and I find myself wondering if I've made some mistake. Maybe he's fine? Maybe I'm the one who's lost her grasp on reality? "She's independent," he continues. "Clever. Better than me. Have you ever met my daughter?"

"No," I barely manage to say. I lean forward to take Raymond's free hand. I don't mind touching him now. And in this moment I decide that I won't tell him about what I've done to Celestial; I'll let it live on inside him as he envisioned it. Because just as much as Raymond isn't Raymond anymore, Celestial isn't Celestial either. If it ever was.

Over the last three weeks I've been very busy. First, I had the driveway cleared again and paved on the steep part so it'll be easier to get up in the snow. Next, the excavator pulled down the rotten cabin, the one my mother died in, the one I lived in all those years, and it was hauled away in a line of dump trucks along with the yurt, the school bus, the old trailer, and the years of trash. Then I had the birches along the cliff edge felled and bucked into firewood—wood I stacked inside a new metal shed that I put together myself from a kit. I even took down the sign at the road. Now the Encampment is just a clearing again. It's bare, much more spacious than before, full of light and open to the valley below. And right in the dead centre is the hole for the foundation of the house I'm going to build. The contractor and his crew are coming tomorrow morning to start the forms. It won't be big, but there will be a spare room for Hugo and his family so they can come visit in the summer, or in the winter months if they so wish. I'm building a home to live the rest of my life in, on the grave of everything that came before. On Doris, on Gloria, on Clodagh, on Raymond. On my childhood. On solid ground. Because that's what we all do, isn't it? We're not just matter. We're not fucking stars in the cosmos. We're one human life stacked on top of the traumas and the tragedies of another.

Raymond is inspecting me very closely. He frowns. "I'm sorry," he says. "Did you say that you know my daughter?"

"Yes," I say this time. "Actually, I do know her. Quite well."

"Oh, that's good. She doesn't come around much, but I don't mind. I got more than I deserved from her already. That girl doesn't owe me a thing. I always made sure of that, from the day she was born, that she'd never owe me anything."

"Nothing?" I ask, and of course I'm crying now.

"It's true, Astra," he says, turning to the window. "Nothing."

Oh my aging heart, I think. Because this is it, isn't it? This is what we've both been waiting for. For him to soften enough to love me, and for me to be open enough to let it happen.

I stay with my father for a long time, hours maybe, until he is deep asleep. Once his breathing is slow and steady, I gently uncurl his fingers from the dice and hold it in my hand while I listen to the rain fall. It takes a little while, but eventually I figure out my final question. I put the decahedron to my lips, whisper the words, and then I roll it on his bed. When I pick the dice up, I do so carefully, and I place it on top of my father's astrology book in the exact orientation in which it landed. And even though the answer to my question is right there, begging for me to need it, I rise from the chair and I do not look.

ACKNOWLEDGMENTS

Oceans of gratitude to:

My agent, Martha Webb, for her belief, and to everyone else at CookeMcDermid for their care and guidance.

My editor, Anita Chong, the all-round fantastic human whose brilliance transformed this book into something much, much more seamless and eloquent than it was.

Jared Bland, Trudy Fegan, Christie Hanson, Kimberlee Hesas, Sarah Howland, Lisa Jager, Erin Kelly, Joe Lee, Ruta Liormonas, Wendy Thomas, Gemma Wain, Daniella Zanchetta, and the whole team at McClelland & Stewart for welcoming me into their family of daring writers.

The community of Galiano Island.

Countless folks, but particularly to these women for the gift of their trust, friendship, and support over the years: Erin Anderson, Nahanni Arntzen, Oracle Arrand, Sarah Craig, Lori Seay, Pippa Davis, Tammy Lawrence, Keltie Miles, Tara Pichurski, Kerri Reid, Tahirih and Josli Rockafella, Meaghan Shute, and, of course, Sheryda Warrener.

My lovely family. Jason, Naomi, Claire, and Martha. David and Linda, always. Thomas, Manami, and Seion. And to my parents, who encouraged me to tell stories when I was small.

Mike, August, and Lake, for their company, humour, and love.